KATIANN
A Novel

J. D. Kiser

ARCHWAY
PUBLISHING

Archway Publishing books may be ordered through booksellers or by contacting:

Archway Publishing
1663 Liberty Drive
Bloomington, IN 47403
www.archwaypublishing.com
1 (888) 242-5904

Because of the dynamic nature of the Internet, any web addresses or links contained in this book may have changed since publication and may no longer be valid. The views expressed in this work are solely those of the author and do not necessarily reflect the views of the publisher, and the publisher hereby disclaims any responsibility for them.

Any people depicted in stock imagery provided by Thinkstock are models, and such images are being used for illustrative purposes only. Certain stock imagery © Thinkstock.

ISBN: 978-1-4808-5813-8 (sc)
ISBN: 978-1-4808-5814-5 (e)

Library of Congress Control Number: 2018901247

Print information available on the last page.

Archway Publishing rev. date: 03/20/2018

Dedication

I dedicate this book to all my family and friends who had faith in me, who encouraged me to do something for myself and the Native American Indian music (Thoughtfulness, The Lonely Shepherd, Blue Sky, Apurimac, Celia, Linda Bella Mujercita, Maht Ichi, and Poncho) performed by Alexandro Querevalú that inspired me. He puts his whole heart and soul into his music that mesmerizes your inner self.

From the author:

I am a mother of two and have six grandchildren. I have been working with young children for over three decades. As my health was failing, I knew that I had to start thinking about my future with my grandchildren. I knew I had to make a change in my life, so I started walking each day. I came across some Native American Indian music performed by Alexandro Querevalú, that inspired me to relate to my inner self. Each day I walked, I listened to the peaceful music that gets down into your soul and takes you back in time; where we were stress free, lived off the land and the people really cared about life.

My heart is heavy thinking about the injustice we put upon the Native Americans back in the day. As I researched customs of the world, my heart grew sad and I cried many times while writing this story. I hope as you read this story, you will drift into another time and place where the love for someone is worth giving your life for. We may not understand their customs, but I feel they had more love for their fellow man, respect, Spirit, and connection with their creator than we have today.

Everywhere I looked, on the News, Facebook and Newspaper, thoughts were sent to me and I had to tell someone. A co-worker encouraged me to write them down, so I did. I am not a writer but felt led to write this story. My story is about what true love is and the sacrifices one will go to protect their loved ones. You will become part of the story and feel the characters as they find themselves. You will laugh and cry. I hope you enjoy.

Chapter 1

The Inheritance

Anna May was a twenty-seven-year-old nurse at a local hospital owned by her grandfather. He was a very wealthy man who owned several multimillion-dollar companies, including May Enterprise—a successful investment company known all over the world. Anna had never faced any money issues. Ever since her parents were killed in an auto accident when she was twelve, her grandfather had taken care of her every need. Anna suffered head trauma in the accident and developed a phobia of driving. However, her grandfather provided her with a limo driver to transport her to and from work or any other place she desired to go.

Having had everything handed to her, she was a little spoiled. Well, maybe a lot spoiled, and she knew it. She always got what she wanted and always had the last word. Anna knew how to handle herself and was able to achieve her goals. She loved caring for people, so she attended nursing school and became a registered nurse. Babies were her specialty. Everyone at the hospital called her a "baby whisperer." There had never been a baby in the hospital that Anna could not calm.

Ever since she lost her parents, Anna had felt something was missing in her life. Losing both of them had devastated her; she felt lost. Deep in her soul, she knew there was something missing, but it was not just losing them. After the accident, she had visions of the crash and her mother's last words: "I will always be with you. Stand tall and never give up on the things you believe in. I love you, Missy." Missy was what her mother had called her.

When Anna told people about the visions, she was medicated to stop them. She had not had a vision in many years and was thankful for it.

There were times when she thought she lived a different life and needed to be somewhere else. She had never lived outside New York City, but deep in her heart, she knew she didn't belong there.

Having been raised in a Christian environment, she was saving herself for her one true love. She didn't go out much, just to work and the supermarket. Her coworkers had set her up with eligible men, but they hadn't worked out. Always cautious when it came to men, Anna had thought that they only wanted her money. She would be a great prize for any man. Deep down, Anna knew she could never have a relationship with anyone who knew who she was, and with May as her last name, that would be very difficult. But that was not going to set her back. She knew he was out there, and she would know him when the time was right. She was searching for someone who would respect her for who she was and not just for her wealth.

Her grandfather passed away a few months ago, leaving Anna to manage life on her own. She was a smart woman, and she knew she could do it. But Anna wanted nothing but to find her true love, her soul mate, just like her parents had. She could not remember them much because of the head trauma she had suffered in the accident, but from the pictures she had of them, she knew they'd had a deep love like no other.

Anna's grandfather had told her how special her mother was and how every night when she put Anna to bed, she would say, "One day you will wake up and the world will be yours."

One morning, Anna got up, took a shower, got dressed, and ate a piece of toast with her coffee. She met her driver downstairs, in front of the condo that she lived in and owned. He drove her to the front door of the hospital, just like he did every day. As she entered the building, Anna spoke to everyone. This morning, when Anna arrived at the nurse's station, she was met by her grandfather's lawyer, Mr. Peterson.

"Good morning, Miss May. Do you have a few minutes to go over the final request from your grandfather's will? It should not take much of your time, but it is time sensitive and needs to be addressed at once."

"Sure, Mr. Peterson. Follow me into the conference room. Is everything okay? How is your family doing?"

"Yes, everything is fine, and the family is doing well. Thanks for asking. There is one more piece of your grandfather's will that needs your attention now that you have celebrated your twenty-seventh birthday. Your grandfather wrote a letter to be given to you once you turned twenty-seven. You need to read it and make a decision today."

Mr. Peterson handed her the unopened letter. Anna looked at him with a tear in her eye. She had a letter from her grandfather. "Did you know about the letter all this time?" she asked.

"Yes, your grandfather and I came up with the plan, and everything is set, waiting on your decision, my dear. This was your grandfather's last wish."

Anna took the letter and began to read.

> Dear Anna,
> My love, you have been such a blessing in my life. Words can never describe the love I have for you. When you lost your parents, it was like a knife in my heart. Your mother was a

special person. She had a spirit within her that no one could explain. Losing my son was the hardest thing I have ever gone through. When I took you in, it was as if I had a second chance; you looked and acted just like him. You are your father all over again. You have always been the apple of my eye, and I would do anything for you.

Now that you are twenty-seven, I need you to do something for me. Many years ago, I traveled around the world looking for land to invest in. I came across the most beautiful place I had ever seen. The people were different, and I learned quickly of their spirit and how they cared for each other. They took me in as one of their own. The leader of these people saved my life after my plane crashed on their land, and I owed him everything.

The land on which they lived was not owned by anyone, so I claimed it, and it now belongs to you. I need you to go to this secret place and see for yourself if it should remain as is or if you want to sell it. It is up to you. No one except Mr. Peterson and myself know of my request. Before you decide, I want you to go and live with them until your twenty-eighth birthday. They are waiting for you.

They are very different from you and your ways. You will not understand theirs at first. As I spent time with them, I learned to understand their way of life and formed a loving relationship with them. They are good people, and I know you will try to change what you do not understand. If changes need to be made, do it slowly. Help them understand. They are set in their ways, and you cannot go into their homes and start making demands. I know how you are, Anna. Take it slow. Do not expect them to go against what they have been taught for thousands of years.

I always felt that you were searching for something all your life. I don't know if it is the need to make a difference or to find a purpose. There, among these people, you will find happiness, love, peace, kindness, hope, worthiness, strength, freedom, and joy. They know how to live off the land. Be open-minded. Respect their ways. Give them a chance to understand you, and you will learn to understand their way of life. They are simple people; they know how to love and respect one another.

Mr. Peterson has a box for you to give to the one in charge. He is expecting you. The box is proof of who you are and why you are there. The leader has the key, and when it is time, he will open the box and explain everything to you.

Do not give the box to anyone else or tell anyone of it. You do not have to stay a full year, but I do ask that you stay for as long as it takes you to understand them.

You hold their future in your hands. Once you arrive, they will know I have passed, and the leader will be expecting your decision. It will mean everything to them. Without this land, their way of life will disappear.

Be wise in your decision, for their lives depend on you. You need to give it great thought. Tell no one why you are there; it is between the leader and you. You do not want to cause panic among the people. They know no other way of life. Your decision is of life or death to them. Tell the people you are there to teach their children. It is a secret place, and not even Mr. Peterson knows its location. I have everything set up for you. My private jet will take you there.

You will need only your personal items for a year and enough clothes for a three-night camp. Once you arrive, a town car will pick you up and take you to a general store. A guide will take you from there. When you reach your destination, all your needs will be provided for. The land is a sacred, holy place. There you will find what you are searching for. You will find your soul. Be safe.

Anna, dear, I love you very much. I have always known that there is something missing in your life other than your parents. Your soul is searching for something, and I truly believe among these people you will find it. All I want is for you to be happy.

Mr. Peterson has been instructed to take care of all the paperwork you need for whatever you decide.

I love you, my sweet Anna.

Would she take a leap of faith, or would she continue to live her life as it is? Working with babies seemed to relax her, but today Anna's life would change forever.

Anna thought hard about what her grandfather had written. What did she have to lose? It might just be fun and exciting, and who knew—she may even find her true love. She needed a change, and what better than going away to a new place.

Anna signed all the necessary paperwork to take this trip and gave Mr. Peterson power of attorney to oversee Anna's interest in her companies. Mr. Peterson finalized everything and gave Anna the little trinket box. It was made of wood and had the most beautiful engravings she had ever seen.

Mr. Peterson told Anna that everything she needed would be provided once she arrived, including clothing, housing, and food. All she needed was her personal items for a year, warm clothes for a four-day travel, and some camping gear.

Anna was excited about her new adventure and invited some friends over to her condo that evening to share the news. She told them that her grandfather's last wish was for her to travel across the country for a year in search of her love. They were understanding and excited for her. After they left, she pondered what to pack. Since she was from the city, of course she just had to take some of her most fashionable clothing. After all, she was going to stay for a year, and she was not sure if they would have her style of clothing. By the time she was finished packing, she had filled a total of nine suitcases.

She flew out the next day on the company jet to an undisclosed location. However, she could tell it was outside the United States. A town car escorted her to the small town where she was to meet up with the guide.

She was so excited that she ended up being too early and had to wait for the guide on the porch of the general store with all her luggage. So she decided to look around and admire the scenery. Snow-covered mountaintops loomed in the distance. Spring was in the air, and flowers were popping up everywhere. She could see some elk and goats on the lower parts of the mountains. She knew that if she did not like the people, at least the land was breathtaking and she loved animals.

Chapter 2

First Night

Eventually, in the distance she spotted a cloud of dust coming her way along the road.

"Finally!" she said to herself.

But as it got closer, she noticed it was just an old beat-up Jeep and knew it was not her ride. She admired the driver as he parked in front of the store and got out of the Jeep. He was about six feet tall and had a dark suntan. He wore a white T-shirt with cutoff sleeves, blue jeans, and a ball cap. He appeared to be a few years older than her, and she could tell by the muscles in his arms that he worked out a lot.

As the man came up the steps and onto the porch, she nodded to acknowledge his presence and said, "Hello."

He sighed as he walked past her and into the store without saying a word. How rude to not even acknowledge her welcome, she thought. *How dare he. He must be stuck-up or something, and that Jeep looks like it is falling apart! I don't even believe he can drive. Thank goodness this is not my ride. I would not be caught dead in such a vehicle!*

Up close, the Jeep looked older than she'd originally thought. It was a wonder it even ran. It looked as though it was on its last ride. It was a shame. As nice as the man looked, one would think he'd have something better to drive. Either he had no taste or it was all he could afford.

Anna continued to wait for her ride.

About thirty minutes later, the man came out of the store with two diet sodas. He handed one to her and said, "You ready?"

Anna was surprised. She looked around the deserted parking lot. Was he talking to her?

"Are you asking me? Ready for what?" She glanced up at him.

He looked her straight in the eye and said, "Ready to go?"

She got a bad feeling as she held his gaze. His eyes were the color of coal, cold, and mysterious. Who did he think he was, being so bold after not speaking to her earlier? He seemed standoffish and was acting like he did not want to be there.

"No, I'm sorry," she answered him. "I am waiting for someone else."

"Are you Miss May?"

"Yes," she said. *How does he know my name? I have not*

told anyone in the store who I am. Anna was suspicious. Could he really be her ride? If so, what were they thinking? This ride was definitely not her style. How dare they put her in a situation like this! There was no way anyone could make it to a destination in one piece in that Jeep! He would probably wreck it before they got too far down the road.

"I drive you. We go now."

"There must be some misunderstanding. I am waiting for someone else in a town car or a camper. I am going camping for three nights."

"Out here?" He laughed. "No one come. I your ride. I take you."

She could tell his English was not good and definitely not his first language. She took a step back and shook her head as she glanced again at the beat-up Jeep.

"Lady, we no have all day. We go now. Getting dark soon. Have to travel long way." He began to walk toward the Jeep.

Realizing that he was no longer waiting for her, she yelled, "Wait! Wait! What about my luggage?" She pointed toward the end of the porch where she had placed her luggage.

"What that?" he said.

"These are my things."

"You no need. We leave now. No time. Get in. Let's go."

"Yes, I do!" she said.

His mouth curved into a silly grin, and he just shook his head at her.

"How do I know that you are my guide?" she asked.

"Out here, who would come?" he said.

"Well, I do not know you, and I am sure my ride would not be something like that." She pointed at the Jeep with a snooty look on her face.

"What wrong with ride? It does the job. Go now?" He looked at her and said, "I go now. You come." He got into the Jeep.

Anna went to stand in front of it and, with a stern look on her face, folded her arms.

"You come!" he shouted.

"Not without my luggage!"

He shook his head and started the engine. "I leave with or without you! Need to get to river before dark."

"I am not going anywhere without my luggage."

He backed the Jeep up, turned around, and drove off, scattering gravel everywhere in his wake.

I can't believe he would leave me here, she thought. *Just wait until I get back home. I will have Mr. Peterson fired for setting me up with such poor accommodations. How dare he!*

Anna was used to the fine things in life, and for being treated in this fashion, someone would pay. Anna got out her cell phone to call Mr. Peterson and complain but quickly discovered that she had no signal.

"That is just great," she said aloud to herself. "I am out here with a crazy man, no place to go, no way to get anywhere, and now no phone. What was I thinking coming out here to the middle of nowhere! How dare he leave me here with no place to go. I have never in all my life been treated this way, and I will not now. He will have to come back and pick me up. And if he thinks for one minute that I am going to load my own luggage into the back of that Jeep, he is mistaken."

Anna watched as he continued to drive down the road. Just before he got out of sight, she saw him turn the Jeep around. He came speeding back, leaving a dusty trail behind him. She did not move as he slammed on brakes and stopped inches from where she stood. Anna stood her ground.

"You get in Jeep now!" By now, it seemed the man had had just about enough.

"Are you going to get my luggage?"

"You get luggage."

"I see you have no use for manners. A man always carries a lady's luggage."

He got out of the Jeep and slammed the door shut.

Well, he will have to get over it because I am not going to get the luggage. I am sure he was paid enough for this job, she thought as he walked past her, mumbling, "White women, lazy, stubborn, weak. No good here."

"I beg your pardon? I'll have you know that I am not lazy, weak, or stubborn. Okay, maybe a little stubborn," she conceded.

He started loading the luggage into the Jeep, looking inside each piece as he did.

"What do you think you are doing? Those are my private things. You have no right to look in them." Anna walked over to him, grabbed the top of the trunk he had opened, and slammed it shut, almost taking his fingers off.

"Just take most important," he told her.

"All my things are important. You need to stay out."

After he loaded the luggage, he walked over to Anna, picked her up, and threw her over his shoulder.

She kicked and screamed, "Put me down!"

He deposited her onto the passenger seat, secured her seat belt, and then slammed the passenger side door shut.

"You ready now? Anything else you need? We go now?"

"Yes, I am ready, but don't you think that was a little extreme? I could have gotten in by myself."

"Woman, I asked you many times. You no come. Extreme? No."

Once they were on the road, Anna tried to put her window up to keep her hair from flying all around her face.

"Can you please put my window up?" she asked as she tried to control her hair against the wind.

"You no need window up."

"I do. The wind is blowing my hair too much. There must be a button somewhere."

"No button. You turn handle."

Anna reached for the handle and turned it, but nothing happened. "It is not working."

"No, never has."

She gave him a harsh look and said, "Why didn't you just say that?"

"You no ask."

"Are you always this rude?"

"I am me. This what you get."

Anna was not too sure about him. What was his problem? She had not done anything to him for him to treat her this way.

After about an hour on the long, winding, dusty, and bumpy road, he started throwing the luggage behind him out of the Jeep.

"Stop!" she shouted. "What do you think you are doing?"

He said nothing and kept throwing the luggage out.

"Stop! Stop! I said you have no right!"

"You no need."

"Yes, I do!" she yelled. "I need all my things. Who do you think you are? Stop now!"

He continued to dispose of her luggage piece by piece. She was so mad, she was shaking. She knew that this was going to be a long, hard trip, and she hoped the other people would not be as disrespectful and rude to her as this man was. She had never met anyone like him before. He was easy on the eyes but had no personality whatsoever.

They had both been silent for a while when he said, "I am Mat."

She still had nothing to say to him. But eventually, she turned to him and said, "You can call me Anna."

He told her they still had a long way to go. He turned down an off-road trail that went deep into the woods. Having grown up in the city, she had never seen a place like this. It was dark, cold, and scary. She suddenly felt afraid that she would never get out alive. But, being a proud woman, she was not going to let him know how she felt. He already thought he was better than her, and she was not going to accept that.

After a long distance, the road led them to a dead stop at a barn and stable. She knew it was the end for her. There she was, deep in a forest with a stranger who already did not like her. What would he do next? She went to check her cell phone. Still no service. Mat got out of the Jeep, opened the barn door, got back in the vehicle, and drove it inside.

I should have never gotten into the Jeep. I knew this man was not my ride and up to no good, Anna thought. Her friends had warned her about people getting picked up, abducted, tortured, raped, and killed, and there she was, in a place like this, with some stranger. Why had she come with him? Why had she not listened to others? She had always done what she wanted, and now it was time for her to learn a lesson.

Mat disappeared further into the barn, and Anna got out of the Jeep to retrieve what pieces of her luggage remained.

A few minutes later, he returned with a saddlebag, which he threw to her, and said, "Here. Only take what you need."

"What do you mean? I need all of this and what you threw out."

"No need," he said. "No time. Must go now. You pick or I pick."

She knew he meant business, so she started to stuff the saddlebags with as many of her personal items as she could before he stopped her.

"We go now!" He grabbed four outfits and handed them to her. "Enough!"

But before she left, she grabbed a piece of her camping gear. He nodded in acceptance.

Outside stood two horses, packed and ready to go.

Anna looked at the horses and then back at him. "What is this?"

"We ride the rest of way."

"I do not think so."

"Yes, we go now."

"I am not riding a horse."

"Then walk. I no care. Will take longer. We reach river by dark."

"I cannot ride dressed like this." Anna wore high heels, a black blazer, and khaki slacks.

Mat took her by the hand and pulled her back into the barn. He went through her luggage and handed her a pair of jeans, a shirt, boots, and a jacket.

"Here, wear this. Dress now."

Anna looked at him and rolled her eyes.

"What wrong now? Get dressed."

"Well, are you going to leave?"

"You dress now."

"I am not going to dress in front of you. You will have to leave."

"Why? I see woman before. I no leave. Get dressed now."

She folded her arms, shook her head, and stared into his eyes. He shook his head in resignation and went outside. When Anna was dressed, she came out of the barn and stood by the horse. She knew she had no other choice and

Anna was setting up the shower. From the river, he shouted, "Stand next to fire. You be safe there."

She looked around to see why he was shouting at her. She did not see any danger from where she stood. "What? What is it? I know what I am doing, and there is no reason for me to be afraid."

Then she saw it, the most beautiful animal she had ever seen. It was a big white dog with blue eyes. Mat started shouting to scare the wolf away. Anna was not afraid of the dog. She got down on her knees and called the dog over. She held her hands out to the wolf, and it walked right up to her and licked the palm of her hand and her cheek. Mat watched in stunned silence.

Then in a calm voice he told her, "Walk away slowly, now. Keep your eyes on hers. Come backward to fire."

Anna looked at him and told him not to worry and that the animal was not going to hurt her. Then she waved the dog away. She shouted to him to let her know when he was about to come out of the water so she would be prepared.

"Come now!" he shouted in a very harsh voice.

Anna turned her back to him as he came out of the river. He walked right past her to get some clothes out of his saddlebag.

Anna closed her eyes and let out a scream. "Why did you not tell me you were coming over here?"

"Had to clothe," he replied. When he was finished, he said, "Done."

Anna opened her eyes. She could not believe what she saw. "What is that?"

"This I sleep in or nothing." He wore a leather flap in front of his hips, one in back, and nothing on the sides.

She was upset and told him that he had just better keep it covered.

He smiled and said, "If you insist."

"I do!" she said.

He walked over to her with a serious face, grabbed her shoulders, pulled her close, and looked straight into her eyes.

"Do you have problem hearing?" he asked. "Did you no hear what I said? You no listen. I told you go to fire. Very aggressive animal tear you apart."

"That dog? She won't hurt a fly. Wasn't she beautiful?"

"No dog, wolf. Spirit wolf. Very dangerous animal. You no get close. You no listen to me. What your problem, woman? If you survive in this place, you have do as I say."

Anna knew it was hopeless trying to get through to him.

Mat released her and then cleaned the fish and started cooking.

"What kind of fish is that?" she asked.

"I think you call it a catfish. Fish good dinner."

into his heart and give him peace. Forgive me for the things I have said or done wrong and for the things I think of in a wrong way. Help me find the strength to do your will. In the name of Jesus, I ask these things. Amen."

He looked at her with one eyebrow cocked and his mouth wide open. "I no touch you. I already told you. I no lie. Why bother you? You no trust me?"

"Mat, I do not expect you to know my beliefs, but try. My body is my temple, and my God tells me that a woman is to save herself for her true love. This love will be like no other, and there is someone out there for me. I have to keep searching. When I choose a mate, it will be for life. He and I will become as one. You would not understand. You seem to be free to all women. And besides, after today with the deer, I don't know if I will be able to trust you again."

"I no ladies' man, as you call it. I am man. I have needs and desires. I no dead. I too believe in true love. I also believe in soul mates. The deer is not up for discussion. We needed food, and the spirits sent it to us."

"Really? Your spirits send food to you like that? And if you are not a ladies' man, why have you been sending messages to me as if you want me."

"I do want you. But I take no woman unless she wants me too."

"I have already told you that you cannot have me."

"Yes, I know. That's what makes it so hard. I know you feel same feeling I have for you. I feel it. Why you resist?"

"Because it would be wrong. It would not be for life, only pleasure."

"What wrong with pleasure?"

"Love stays forever. Pleasure ends when you find another."

"I have true love."

"Really?" she said, surprised.

"Yes, my wife. We loved much. Grew up together, played together. When became of age she mated and we married. She died bringing child into world. We have son, now fourteen, soon to be man."

"How so?"

"When boy fifteen, he no longer child. He leaves mother go with men hunting and fishing, trains to fight, takes a wife. Every woman promised to man."

"Were you promised to your wife?"

"No. This why spirits punish me, for breaking rules. They took her from me. With her, different. We close. Everyone knew we soul mates. I miss her much. I no take another. She my one and only but still have needs. I think of her always."

"You said your wife was mated. What did you mean by that?" Anna asked, looking puzzled.

"You no understand."

"Try me," she said.

"Our life different than yours. You no like what I say."

"Try me anyway."

"When girl begins bleed, she taken to mating ceremony. Here she opened up by the maker in front of tribe."

"Opened up? I do not understand."

"The maker enters her body, make way for her man."

"Are you serious? Do you mean when a young girl starts her first period?"

"If that what you call bleed, then yes."

"That is rape and wrong," Anna said.

"When bleeds, the maker enters her. No wrong. She agrees. Rape forbidden, punishable by death."

"What if she does not agree?"

"She protected from all men until she bleeds again."

"So you let another man enter your wife to make it easy for you to have sex with her?"

"Sex? I no understand."

"When a man enters a woman or, as you say, has his way with her, that is what I call sex. That is crazy and wrong. You let it happen? A man should have an untouched woman, and he should be untouched until they unite."

Mat did not tell her everything he knew, for she would not understand and it was not the right time. He knew she would find out in time. He would deal with it then.

"How old was your wife when she was mated, and who is this maker?"

"My wife was eleven when mated and married. The maker is the chief or acting chief."

Anna's jaw dropped. "Eleven? She was just a child! She should not have anyone touch her until she was at least sixteen. She became with child before age twelve?"

"You no understand. She bleeds," he said.

"I understand that your wife was a baby and too young. Her body was not mature enough for this mating. I understand that your wife died during childbirth. She was too young. It takes years for a woman's body to prepare for childbirth. I feel your sorrow. It is heavy on your heart. You blame yourself even today."

With a tear in his eye, he whispered, "Every breath I take."

Anna could feel his pain and felt bad for scolding him. She said in a calm, compassionate voice, "I am sorry about your wife. I should have been more sympathetic to your feelings. I had no right. You cannot blame yourself. You could not have known that she would die. I am truly sorry for your loss."

"Me too," he said quietly. "Spirits took her away from me. I no obey the spirits. I am punished all my days."

"You cannot believe that. It will take time for your heart

to heal," she said. "The chief is a grown man and is too big for a girl that young. How old is the chief?'

"Father, the chief, is over sixty."

"He is too old for a girl's first time."

"When Father's firstborn son turns fifteen, he becomes maker. When his first son turns fifteen, he becomes maker and so on. The maker usually between fifteen and thirty, unless the maker is unable to perform his duties for some reason, and then goes back to the previous maker. He no mate now. Once firstborn male becomes man, takes over until his first male child becomes man."

"What if they become with child during the mating?"

"Once they opened, they now women, send to women's hut. She protected from all men until bleeds again. If bleeds, she returns to family and mate chosen for her. If no bleed, she stay until child born and both branded with the maker's brand to prevent intermarriage. The maker's firstborn male comes from wife. Only maker has right to take on important ritual. Child created from love. Mating duty of maker; there no lovemaking. Quick and cold when opening a girl as she become woman."

Mat continued, "The maker helps man better passage with wife after healed. If father still living, boy turns fifteen, becomes acting chief until he takes on role of chief. He trained hard to be leader. Father highest of power. Acting chief second in line for control of tribe. Both respected and powerful. You no cross them. Will be punished. I no stop that. You no go against our way of life."

"What will you do to me if I do? Spank me?"

He gave her a serious look. "No, not I. Elder put you on whipping pole. Do what Father say. He sets punishment."

"Like what?"

"Lashes with whip. Not pleasant, even take life. I no expect you understand. Our customs been part of life for generations. You no change our customs. We do as taught. We no want make spirits mad. We honor spirits. Our land sacred. Woman, I fear you no survive long stay with our tribe. You need go back home."

"I am a big girl, and my mission in life is to make the world a better place. If I have anything to say, these customs of yours will stop."

"Good thing you have no power in tribe."

"We will just see about that," she said. "Listen. Did you hear that? What is it?"

"Wolves. You hear them at night. I have only seen one three times. No, five times, counting last night and today. I saw one when my mother died, when my father died, when my wife died, and two times with you. I have never seen one up close, yet you had one lick your hand. The white one special. Alfa female. She rules the pack. We believe she has spirit."

"Ha! Man not over female in wolf pack. Just something to think about," she said politely.

"We talk enough tonight. We have lot travel tomorrow. You lie with me now."

Anna did not resist this time, but she did, however, leave her bra and panties on, and he wore his flaps. She lay down in his bed, and they lay together, holding each other. Her head rested on his chest and her arm was draped across his waist. She could smell his scent, sweet and musty with a hint of leather. It made her weak.

It was not long before she drifted off to sleep. But not him. Mat held her tightly. He knew he was falling for her, and he felt the danger that lay ahead for them if she stayed. She had a strong will, and once she made up her mind, there was no persuading her otherwise. Not only would it be bad for him, but it would also be bad for the tribe. But change was coming, whether they liked it or not, for them both, not to mention the feelings he had for her. He knew she felt the same. They were feelings he knew he was not willing to give to her in order to save his soul.

He lay awake as he held her close. Anna was in a deep sleep. He could tell she was dreaming. She began to rub his chest and then her hand slowly went to his front flap. He didn't make a sound for fear of waking her and because he had not felt a woman's touch in nearly fifteen years. He felt great joy and pleasure as she touched him. He tried to be quiet, but it was more than he could handle.

He knew not to betray her trust, so he refrained from touching her. He wanted her to come to him on her own and not in sleep. He did nothing and lay still. He experienced such pleasure that he gasped. Just as he was about to reach his peak, Anna opened her eyes and jerked her hand back.

"I am so sorry," she said. "I had no right."

"No! Don't stop," he said, gasping for breath. "You no stop."

She could tell he was about to reach his release. He was holding his breath, sweating, and making sounds.

"No! Don't do it," she said.

He tried hard to speak, catching his breath after each word. "I ... can't ..."

"Yes, you can. Stop," she said and elbowed him in the side.

"Ouch! Why do that? That hurts."

"It made you stop, didn't it? You should have not let me go that far. You should have stopped me."

"Why? You enjoy. I enjoy," he said.

"No, it is wrong."

"I no complain."

"You should." She apologized once again and turned her back to him. "Now, do not let me do that again."

He whispered, "You will be mine."

She whispered back, "Men are so weak."

Then they both fell asleep.

Chapter 4

Day 3

It took great strength, but they kept their hands to themselves for the rest of the night. Since they both wanted each other, they knew it would eventually be impossible.

Mat still grieved for his soul mate, Kati, and this girl, Anna, would only be staying for a short period of time. He had no hopes of having a relationship with anyone other than his soul mate. Yet there was something about her.

Anna could not get what had happened that night out of her head. How and why had she done that to him? She was going to have to be stronger, but there was something about him—his scent, his stature, his beautiful long hair, his voice, his strength, his authority—that kept drawing her to him. She felt as if she had known him at one time. But that was impossible; she had never traveled outside New York.

Mat woke just before dawn. He had an uneasy feeling that he was being watched. He knew this part of the trail would be difficult because it went through land inhabited by another tribe. They were not like his tribe. They were more aggressive. He knew he would have to be alert if they were going to survive.

He slowly nudged Anna to wake her up. She rejected his gesture and rolled over to go back to sleep. But the feeling of being watched was strong, and he knew they needed to leave soon.

He put on his clothes and started packing up. Then he whispered to Anna, "Wake up."

"No! It is too early," she said.

Mat insisted in a stern voice, "No, we go now!"

She could feel the tension in the air. "What is it?"

"Nothing. Get dressed. We leave now."

He continued to look around and listen intently to their surroundings. She started to get concerned. He had never acted like this before. He knew something and was not telling her.

"What is it?" she asked.

"*Sh*. Dress now," he said.

He went to the saddlebags and removed a leather pouch. Inside the pouch was paint. He painted his face from his forehead down to below his eyes black. Directly under the black, he painted a strip of white that ran from ear to ear. Below the white, he added red stripes that ran down his cheeks and neck.

"What are you doing?" Anna asked.

"I put on war paint."

"War paint? Why?"

"These parts of trail dangerous. If meet another tribe, they know where I stand."

"And where is that?"

"Black means death. I strong warrior. No 'fraid to die. Strong, worthy, powerful, and aggressive. Have power, high rank. Red means blood. No 'fraid to shed blood. Fight to death. White means come in peace. All together show I no 'fraid to shed blood today. We come in peace."

"Wow! That is what the paint means, that you are a great warrior and not afraid to die today? Should I be worried?"

He went to her and placed his hands on her cheeks. "Anna," he said in a soft, compassionate voice. "I need you listen and obey me. Must do as I tell you. No talk to them. No resist. Follow what I say. No speak. I mean it. Very bad people. They hurt you. You white woman. White meat good. They take you away, have way with you, then roast you."

"Can they do that? Roast me? Like for dinner?" she said.

"Yes. I no lie. Bad people. Please do as I say. If things get bad, you may do something you feel strongly against. We live if you obey. Please do as I say."

"Will it hurt?"

"No, you enjoy. Please, Anna. For once, do as I say. Only hurt pride. Will get over it and we live."

She knew he meant business, for he had never called her by name before. "What do you need me to do?"

"Obey. Keep mouth closed."

"I don't like this," she said.

"No do I. If want to see another day, we must. In this life I live, we make sacrifices to maintain our lifestyle. Today you sacrifice to live."

He looked up, listened closely, and sniffed the air. "They here. They watch closely. If we lucky, they come talk.

"If we are not?" she said, now beginning to feel scared.

"They attack. Anna, forgive me now. You hate me when over. We need higher powers to work together so we live. No look. We know they here. Pray."

They both got down onto their knees, and he did his chant while she prayed quietly. Then he looked at her and said, "We look as we are one. No fight with me. They watching. Anna, you kiss me, and mean it. They see us together."

Anna looked at him and said, "Is this a trick to get close to me? I knew it. You will do anything to get me."

"No, Anna, please. You make advances. Otherwise, they think I force you. You know I no do that. You must be genuine."

Anna knew if she kissed him she would not be able to

stop and he would want her even more. "Please, Mat, do not ask me to do that," she said in a soft voice.

"You must if we have half a chance of getting out unharmed."

Anna pulled herself together, closed her eyes, and said a little prayer to herself. Then she placed her hands on the sides of his face and kissed him. It was long and deep; she could not stop. He kissed her back with just as much passion. She pressed herself against his chest, and her hands traveled all over him, as did his on her, until he whispered in her ear, "Stop, Anna, before I take you right here."

She had to force herself to stop. As she pulled away, she looked into his eyes.

They mounted their horse and rode off. They had not traveled far before five men appeared on horseback. Anna gasped. They were the most frightening men she had ever seen. The one in charge looked like the devil himself. His teeth were sharp, he had a bone through his nose, and his fingernails were long and black with dirt. They were all covered in red paint as if they had rolled in blood. To her it could have been blood, for they smelled of death.

Mat held her tightly. "Please, Anna, do as I say. No speak."

She was so frightened that she began to shake all over and gag from the smell.

"Be strong," he whispered softly in her ear.

The leader came up to their horses and spoke in a language she did not understand. He and Mat exchanged words, loudly at times, and once, weapons were drawn. She knew there was going to be a fight and she and Mat were going to lose.

The one in charge looked Anna up and down and sniffed her. "You his?" he asked in English.

Mat spoke up, "Yes, she mine."

Anna looked over her shoulder and into his eyes. "Yes, I am his and he is mine."

The leader of the band of Indians turned to Mat and said, "Prove it. Drink her wine."

Anna was confused. She knew she did not have any wine. If Mat did, how could he not share with her? She looked back at Mat. "You have wine?"

"Anna," he said gently, looking into her eyes with sadness. "Not that wine. Forgive me." Then he whispered in her ear, "No object or rebel. Let happen. We talk later."

Anna knew something was going to happen that she was not going to like, but what choice did she have? She started to feel sick to her stomach.

"I sorry, Anna. Forgive me," he whispered again.

Mat leaned her back softly to his side as they sat on the horse and unfastened her jeans. Anna started to reach to stop him and gave him a cross look, but she knew his eyes were telling her no. He slipped his hand down the front of her jeans and pressed two fingers into her body. She gasped.

"*Shh*," Mat whispered.

He pushed his fingers deep inside her, all while watching her eyes. Her eyes widened.

He said, "Relax. Let it go. Let it come." He knew this was her first time and he needed to go easy.

Her breathing became heavy, and her heart raced. She could not be still; she moved at the pleasure. She had never felt anything like it before. She began to sweat. She could feel him inside her. He moved his fingers in and out, all around, fast and slow. She did not know what to do. The intensity continued to rise for Anna.

Mat whispered, "Let it come, Anna. Let it come. You can do it, and it will be over."

She did not know how. She tensed and squeezed his leg, hard.

"Anna, you hurt me. No so tight. My leg."

But she could not hear him. Then it came over her, the most pleasurable moment she had ever experienced. Her body went limp.

He removed his hand and cleaned his fingers with his lips. Then he reached over and kissed her to share the wine with her. All Anna could do was look at him; she was frozen.

He could still feel her heart pounding as she shivered, still trying to catch her breath.

What just happened? she thought. She could see how sorry he was for doing that to her as a tear fell from his face.

The one in charge nodded. Mat returned the nod, and they left.

As they rode along, Mat looked at Anna and said, "I sorry. We talk of this no more."

Anna refastened her jeans, leaned back against his chest, and began to cry. Mat did not know what to do.

"Please, no cry. That hard for me too."

"Sure it was," she said.

"No harm done," he said to her.

"Maybe not to you. You have ruined me." Anna felt sick to her stomach. "Do you have any idea what you have done to me? Now I am a touched woman."

"Anna, you understand what they do to you if I no do that to you."

"Yes," she said. "But it does not erase the fact that I am now a touched woman."

"Anna." He held her tightly. "You were already touched woman."

"I was not! How dare you say that!"

"Yes," he said.

"What makes you think that?"

"You open."

She looked back at him sharply. "What do you mean open?"

"You open, no tight. Untouched woman very tight. You not. Anna, you have had a child."

"I have not!"

"I 'fraid you have. Once open, still some tight. Have child, completely open. You completely open. Trust me. You had child."

"How is that possible?" she asked. "If that was the case, would I not know that?

I have not been with a man before, and what you just did was my first time, I promise."

"I 'fraid not," he said.

"Well, maybe it is because I am white. White women may not be as tight as Indian women."

"I have been with white woman. They are same."

"You have been with a white woman?"

"Yes, just one white woman."

"Is that how you learned to speak English?"

"Yes, and I went to white school for two years."

"So that is how you learned to drive that piece of junk?"

"Yes. No piece of junk. It does job. And I teach tribe what English I know. I am what you call liaison from my world to your world. I go into town sometimes to get supplies and sell goods."

Anna thought about what he had told her. Then a she sat perfectly still, as if in a trance.

"Anna, Anna, Anna, are you okay?" She could not hear him. It was as if she had drifted into another place and time. Finally, she jerked. Mat held her tightly to keep her from falling off their horse.

"What just happened?" he asked.

"I do not know," she said. "I saw my parents, their faces, both covered in blood. I could not see the car. I know they were killed in a car accident, but I cannot remember. I saw myself as a young child. I have been with my grandfather ever since."

"How old were you when parents died?"

"I was twelve. But I just saw myself as a small child. How could this be? I remember my grandfather taking me home when I was twelve but nothing before the accident."

"You no remember?"

"I do not. I was in the car with them, and I got hurt. I was told that I was out for many days. I do remember being there when they died, but nothing else. I had some head trauma. Do you think someone took advantage of me before the accident?"

"I not know, Anna. Something happened to you. It very obvious."

"I have been living in a fantasy world all my life. How could no one have told me?"

"No, Anna. You have dream and high standards. You were child. No man reject you for that. You still search your dream of soul mate. I know there of such thing. You no give up or lower morals. This I admire you for. Stand up for what you believe. This our way of life. We too stand up for our beliefs and take great honor in it. You are survivor. Stand tall."

He thought he would never say those words to her, but he had, and he realized how unfair he had been to her, not understanding her ways. Her beliefs were much like his; they would both fight for what they believed was right.

"I not know why you been touched," he continued. "It no matter. If it true love, nothing will be able to keep you apart."

"But how do I explain it to him?"

"Just as you did to me, Anna. It would no matter to me. I would take you as you are."

"Sure, you would. But I feel unclean. How am I to get over that feeling? I am damaged goods now." She began to cry.

"Anna, please no cry. I no stand you cry. It be okay."

"No, never! I will never be okay again," she said. "What if I have a child out there?"

"I not know," he said.

"How would I find out?"

"What if you do? Will you take the child and destroy what he knows his entire life?"

"No, but I would like to know what the child was and if he or she was happy."

"You pray to your God to take good care of child."

"You are right. If I was meant to have a child, my God would see that the child was safe. Why would my family do this to me?"

"We not know for sure. Your grandfather did best for you. At that young age, baby may not make it. We lose many babies from young mothers. You need not worry yourself."

"You are right. Are you sure a man would want me now?"

"Yes, Anna. No question about that."

That afternoon, Mat once again got the feeling that they were being watched. He slowed the horses to a stop when the savages reappeared. Anna knew she could not do it again.

"Let me off."

"No!" he said.

"Please. I will not do that again. I will die first."

"You just might and take me with you. I no want to die today."

"I will take my chances. Trust me," she said.

He put Anna down, and the leader of the group got off his horse as well. He walked over to her to take her with him.

"We want white woman. We will fight for her," he said.

"No!" Mat said. "I will fight to the death."

Mat got off his horse to defend Anna. She held out her arm to hold him back.

"Anna, they no take you. I fight."

"No need," Anna told Mat. She looked into the eyes of the Indian in charge with a vacant look.

Mat watched her closely. *What is she doing?* he thought. She just stood there. He remembered the look on her face when had she talked to the deer, but this was not as compassionate. The one in charge stared back at her. The savage reached to take her hand and then realized he had better not. Anna seemed to be talking to the savage in his mind. He nodded as he backed up until he reached his horse, facing Anna all the way, and off they rode. He looked as if he had seen a ghost.

Anna turned to Mat and said, "Let's go. They will not be back today."

Mat said nothing, but he could not shake the questions running through his mind. What was it about Anna, and what powers did she have? He knew she was special. He didn't ask her about what happened that afternoon, and she didn't speak of it either.

Soon it was time to make camp. Anna ate apples again, for she still would not eat the deer he had dried.

"Anna," he said. "You must eat to keep your strength for travel."

"I will be fine," she said.

She did not have much to say to him the rest of that day. He knew it had been a traumatic day for her, so he left her alone with her thoughts. There was no way they would lay together that night, he was sure of it. After their nighttime prayers, which they did not share with each other, he made her a bed with all the blankets except one for him to sleep on.

She wore her sleeping clothes over the clothing she had worn that day. He too put on extra layers of clothing to keep warm. He went to the woods to sleep, knowing he needed to be as far away from her as possible.

Mat knew he could not sleep next to her again after tasting her wine. She was more attractive than ever, and there was no way he was going to be able to keep himself from taking her. She was going to have to leave and soon. How would he get her to leave on her own? He was going to need Mother's help. He did not know if he was strong enough to stay away on his own.

Before he was out of sight, Anna said, "Thank you for saving my life today."

He nodded in acceptance.

It was very cold again that night. Anna could not sleep after all that had happened that day. Her body had been violated, not just by Mat but also by some unknown person her grandfather had neglected to tell her about. She hadn't been an untouched woman, and now she felt unclean.

She prayed and cried for an hour before she started feeling very cold. But how could she be cold? She had plenty of blankets to keep her warm. *Mat!* she thought. *He is cold. I must go to him.* It did not take her long to find him. It was as if she was led by the spirits. She brought all the blankets and lay with him to keep him warm. He put his arms around her and held her tightly.

Half-asleep, he whispered very quietly, "I love you."

"I know," she whispered back. "Go to sleep now."

Anna still could not sleep, thinking about what Mat had done to her. She would never forget it. How could something she felt was so wrong feel so good? She felt even closer to him now. What was she to do? She knew he was sorry, but in the back of her mind she knew he had wanted to do it.

In the distance, she could hear the wolves howling and could tell they were getting closer. When she looked up, Missy stood next to her. The wolf lay beside her as if to comfort her and stayed there all night.

Chapter 5

Poison

The next morning, Anna woke to the sound of the eagles whistling in the morning sunshine. Missy had already gone back to her pack. Mat had been up for a while, building a fire to warm Anna when she got up. The mornings were always a little nippy for her.

While searching for wood, he had discovered some bird eggs and thought she might enjoy them, since he knew she was not going to eat the dried deer. She needed some protein; she had not had any over the last few days, and they still had many hours to travel today before reaching the village.

Mat had noticed the wolf prints around their bed and a spot where a wolf had slept when he first got up. "Anna, did you know wolves were here last night?" he asked.

"Yes, but just Missy. She slept beside me all night as if she was watching over me. How long before we get to the village?"

Mat just shook his head in disapproval and said, "'Bout

three hours. Come eat. I have something special this morning. I made eggs."

"Eggs? Oh yes, that sounds great. Thank you. You made them because you knew I was not going to eat the deer, didn't you?"

He smiled at her and fixed her a plate. Anna ate almost all of the eggs; she did not ask where he got them because she was so hungry. This pleased Mat.

"Tonight we celebrate your arrival. Anna, it going to be hard for you to understand our ways. We have many customs, we do things different. Try understand and not make a scene?"

"Yes, my grandfather warned me and asked me to be open-minded. I will do my best, but I will fight for what I think is right. You know I have strong beliefs."

"I am sure of that," he said. "That what worries me." He did not know how far she would go to protect the ones she loved and how strongly she felt about her causes. He knew she would want to change their way of life, and he did not know how his people would react.

"You need not worry about me. Remember I am a big girl now."

Anna walked around while Mat loaded the horses. She spotted a field of flowers in a clearing along the edge of the woods. They stood about four feet tall and had large yellow blossoms hanging down. She thought she would go check them out. She and Mat hadn't had a lot to say to each other after what happened the day before, so she did not tell him where she was going.

Mat always had an ear out to listen and make sure she was close, but suddenly all he heard was silence. He turned around, and she was gone.

Where did she go? he said to himself. His first thought was that the savages had snatched her. His heart fell from his body. Then he spotted her. She had wandered into a patch of flowers. His eyes widened and he shouted loudly and sternly. "No!"

Anna turned around and could not figure out what was going on. She had picked a handful of the flowers and raised them to her nose to smell them. They smelled sweet.

"Anna," Mat said in a calmer voice. "Put them down and come."

She just stood there.

"Walk quickly, drop flowers, come now."

"Why?" she said as she walked out of the field. She stopped and then she felt it. The flowers were burning her hands. "Oh, it burns!" she cried as her hands began to shake.

"Drop them," he said again.

"I can't move my hands. I can't drop them."

Mat took a blanket and covered her hands to help her

release the flowers. Even when he'd removed the flowers, she still held her hands out, shaking.

"They are poison," he told her.

"My eyes burn."

Then it was inside of her. The pain was so bad, she could not stand straight. She was shaking and crying out. He grabbed her, placed her on his horse, facing him so he would have a better hold on her, and rode off as fast as the horse could travel.

He prayed to Anna's God in his language. *Anna's God, please hear me now. I know you do not know me, but you do know her. Help us get there in time. If there was ever a time she when she needed you, it is now. In that Jesus guy's name she prays to, amen.*

He was so scared. Because of the feelings he had for her, he could sense her pain. It made him sick to his stomach. He could not stand seeing her this way. The flowers were deadly if inhaled, and she had smelled them. He knew he did not have much time if he was going to save her. He had to get her to Mother, and fast.

Why does she do these crazy things? he thought. *Anna, you will be the death of me.*

As they rode, she was crying and screaming. Then she started convulsing. Mat knew he was going to have to go faster if they were going to get to the village in time. He needed to get her to Mother before she stopped breathing. She held on to him very tightly as the pain coursed through her body. He did not know what to do.

"Anna!" he said. "Be strong. Hang on. You no die on me, you hear. I no let you. Stay awake. Anna! Anna!"

She did not respond. Then her body went limp. He looked down at her. She had stopped breathing.

"No no no!" he cried. He breathed into her mouth. "Come on. You have work to do in village. Breathe! Breathe!" he shouted. Still no response. "Anna!" He shouted and breathed into her mouth once again.

She gasped.

He held her tightly and began to cry. "Anna, please hang on. I need you, we need you, and our children need you."

She could hardly speak, but she had something to tell him. Her voice cracked as she whispered, "I know I am going to die. I need you to do something for me. In my things, you will find a box and some papers to give to your chief. They hold the key to everything. He will know what to do with them. Do not tell anyone about them or show them to anyone. The box and papers are for his eyes only. Promise me. I am dying, Mat."

"No say that. You no going to die. We have no come this far for you to die before we get there. You see chief and give to him on your own."

"Mat, be realistic. I am dying. Do as I say. Please promise me."

"No. You do yourself. Why you so stubborn?"

She started to scream again. "Mat, it hurts so bad. I am not going to make it. Promise me that you will do as I ask."

"I know it hurts. Hang on. I am sorry, Anna. I should been watching more closely. Have you not heard a word I tell you? You were told no to touch plants and flowers. Too many dangers out here."

"I am my own person, and no one is over me!"

"Anna, please, this no funny. I scared for you. You no die. Do you understand? You will not die."

Her body went limp again.

"Anna! Wake up! Wake up!" He shook her, but she would not respond, and again, she stopped breathing. He breathed into her mouth once more, and she began to breathe. This time she screamed louder than ever with pain.

"*Make it stop! Please!* I am sorry. I feel I have misjudged you," she said. "You are a good man."

As they neared his village, Mat sent out a bird call. He received a response and sent a reply alerting his people that he needed medical help and that they should get things ready because they were coming soon.

When they arrived, Mother and Teka, along with some other men, met them at the edge of the village. The men carried Anna to Mother's hut and placed her on the bed in the middle of the room. Mother was the chief's wife and a medicine woman. She instructed Teka in their language to take off the girl's boots and hold down her legs and told Mat to straddle the girl's waist and hold her body and arms down.

"It is devil's weed. She picked some and smelled them, lots of them. It happened so fast. I looked, and she was gone. There was no time for me to warn her. She inhaled a lot of it." Mat was concerned and scared. His eyes were full of tears.

"Son, what have you done?" Mother could tell by Mat's expression that something else had happened. She knew he was hiding something because he had not cared about anyone other than his family since his wife died, especially another woman.

Yet Mat seemed sincere and concerned about this girl. But why? They had not seen this girl before. Why was she here, and where had he found her, Mother wondered. Then Mother felt it, the spirit.

"This girl has spirit."

Somehow spirits found each other. Mother knew then she would have some explaining to do. Now was the best time to do it, while he was occupied with another and would not get mad at her for what she had not told him growing up. She hoped she would never have to tell him, but she was sure it would come up.

"She did this on her own. She no listen and does what she wants. I told her not to wander."

"Who is she?"

"Her name is Anna. Father sent for her. I do not know why."

Mother proceeded to pour medicine she had mixed into Anna's mouth, but Anna did not swallow, and more came out than went in.

Mother looked at Mat. "What have you done, son?"

"I have done nothing."

"Anna's body is resisting the medication."

"Mother, please, help her. Do not let her die."

Mother looked into Mat's eyes. "You have bonded with her. How could you do this? Do you know what that means?"

Mat looked at Mother. "Please save her."

"Son, it is not in my hands. It is in the spirits' hands."

"What you mean?"

"This girl has spirit. Somehow you two bonded. Mat, what did you do?"

Mother danced around Anna with shakers and lit a pipe to puff smoke on her body. Then she chanted to the spirits to heal Anna and spare her life. Smoke filled the room.

Chapter 6

Spirit

Mat looked ashamed. "I drank her wine."

"Why did you do that?"

"I had to. We met savages. They were going to take her and have way with her. Our lives in danger. I told them she mine. They no believe me. They make me prove it by drinking her wine."

"Did she resist?"

"No, I believe she enjoyed it."

Mother looked at him and said under her breath, "Who wouldn't?"

Mat sent her a disapproving look.

"The truth is truth. What woman not want you, son? Don't tell me you sealed the deal."

"How so?"

"With a kiss."

He said nothing.

"Mat, what have you done?"

Just then Anna became very hot and started shaking all over, fighting to get away. Teka was having a hard time holding her legs down. He noticed a birthmark on her left leg and foot that he had not seen before. Teka's mother had been white, but she had died at his birth. This was the first white woman he had seen, and he became very interested in Anna. He felt some type of connection.

"She is too hot," he said.

"We must undress her to cool her off."

"No!" Mat shouted. "She no like. She made it clear her body no be bare."

"I see, son. I fear she is of spirit, and her body is her temple. She will have to depend on the spirits to save her. When with spirit, the spirits decides if she lives or dies. All we can do is put cool cloths on her body. We can leave her clothes on. Teka, you cover her legs with cool cloths. Mat, you cover her arms. I will cover her face and neck. Now we wait. She is bonded to you and you to her."

"Mother, I cannot be bonded."

"She feels for you, and you feel for her. I can see in your face. The bond cannot be broken."

"You must break it, Mother. You must know of something to break the bond."

"Only the spirits can break the bond. Teka, run along. We have done all we can. Now it is in spirits' hands. Mat, if she did not resist you drinking her wine, the spirits allowed it to happen. Anna will believe you have ruined her and is no longer pure, now a touched woman."

"How so?"

"Her body sacred temple forced upon will surely send her to death."

"Death!"

"Her soul will die. By not resisting, the spirits allowed this act take place, therefore allowing you two to bond. To break the bond, she will surely die."

"Mother, is it not true that spirit must mate another spirit?"

"Yes, it has been said for thousands of years that spirit must mate with another spirit. If she rebels against spirit, then soul will die. I do not know what will become of what you have done; only Spirit will tell. She is young. It has been written that spirits are not fully matured until their thirtieth year."

"She is twenty-seven, Mother. She still has time to grow."

"If she already protecting body, she is maturing early."

"Mother, she been touched by man before."

"Are you sure?"

"She opened."

"How do you know this?"

"Mother, really, when I felt inside her, she was open all the way."

"You no tell her?"

"Yes."

"Mat, what did she say about it?"

"She said she not been with man before. She saves herself for soul mate."

"The spirit must have subdued her memory. Whatever happened, the spirit allowed to happen. We never question the spirits. She believes it; that's all that matters. If she believes she has been violated, she would have no reason to live therefore her spirit will die. Son, why tell a woman that? Now she feels unclean. No one want her this way. If I am right, she has strong feeling about that."

"She does. Mother, I felt life come out of her when I told her."

"Son, you have much to learn. There some things you no tell women. Women have a sense of pride. They want to be their best for their men. Here you told her she will never be."

"How do I fix what I have done, Mother?"

"I not know if you will ever be able to, son. The damage already done."

"How was I to know?"

"Son, you have feelings for one's well-being."

"I do have feeling for her, and I do not understand. I have

only known her a few days, but it feels like I have known her all my life. How can this be? I know nothing of her."

"Not that kind of feelings. You need to feel her spirit, keep it safe. Men think women have no feelings, but we do. She proud woman. Not being touched by man is an honor. Now you take away from her. What does she now have to live for? She feels unwanted, never to be wanted by another. In other words, son, she is dying inside. In time, so will the spirit. We encourage her, build her back up, and let the spirit do its job."

Mother continued, "Son, you must learn be more sensitive to feelings other than yours. Men very selfish, think of self, believe only matters to them, no think of others first. This girl thinks others first and then herself. She has high expectation for others and herself. She will stand up for what right and for others' rights. She will sacrifice herself for another. She feels strongly about happiness of others over her own. Tell me other things she do."

"She no listens. She hardheaded. She talks to animals."

"How she talk to animals?"

"Mother, she had the white wolf lick her hand. A deer was trapped, and she talked to deer with ease. The deer responded to her every word. She rubbed deer's back and had me come to deer too. I killed it. It devastated her. She refused eat the meat."

"She one with deer, my son. You destroyed connection by breaking her trust, her promise to animal that it was safe. The white wolf watches over her. Spirit could be past family's spirit. Very special. I feel you will see more of the wolf as long as she here. What else she do?"

"She connected to all animals, birds, even a spider. She no kill it but placed in safe place and then apologized for invasion of home. We met up with the savages again. They no believe us and returned to take Anna. Anna got off horse and stood there looking at them. Nothing was said, but they nodded and left. But look on her face is one I no want sent at me."

Mother became very quiet, deep in thought, and then whispered, "Great spirit? They can talk in one's mind. She has the spirit of life. Life very important to her. Quality, happiness, caring, and love mean a lot to her."

"Her scent is unbearable to me, more now than before," Mat said.

"You smell her?"

"Yes. It takes all I have within me not to take her. It hardest thing I have ever done, to withhold myself from her. It drives me insane. I have to keep my distance before I lose control. She is dangerous for me."

"You can smell her?"

"Yes. I can't get it out of my head. I have smelled it before but cannot remember where. It draws me to her. Like she put a spell on me. I have to be strong and pull myself together to resist her."

"When did this start?"

"The moment I saw her. I could not speak to her. I went into store for quite some time to pull myself together before I could be near her."

"Does she smell you?"

"Yes," he whispered. "While we lie together to keep warm only, Mother, I felt her smelling me, my skin and my hair."

"How did she react when she lie with you?"

"She no happy but accepted it."

"She is not all disobedient. She knows when important and make sacrifice for better good."

"What do you mean?"

"She will give her life for the ones she loves, will take pain from others if need be. From what you described, this could be great spirit. Taking pain is next to the greatest spirit. The grand spirit has more power than you can imagine. They return life and heal."

"I have heard of this. I thought it just a myth."

"It has been passed down through many generations that two great spirits together, their child could have great powers, the grand spirit."

"How is this possible? She is white."

"Spirit passed by a parent. One of her parents must had have some type of spirit in the bloodline. No have to be great spirit. Somewhere there was great or even a grand spirit. Someone in family, even thousands of years ago, had the spirit. She will sniff out another great spirit to mate with."

"So that is why she smells me. She is trying to see if I have spirit. But I no have spirit in my veins."

Mother was very quiet.

"Mother, why you so quiet? What you not tell?"

Mother looked at him and said, "Your mother was of spirit."

"No told me that. How could this be? I no have the spirit."

"But you do. It dormant in man unless grand spirit. Males can only pass to another with spirit. I have spirit of medicine. I no pass to your father. Father and I spirits too weak. Your mother had spirit. She passed it to you."

Mother knew she had to keep to her story about his father not having spirit even though he had and had passed it to Mat. Mat did not need to know that it was his mother who had had the great spirit. All he needed to know was that it was some type of spirit for now.

"If your mother had spirit, you must mate with spirit or your soul dies."

Mat thought about that for a minute. His wife had not

had spirit, which is why spirit was mad at him. His soul was dying. He had loved Kati so much that it would not have mattered to him whether or not she had spirit. He would have given his life to be with her for as long as the spirits allowed. His love was that strong, just as his father had loved his mother.

"You do have strong belief, bravery, and courage. You no 'fraid to die. You have way of knowing what needs be done and what lies ahead, just as you knew savages were there. You smelled them. Yes, the spirit with you. Your mother no understand spirit. Married your father without the spirit's consent. Her soul died many years later. She could no bond with your father. Her soul just drifted away."

"And my father?"

"He died of broken heart. He loved her much, just as you loved Kati. If Anna has the great spirit, she mates with another great spirit, and they create grand spirit, one that can return life. If Anna has great spirit, she will see future, see past, take pain away, stop you in tracks, talk to animals, calm the soul, get into your head."

"Kati could get into my head. She could talk to me even when I was away. Did she have spirit?"

"She could have, but she was so young, it would be hard to tell what spirit she had. If she did, then you are safe from spirit; you mated with spirit, and that is why they blessed you with child. It has been told throughout all generations that a day will come of grand spirit. This is the only time male can actively use powers. It is very important that a child, male or female, usually the firstborn, be raised in positive, loving environment. Their power be used for good. One who raised by evil has devastating powers. It like the evil spirit came to life, very powerful and destructive. This Anna needs to be careful of who she mates with."

"Mother, I feel she is good."

"Yes, I sense that, but she not been told what do if she rejects spirit. I fear she be trouble if stays here. She try to change things."

"She has already started a list, Mother."

"A list of what?"

"The mating ceremony, she said that will be gone. I am sure bare skin be gone."

"She has passion and respect; she will do as spirit tells her, my son. She strong beliefs. Will fight even if punished."

"I am sure she plans do away whipping pole."

"This why she must go. You need to stay far from her. Her spirit getting stronger. Her life in danger and ours, too, if she stays. You in danger of falling into her spell."

"How am I to stay away? She has hold on me I cannot resist."

"It is a hate-love relationship. She teases you," Mother

said. "You will find a medium. If you stay with her, she will have power over you. You will have to make her yours to protect her from the other men."

"How am I to stay away if I am going to be her protector? You know I cannot protect her that way. I already told her she will be mine. She tells me she is her own person and belongs to no one."

"She is right, but for protection, you make her understand. As a free woman, there is a power struggle between herself and spirit. The spirit must win. Your mother did not let spirit win."

"How do you stop it?"

"You don't want to stop it, for it was written many years ago. Your mother broke all the rules and gave her life for it."

"Mother, I do not want to take her life away."

"It important you keep her safe. You must make her yours, but must be at her own free will."

"I do it tomorrow. We let her rest tonight and celebrate tomorrow night."

"Be careful that she is not taken by another man, with or without her consent."

"What about our bond?"

"You will just have to handle it. Stay away much as you can. The spirit wants you there; there nothing you can do to stop it. As far as we know, spirit is using you to protect her until she finds her mate. She know not of her spirit. Has she said anything to you about having powers or spirit?"

"No. The only thing she said was that she had vision when her parents died."

"When did her parents die?"

"When she twelve, in a car accident. She was with them."

"Poor girl. To lose her parents so young must have been hard on her. I stay with her today. You will stay the night and all day tomorrow. Mat, this going to be one of hardest things you have done, other than losing Kati. You may be forced to do things you no want to do. I test her today to see if I right about the great spirit."

"What you look for, Mother?"

"Can she calm? Does she drift off into spirit world as in deep thought? She no tell you she sees visions other than the one about her parents?

"No."

"By what you have told me, she can see visions awake or in dreams. She no knows how to control or use powers she has."

"Mother, how she not know all this time?"

"In her world, they have medications for these type of conditions. The white people no understand spirit world. She could take something to suppress the spirit."

"Her medication," Mat said. "That explains why she upset when I threw away luggage."

"Why you throw away her luggage?"

"Mother, she had too much. No need for all that luggage."

"But to her, she did need her luggage. You have to understand you two from different worlds. You need to respect where she coming from; she has do same with us. We all have to work together to protect her."

"She did tell me I threw away medication she was stopping anyway."

"That would be the spirit talking. The spirit ready to come to her. She need time to understand the spirit. I fear we all in for awakening. This not going be easy for any of us."

"She needs go back, leave us alone," Mat said.

"It not that simple, son. The spirit may have other plans. The spirit pulling her here for some reason. I speak to Father, see why he summoned her. Look, her temperature is down. She calming down. Son, I like to try something. Go get a pan flute and play this old tune for her."

Mat was the music man in the tribe. He could play all types of flutes, drums, and many other instruments. He had different callers, rattles, and shakers. He was very good.

"If she has spirit, any spirit, it will wake her. She will know not of what she does and will not remember until the spirit is fully developed."

Mat left and came back with his flute. He stood by Anna's bed and began to play a slow, soft tune, one that touched the heart. It was an old tune that had been passed down for thousands of years.

A minute or so after he started to play, Anna's eyes opened. She stood up, went to him, and admired his attire. He was dressed all in black. He wore no shirt, only a bone breast-plate with many necklaces and a choker. He wore matching arm- and wristbands. Mother just stood back and watched.

Anna smiled a very gentle smile and stood in front of him. She wiped a tear from his eye and then turned her back toward him, pressed up against him, and laid her head on his shoulder. They danced together as if they were one being. Every inch of their bodies moved the same way. He wrapped one arm around her waist, pulling her against him as they swayed from side to side. He only needed one hand to play the pan flute, leaving his other hand free to hold her. He could tell she was lost in the moment. Her scent was stronger than ever. He knew that staying away from her was not going to happen; he was going to have to come up with another plan.

When he stopped playing, she sat on the bed. He could see in her eyes that she was not herself. She had that faraway look, as if she had drifted off into her own little world.

"It's the spirit," Mother explained.

All of a sudden, Anna closed her eyes and then opened them again and said, "What happened? Where am I?"

"This Mother, medicine woman," Mat said as he tried to speak English. "The flowers you picked were poison. You no listen. I warned you no wandering. You could have died."

"Good thing I had you to watch over me," Anna said.

Mat turned around, shook his head, said to Mother, "See, she is impossible," and left.

Anna looked at Mother. "I think he is a little upset with me. Hello, my name is Anna. Are you Mat's mother?"

"No, dear, I am the chief's wife. I am medicine woman. Chief is Father to all, and I am Mother of all. You will call me Mother."

"Thank you, Mother, for caring for me. Mother, are you like the doctor here?"

"Yes, honey, I am."

"Can I ask you something? Can you tell if I have been with a man before?"

"Yes."

"Could you check for me?"

"If you want me to, I can. Mat told me what happened with the savages."

"Savages? Ha, more like the devils."

"Yes, they can be. What Mat did different from being with man.

"Can we do it now? I need to know."

"Sure, if like."

Anna removed her jeans and positioned herself on the table. When Mother went to examine her, she noticed the mark on Anna's leg. Mother paused.

"Anna, how did you get this mark on your leg?" she asked.

"I was in a car accident. My parents were killed, and I hurt my leg. It has faded. All that is left is the impression. It does not bother me, except it produces scar tissue and shaving makes it smooth."

"Shaving? I no understand."

"I scrape, or cut off, the raised sections of the scar. It does not hurt or bleed."

Mother examined her. "I no see any evidence of you being with another man. You fine and healthy."

"But Mat said—"

"What do men know?" Mother interrupted her. "You have no been touched by another. We have cleansing ritual if you like for me to perform to ease your heart."

"Yes, you can do that. I think I need to be clean."

Mother gathered her materials and asked Anna to completely undress. Anna felt comfortable and did as Mother asked.

"Anna, I need you relax. Let all negative thoughts go.

Release them into spirit world. Let the spirit take over your body. Say nothing until I am done. You may even want to sleep."

Anna nodded, though she was way too anxious to see what was going on to sleep. She relaxed, and it felt good. Anna tried to keep her eyes open to watch what Mother was doing. She saw Mother place several clay bowls and some large shells around the room. She filled them with different herbs and plants. She also saw some stones. Anna watched Mother burn the plants in the bowls; they started to smoke.

Mother took an eagle feather and fanned the smoke toward Anna's naked body. She shook her rattles and shaker and reached skyward. Anna knew she was sending a blessing to the spirit to cleanse her. Mother took the stones and heated them until they were just warm enough to put on the skin without burning. She placed the stones around Anna's navel and between her breasts. Mother worked slowly and calmly throughout the ceremony, speaking in a language Anna could not understand, but that did not matter. Anna knew Mother was blessing her.

Mother spoke occasionally in English to tell Anna what she was doing and said the bowls represented water, the herbs represented earth, the feathers represented air, and the flames represented fire. Mother tapped Anna with the feather from head to toe.

Soon after Anna fell asleep, Mat walked in. He froze in the doorway at the sight of Anna's bare skin. Mother went to him and led him out.

"Son, this no place for you at this time."

"What are you doing to her?"

"I am performing a cleansing ceremony."

"We have no cleansing ceremony."

"Yes, son, you right, but she does not know this. We must make her feel pure again. If she is to continue to live, she must believe."

Mat shook his head and walked away.

Shortly after the ceremony was finished, Anna woke up.

"Thank you, Mother" she said. "You know I will never forget."

"I know, dear." Mother shook her head and began dressing Anna in tribal clothing. "You dress like us from now on, be part of tribe."

Anna wore a brown dress made from some animal skin. Tassels and beads were sewn onto the bottom of the dress and the sleeves, as well as around the neck. She looked quite pretty.

"Thank you. It is lovely."

Chapter 7

Father

After the cleansing ceremony, Mother took Anna for a walk to introduce her to the tribe. When Anna walked outside, she had to shield her eyes at the sight of the tribes people.

"Mother, they have on so little. I cannot look at them."

"We have no use for clothing. We not 'fraid to show ourselves to others."

"Mother, it is wrong."

Mother looked at Anna with disappointment.

"I am sorry," Anna said. "I do not mean to be disrespectful, but I am not allowed to look at a body that does not belong to me."

"I understand, dear. You will have to take this matter to Father. First, we visit the village. You need to know where things are so you can get around. You part of our tribe now, for as long as you stay."

"Sure."

Anna hid her eyes as much as she could to prevent herself

from seeing the people's nakedness. She visited huts and teepees; a person's rank in the tribe determined their type of housing. Men who lived alone usually lived in small teepees. Men of power, high-ranking warriors, and those who ruled the tribe lived in long huts. Mother had a large hut for her work as the medicine woman and lived with Father in the chief's large long hut.

Next they walked by the women's hut.

"Anna this is women's hut," Mother told her, "where all young girls stay once they become women and are ready to take on husbands."

Anna noticed how young the girls were. Some looked younger than ten. This bothered her, as she remembered what Mat had told her about the mating ceremony.

"Is this where the girls stay after the mating?"

"Yes. Mat told you about that? They stay until bleed again, and then they return to their families to take on mate. It is a custom that has been passed down for thousands of years."

Mother then showed her the food storage hut and the hut where they made clothing. There were also sheds where woodworking was done and where they made weapons. Anna noticed that there were no bathrooms.

"Mother, I did not see a place for personal hygiene."

"I no understand hygiene," Mother said.

"A place to bathe, a bathroom."

"We have none. We use river."

"Mother, where does one go to relieve themselves?"

"Down that path"—she pointed—"around the bend is where, as you would say, we relieve ourselves. We bathe in river every day."

Anna knew she could not do that in public, so she decided that she would take some blankets and rig up a spot that would give her privacy while she showered. All the women were topless and a few men had nothing on at all. Mother tried to assure her that it was okay to look, but Anna refused. She closed her eyes as needed.

"Can I see the chief now?" Anna asked.

"Not today. He out hunting will be back tomorrow. You see him then."

Lastly, Mother took Anna to a hut out by the edge of the village.

"What place is this?" Anna asked.

"This where the sick stay."

Anna's heart fell. She could not stand to see people suffer. Anna knew then where she belonged. She would help the sick and weak.

"Why do you put the sick way out here?"

"Many cry, upset villagers."

"How sick are they?"

"Some dying. Children won't stop crying. We believe spirit upset, causes one be in pain."

"Can I see them?"

Mother took her to see the crying children. Anna was heartbroken at the sight.

"Mother, may I stay here awhile?"

"Yes."

Anna spent only a few minutes in the sick hut before she went to get something from her personal items in Mother's hut. She returned with paper and a pen and drew a picture of a rocking chair. Anna went to the workshop, hiding her eyes so she did not catch sight of the indecent men walking around.

"Can you build?" she asked the craftsman.

The woodworker looked at the drawing and nodded. Anna stayed and helped him the rest of the day. It was getting dark when Mat came to fetch her for dinner and so she could get ready for bed.

"Anna, time to go," he said.

"No. I need to finish this tonight."

Mat stayed and helped. "What this?" he asked.

"You will see soon."

When it was done, Mat took her to get some food. Anna was impressed by the food they served and how good it was. They had a system. It was like a cafeteria. Each person went through the line and got all he or she wanted. As Anna looked around, she noticed that no one took too much, and they ate everything they served themselves. There was no waste.

After the meal, Mat took her to his hut. When entered, she knew he was special because it was one of the largest huts in the village.

"Do all warriors live like this?" she asked.

Mat felt bad for not opening up to her about who he really was. But it was not a lie, he thought, if he did not tell her the whole story. He knew she would not take the news very well and that he needed to handle her with care. So he only told her what she needed to know.

"No. I great warrior with high rank. I live here with my son, Teka." Teka had already gone to bed when they arrived and presumed asleep. "He sleeps in corner." He pointed toward the end of the hut. "You sleep this corner at other end of the hut."

Anna looked around the hut and saw that the walls were covered with all types of Indian attire—black, white, and brown leather and painted animal skin, some covered with lots of beading. There were also beautiful headdresses and matching arm- and wristbands. The headdresses were decorated with different feathers; some had just few feathers while others had many. One headdress was so long that looked like it would drape from head to toe. It was magnificent.

On another wall hung different breastplates made with beads, shells, feathers, stones, and bones. There were also all kinds of necklaces, and a bearskin robe that still had its claws. It looked scary.

He must be important to the tribe to own all this, she thought.

She also saw two white shirts and two pair of jeans like the ones he had worn when he picked her up. *I guess he does not have much use for them.*

She went to touch the headdress that hung all the way to the floor; it had hundreds of feathers on it.

Mat stopped her.

"Wow! Did you make these?" Anna asked.

"Most of them. Women help some but not too much."

"It took skill to make all these things; your people are very talented," she said.

"We learn for hundreds of years, passed down by our forefathers. This one used for special ceremony. No one touch. It with Spirit. I am music man for tribe. Have to wear for different ceremonies, war and pleasure."

Anna continued to look around and admired the hut. She could not believe how much work and love had gone into creating all the items. She knew he must be important to these people, but how important? She could tell that he had not told her everything. She knew that she needed to be patient and give him time. There was more to all this than he had led her to believe.

"Mat, where do you sleep? And it is not in that corner," she said as she pointed to her bed.

"I sleep in front of door for now, and when it safe, I sleep across from your bed."

"Why do you sleep there?"

"Anna, many men want you. They take you from bed. I sleep here, protect you. You a free woman for the taking."

"No, I am not."

"They know not and have right to claim you. I protect you tonight. Tomorrow we talk to Father, make pact, keep you safe. Tonight it is I. You no want be claimed tonight?"

"No, I do not, not ever. So you can tell them all what I said."

"Tomorrow we celebrate your arrival. Big party, lots of music. You dance all night."

"We will see," she said. "I am not much of a dancer."

"I teach."

"Is this another one of your games you play to get close to me?"

"No game. We dance."

"I would like to see Father when he comes in."

"Father sees you when he wants to see you. We no get him. He comes to you."

"I will see him tomorrow one way or another."

"Anna, please try understand our ways. Push far, get punished."

"On the whipping pole, I presume," Anna said, smarting off.

"Anna, this no lie. You need be careful."

"I am."

"I know, big girl. You no let me forget."

Since she had not bathed in two days, she asked Mat to put up her shower. He did, and this time she knew where to put the light so that she did not put on a show for anyone.

That night, they slept apart. In the middle of the hut, a small fire burned. She was glad to have heat for once.

"Anna, we sleep now. Big day tomorrow."

"Goodnight, Mat. I had a good day, and thanks for saving my life."

"Anna, sleep now."

Anna had just closed her eyes when she heard a sound outside. She whispered, "Mat, Mat, did you hear that?"

"No. I hear nothing but you talking."

"Listen. There it is again. Did you hear it?"

"Anna, please. We need sleep," he said.

"There it is again. Someone is out there making noises. Mat, I know you heard it."

Teka spoke up from his corner with a little giggle, "Yes, Father, what is that noise?"

"Teka, go to sleep," Mat snapped.

"Mat, what is that sound?" Anna asked again.

"Anna, it is night. People sleep."

"How can they sleep with all that noise? It sounds like someone is in pain."

"Trust me, they no in pain. Those sounds of pleasure."

"How can that be the sound of pleasure …? Oh, that pleasure."

"Yes, Anna. We make pleasure sounds one day."

"In your dreams. With all that noise, I don't know if I will ever go to sleep."

"Try, Anna. No more talk."

Anna tossed and turned all night, listening to the sounds of lovemaking. She could not see how anyone could sleep. She looked over at Mat. He did not have trouble sleeping. Neither did Teka. She had never heard sounds like this before. The more she listened, the more it sounded like music. Each sound was different. It was like they all had their own lovemaking calls, either in a chanting yell, a cry, or a song. Then she wondered what Mat's lovemaking call would be. She was sure it would be different from all the others. Mat seemed to have more prestige, power, and respect than the other tribe members.

After just a few hours of sleep, Anna could hardly wait to get dressed and get the chair over to the sick hut. She had Mat carry it for her and asked him to position it outside the hut door. She went inside and picked up the loudest and fussiest baby she could find. Then she took her outside and rocked her to sleep. Mat could not believe it.

"This baby cries all time and no one able to calm her."

Anna had an apple with her. When the baby woke, she took a bite, chewed it up, and spit the mush out into her hand and then fed it to the infant. The baby was about six months old.

"This baby just needs love and food. Not enough milk," she said.

Anna went to the baby's mother. She was so young. Anna showed her how to rock the child and how to prepare the baby food. She told Mat that this baby was not getting enough to eat and that her mother's milk was too weak. Anna asked for a piece of thin leather and a cup. She placed the leather over the cup, pushed the leather into the cup, filled it with some goat's milk, and tied the top. She then cut a very small hole in the leather to make a bottle for the baby to drink from.

"This baby is not sick," she said. "The mother and child can go home now."

She had learned a lot on how to care for babies from her work at the hospital. There was not one crying baby left in the hut when she finished her work that day.

Mat could not believe his eyes. At one point, Mother came by to check on Anna and saw what was going on. Mother gestured for Mat to come outside so she could talk to him.

"What is it, Mother?" he asked when they were outside the hut.

"See, she soothes the little ones. She has spirit to calm."

"Mother, how many spirits she have?"

"You told me, talking to animals, speak in mind, see the past, and now calming."

"How many can one have?"

"Depend on type of spirit. Most people with spirit have one or two. We see four so far."

"What others are there?"

"The spirit of taking one's pain, see future, bring one back from dead. Many, my son, many."

"Can one bring one back from dead, Mother?"

"Only grand spirit. The grand spirit is the most powerful of all spirits. No one knows how much power. Never been seen before. It said that one day grand spirit will come save us all. Oh, Mat, Father is back. I need to speak to him before you bring Anna."

"How long you need, Mother?"

"I will send for you."

Mother went to Father's hut and asked, "Father, what have you done? Why did you send for this girl?"

Father said, "I made an agreement with her grandfather. She has important news. If she is here, then he has passed."

"Is this the man who lets us stay on this land? Does she know this?"

"Yes, Mother. This girl holds future of tribe in her hands. I am sure she does."

"You know she has spirit."

"I thought she did. She still has years to mature."

"No, she does not. You must tell her truth. She is more powerful than you think. Mat and I have already seen four spirits so far. She is starting to see the past, and I fear once she does, you will have some explaining to do."

"She is not there yet. I will talk to her when time is right."

"Father, time is now."

Father became stern and raised his voice, "Time is when I say it is."

"Father, please no wait long. I fear you only have a few days or weeks."

"Can she take pain?"

"I do not know. She has not had pain to take. From what I know of her, it won't be long before she does. We are all in danger while she here. You must send her back."

"Does Mat know she has spirit?"

"Yes."

"Anything else?" he asked.

"No. They no get along. Their spirits are fighting."

"Good. Spirits know what needs to be done. We must respect that. Leave it alone."

"But she has the—"

Father held up his hand, silencing her. "Enough, woman. No more tonight. We have party to go to."

"She wants to talk to you now."

"I have no time for this. Talk later."

"Father, she will not accept that. She is very strong willed."

"I will give her a short moment."

"Good luck."

"I will send for her. Go."

It was not long before Anna found out that Father was back. She went to his hut and demanded that he see her. She was not going to wait any longer, and it did not matter to her what the guards told her. She was going to see Father now.

"Father, I need to see you now. I cannot wait any longer. I demand your attention."

"Who you to make such demands?" Father asked her. "I no be told who to see. I see you when I ready and not before."

"I have been stopped from seeing you since I arrived, and I will not stand for it any longer. I apologize for my rudeness, but it is of utmost importance that I see you at once. Please forgive me for my straightforwardness. May we talk now?"

"Please continue."

"I am Anna May. My grandfather has passed, and his last wish was for me to come teach your children and return this box to you." She handed him the box. "He said you will have the key and that you will explain to me what it is."

"No," Father told her. "I open box when time right. No today."

"Fair enough," she said.

"If your grandfather is gone, then you here for something else as well. I am sure it is about our land."

"Yes, Father. I now own the land, and I have been sent here to decide what to do with it, keep it or sell it. If I am to leave it as it is, I will need to see some changes. I do have one request that I ask right now."

"What kind of changes?" he asked.

"I am very offended when I walk out and see naked people. I was not brought up that way. I want all men and women clothed. Men can go without tops, and so can children, but not women. I will help the women create clothing for this."

"This I do," he said.

"Then I heard of this mating ceremony and the whipping pole."

"No. Your time up," Father said. "No. No more talk! We hold party in your honor."

"But, Father—"

"No more talk. One request today."

"Father, please."

"No. Go before I send to whipping pole."

Anna decided it was time for her to leave. Mat met her outside the hut.

"Is he for real?" Anna asked. "He is unbelievable."

"What he say?"

"He told me to get out or I would go to the whipping pole."

"Anna, he our leader."

"Well, he has not had to deal with me before. He will see it my way. Watch and see."

Anna went back to Mat's hut and ran into Teka, Mat's son.

"Hi," she said. "I am staying with you and your father for a few days until I get my own place."

Anna studied him; he looked just like his father, tall and

strong. His eyes were not round and black like his father's, but he was just as good-looking. Teka was stunned. He remembered how sick she had been just yesterday.

"You better I see."

"Yes."

"I was there when you came to village. You very sick."

"Mother fixed me."

"Mother no fix. The Spirits did. I am glad. I thought you going to die. I am getting ready for your party. We have great time tonight."

"My party?" she asked.

"Yes. We have good time tonight."

"Sounds great."

Mat entered the hut. "Are you okay?" he asked her. "You seem in better spirits now."

"Yes, Mother cleansed me yesterday. She said you had no right to tell me I was unclean."

"I no say you were unclean."

Teka looked at the two of them and decided this was not for his ears, so he went outside.

"I believe you were just saying those things so I would come to you."

"I no did. I tell truth."

"No. Mother examined me and said I had not been touched by another man. You were wrong."

Mat did not say a word. He just left and went to see Mother.

I do believe he said that to me to make me think no one would want me so he could have me for himself. He is a tricky one, and I have to be more careful around him, Anna thought.

She decided to take a short nap if she was going to party all night. She fell asleep as soon as she laid down her head.

Left all alone and unprotected, she was free for the taking. Little did any of them know, one of the savages they had met on the trail had followed them back to the hut the night before. He had hidden in the woods all night and day, waiting for the right moment. This was it. He went into her hut and saw her asleep on her bed. Before she knew it, he was on top of her.

She tried to fight him off, but he was too strong, and the smell of him made her sick. She had the opportunity to kick him where the sun did not shine, so she did. He doubled over in pain but still managed to grab her by the hair before she could get away. She screamed.

Mat had a feeling that she needed him and was already on his way to her along with Mother. He entered the hut just in time to pull the savage off her before any damage was done.

Teka came in as Mat struggled with the savage. She could see how strong he was. He was a great warrior. She had never seen him react that way before. He would fight to the death to save her.

Mat managed to break the man's neck; the savage fell to the ground, dead. Anna screamed in pain.

During the fight, the savage had stabbed Mat with a knife, and he was bleeding. Mother and Anna went to him.

"Anna, he is dying," Mother said. "The cut is too deep."

"No!" Anna cried. "No! No! Do something."

"I can't. Teka, come. You and Anna can save him."

By then Mat, had passed out on the floor from the blood loss.

"What you mean, Mother? We no save him!" Teka shouted.

"Yes, two of you can. If I right, it take both of you working together. It take both your powers to save him. Hold hands and touch his wound. Concentrate. Concentrate as hard as you can. Close your eyes and think of healing him. Bring him back before it too late."

Teka and Anna did as Mother told them. They held hands over Mat's wound and closed their eyes, and the spirits started to shine. Teka and Anna began shaking with the effort and soon both passed out on the floor beside Mat's body.

Mat was healed as if nothing had happened. When Mat awoke, he saw Anna and Teka on the floor. "Mother, what happened?"

"They both were knocked out in the fight, just before you killed the savage and passed out yourself. They should be fine in a few minutes."

When they woke up, neither could remember what had happened. Mother's suspicions had been confirmed, but she was not going to tell anyone. One of the two was a grand spirit and the other was a great spirit. It was hard to tell which one was which. Either way, they would both be in danger if the news got out. Everyone would want them for their powers. They both still had to grow and were not matured fully enough to protect themselves.

Teka and Anna were so tired that they slept until party time. Mat stood guard over them both.

Chapter 8

The Dance

After a few hours of sleep, it was time to party. Teka dressed in some fancy clothes, and a dress for Anna to wear lay at the foot of her bed. It was beautiful, with lots of tassels and beading. She knew it had taken someone a long time to make; she wanted to learn how to make something like it one day.

The all-white dress was hemmed to just below her knees, with tassels that hung to her ankles. The sleeves fell just past her elbows, with fringe that hung to her wrists. Halfway up the skirt of the dress was another row of tassels, each about three inches apart with two turquoise beads and quill feathers at the end; this layer of tassels hung down to the skirt's hem. The neckline was high and had a V-shaped row of matching tassels.

After pulling the dress over her head, she wrapped a braided brown leather belt around her waist. Tiny turquoise beads were sewn into the length of leather, and the beaded tassels and quill feathers that adorned each end hung to one side when she tied it. There was also a pair of off-white rabbit-skin boots with the same tiny beading in the shape of flowers that ran down the entire front of the boot.

The matching headdress was all white with tassels on each side that hung in front of her ears. The white feathers at the ends of the tassels touched her shoulders. Anna could not believe Mat had given her such a beautiful dress to wear to the dance. But she was not complaining.

Anna looked at Teka and complimented him on how sharp he looked. He smiled at her.

"My father gone to stomping ground. Asked me take you," he said.

"Why did he not take me?"

"He music man. Had things to get ready."

"Yes, he told me yesterday. Is there anything he cannot do?"

"No, not really."

"I get that. He thinks he is above all."

"He is," Teka said.

"Like father, like son, I suppose."

"I hope so. I would like nothing more than be half the man my father is."

She smiled. "He is pretty good, and I am sure you will be too."

"Yes, he is."

Down at the stomping ground, Mat met with Mother to discuss the musical arrangements.

When Mother saw the list, she protested. "The last two songs, son, I rather you not play tonight."

"Mother, you know I always close with them in memory of Kati. Tonight no different. I will play them as always."

Mother knew not to argue with him. He was serious about dedicating his performance to Kati even though she had been gone for almost fifteen years. Mother feared he would never get over her. It saddened her heart.

After Anna was ready, Teka escorted her to the front row, next to the stage. Anna noticed that Father had done as she asked; everyone was clothed. Maybe she could make a difference here after all.

Anna got herself some punch. She tasted it, and it was good. She could drink it all night. Some other girls came to sit with Anna. Their dresses were much like hers except they were brown. She did not know their names, but they seemed pleased to be sitting with Anna. Then it was time for the music to start.

Mat came onto the stage with all kinds of instruments. He looked down at the front row and saw Anna dressed in the white dress he had laid on her bed. He smiled at her and mouthed to her, *Nice*. He motioned for her to come onstage. She refused, and he smiled. She drank another cup of punch.

The music was fast at times and then slow. It was the sweetest sound she had ever heard. She started feeling the punch and began to sway to the music and have a good time. She reached to drink another cup of punch and then another. Mat motioned for her to stop drinking. Then he waved for her to come to him again. This time she did.

She was laughing. He took her by the waist and pulled her close to him so that their faces were inches apart. He began to sway back and forth and side to side, holding her in a way that left her no choice but to move with him as others took over playing the music.

He whispered in her ear, "Are you having good time?"

"Yes, you play so well. I could listen to you play all day and all night. I like what you are wearing."

He wore white pants and no top. The pants were covered in small beading that matched the beading on her dress, and lots of tassels. He wore three different necklaces, plus a choker and a bone breastplate. His headdress had white, yellow, and red feathers all over it.

"I like what you are wearing. Do you like?" he asked.

"It fits perfectly, and it matches yours."

"I glad you have good time. You seem to like drink."

"Yes, Mat, it is good. I could drink it all the time. It is sweet like honey."

They danced to a few tunes. There was a lot of chanting

in a language that Anna could not understand. Then the music stopped. Mat sent Anna to her seat.

"Anna, tonight I be honored with a feather for saving your life and killing the savage. Stay in your seat and do not interrupt. We have strict rules about showing respect."

Anna watched Mat stand tall in the middle of the stage as the elders and the chief chanted and danced around him. They shook shell shakers and puffed smoke at Mat. Everything was spoken in their native tongue. It was very impressive.

When they were finished dancing around Mat, the chief stood in front of him and presented him with a large feather. Mat knelt on one knee in front of the chief and bowed his head. The chief touched the feather to each of Mat's shoulders and then held it in his upturned hands, lifted it to the sky, and blessed both it and Mat. He handed the feather to Mat. Mat nodded as he accepted the feather. Then he too held it in his upturned hands, lifted it to the sky, and blessed it.

This is how he received all those feathers on the walls of his hut. I wonder if it means he has killed that many people. There were a lot of feathers, especially on the headdress that reached the floor, Anna thought.

Once the ceremony was over, the music started again,

and Mat motioned for Anna to come join him in the dance. She had been sipping punch throughout the ceremony.

"Anna, drink no more," Mat said.

"Mat, we have discussed this before." Anna was getting upset because he was trying to tell her what to do as if he owned her. "Who do you think you are? Do you think you can stop me? If I want to drink, I will drink! If I don't stop, what are you going to do, take me to the whipping pole or turn me over your knee like a child?"

"No!" he said. "Enough drink. I no playing. You have had enough. You will no like how you feel tomorrow. You have had enough, Anna. Trust me. I know what I say is true."

"I will decide when I have had enough." She broke free of him when the song was over, went straight over to where the punch was, and drank a full cup in front of him to prove her point. He shook his head at her and smiled.

The next song began, and again he motioned for her to come up with him, and she did. This time she danced around him, shaking things she had never known she could shake. He had a good time watching her. Then they started to dance together in the most erotic way. She closed her eyes and let the music take her. She'd had so much to drink that she had no clue what was going on.

Mat took Anna by the hands and stood face-to-face with her in front of the tribe where all could see. He took out two necklaces. He handed one to Anna and then he placed the other over her head and had her do the same to him.

Then they exchanged bracelets. The entire tribe was chanting and yelling. Anna was confused; she did not know what was going on, so she just went through the motions. After the gift exchange, they continued to dance.

"Anna, you need go back to hut." He motioned for Mother to come help.

Anna whispered in his ear, "Make me. I am a big girl, and you cannot make me do anything. If I want to dance or drink, I will, and you cannot stop me."

"I no responsible for what happens tonight," he told her.

"No, you are not. I am my own person. I can take care of myself."

"Like in hut today?" he said.

"That's not faaair." Anna could hardly say her word correctly at this point. "I was sleeeeping, and where youuu anywaaay? Were youuu not my protectooor?"

"I did protect you."

"I guessss better sorry late than … What?" She was getting her words all mixed up.

Anna danced some more. Then she said, "I nooo feel sooo well."

Mother was there to help her back to the hut. Anna could hardly walk, and she felt sick to her stomach. She stumbled and waved her arms as she tried to stay upright. Everyone was watching her and laughing.

Mat spoke to his people in their language to explain that she was not used to the drink and would be okay tomorrow. Just when she and Mother reached the edge of the stomping ground, Mat began to play the two special songs he had written and dedicated to his late wife, Kati, as he always did at the end of his performances.

Anna heard the music and stopped. Not staggering, in fact standing as if she had not a drop to drink, she started to dance toward him. She got close and gently brushed his arm from the wrist of one hand to his shoulder, across his back, and down the other arm—all to the time of the music as if she knew the song. It sent chills throughout him. He had not expected her to know the song or to touch him. He was not prepared.

He was on his knees, so she got down on her knees in front of him and sat eye to eye with him. Then she sang the song with him as if she had been the one who had written it. Word for word, not missing a note, she sang it.

How can this be? he wondered. He had created that song, and no one outside the tribe had heard it before.

He played the second tune, and she did the same dance around him. He was shocked. How was she doing that? She was serious, calm, and sexy. She kissed him on the neck, shoulders, and his cheeks.

He did not know if he should be mad at someone for teaching her these songs that meant so much to him or take her home to bed right then and there. At the end of the song, she danced backward, away from him and back to where Mother stood. When the music stopped, Mat ran to her and grabbed her arm.

"Where you learn songs? Who told you them?" He turned her so he could look into her eyes. "I demand you tell me now! Tell me!" he shouted.

"Stop, Mat!" Mother said. "Stop! Look in her eyes. She is not there. It is the spirit that knows the songs. Catch her. She is going to fall."

Mat reached just as Anna started to fall and caught her.

"Mother, you asked me not to play those songs. Why? You knew something was going to happen. I need to know. Now, woman."

Mother did not respond. Mat picked Anna up and carried her toward his hut. On the way, she threw up all over him. Once they were inside the hut, he placed Anna on her bed. Mother sent Mat outside while she undressed Anna, cleaned her up, and put her gown on. He went to clean himself up. When he got back, Mat put Anna to bed. Again, that night he slept by the door to prevent anyone from taking advantage of her. As he lay there, he listened to the wolves in the distance.

The next morning, Mat and Mother were standing over Anna when she rolled over and woke with the worse headache. She thought she was dying.

"Good morning, little princess," Mat said.

"Are you calling me a princess? You know better than that."

Anna started to get up but all of a sudden threw up. Thank goodness Mat had placed a bucket nearby for her to use. He held her hair out of the way as she threw up again. Mother wiped her face with a cool towel. Anna could not say a word and threw up again.

Mat said, "So how do you feel now?"

"Oh, shut up. Did you drug me?"

"You said, 'I am a big girl and you are not going to tell me what to do. I will drink whatever I want to drink.'"

Anna stopped him, holding her hand up in the air as she threw up again. Then she said,

"Yes, that sounds like me. Okay! Okay! I suppose you are going to tell me it is my fault entirely."

"You guessed it."

"Shut up. I thought it was only sweet fruit punch. The best I have ever had."

"Honey, it spirit water," Mother said.

"Spirit water? What is spirit water?"

Mat said, "Punch? Where you get that idea? I think it what you call moonshine or white lightning with fruity taste."

"Moonshine! White lighting! That stuff will kill you," Anna said.

"Yet here you with wonderful aftermath. I told you stop. Anna, you just no listen," he said.

It took Anna quite some time to get over her hangover. She knew she would never do that again. She could not believe he had let her go that far. But then again, he had warned her.

Mother helped Anna shower and get dressed. Some women were admiring the shower, so Anna showed them how to use it and let them bathe. Then all the ladies in the tribe started lining up at the door of Mat's hut. They showered her with gifts.

How sweet, she thought. They gave her a party last night and now gifts. What had she done to deserve this?"

She looked around and saw that there were no men. That was strange. *Yesterday men were everywhere and now not a one. What is going on?"* she wondered.

"Where are the men?" she asked the women.

"They with Mat, celebrating you becoming his last night. We excited that he has chosen someone after all these years.

You are blessed with the spirit to have Mat as your own. We have tried many times, but he no interest. The spirits on your side," said one of the maidens.

"What do you mean I am his?"

"Last night you danced with him. You exchanged gifts that joined the two of you together. Now you are his and no man claim you."

The look on Anna's face could kill. "He did what?"

"You his now. We bring gifts and celebrate."

That devil. Wait till I get my hands on him, she thought to herself.

She accepted the gifts and thanked them all for coming.

Just wait till he gets home, she thought. *He has yet to see my wrath. He tricked me and now he is going to pay for making me his.*

She saw him coming toward the hut, but he stopped to talk to some men who were walking with him before they parted to go into their own teepees. She marched over to them and got right in Mat's face.

"You tricked me! How dare you!" she shouted and tried to slap his face, but he caught her hand just before she made contact.

He picked her up, threw her over his shoulder, and carried her back inside the hut.

She kicked and screamed the whole way. "Put me down!

You have no right! You hear me? Put me down now! Stop this, I said! Put me down!"

Mat set her down on her bed as she pounded his chest with her fists and kicked at him.

"Anna, calm down," he said as he grabbed her wrists and held them.

"No. You tricked me. You did just what you wanted to do. You know how I felt about belonging to someone, so you tricked me to be yours anyway."

"I no force you."

"No, you just got me drunk so you could take advantage of me."

"I no touch you."

"Why not? Don't you like it that way? Women giving themselves to you? Isn't that what you like?"

"No, Anna, I no do. Calm down listen to me."

"No! You think I am damaged goods, so you took me as yours because no other would want me. Did you do that to make me feel better? Or did you just take what you wanted without any consideration of my feelings? How could you do that? I trusted you."

"Stop, Anna. Where this come from?"

"You told me the first day we met I would be yours. Okay. So now I am. Are you happy now?"

"Anna, stop!" His voice was stern. "Listen to me once.

Just listen. All women belong to someone. If no belong to man, anyone can take. I protect you. You no wife. I promise to look after you, keep safe, and keep in line. No man allowed to touch you now."

"Oh, only you," she said. "You have been all over me ever since you picked me up. What am I to think?"

"No, I no touch until you come to me. Not before."

"So this does not mean we sleep together?"

"Not unless you decide to. I no touch you without your consent. I claim you to keep others away. Trust me."

"I did trust you once, and you betrayed that trust. Are you sure?"

"Yes, Anna."

"And what did you say about keeping me in line?"

"What you just tried to do in public would cost you lashes. I bring you here. You no disrespect me in front of others. I guide you, but you have to listen and understand. I help you."

"Sounds like marriage to me. You had me dress in all white, and you wore white. What am I to think?"

"No, Anna. No. You think you protect yourself. You cannot. Look what already happened. Savage came into hut. He could have way with you. Nothing we could do to stop when free woman. Free women free to all, Anna. I no think you like."

"Okay, you are my protector. You cannot tell me what to do, what to wear, what to say? I am still my own woman? You cannot touch me in any way unless I tell you it is okay? You cannot force yourself on me? I can come and go as I please, and all other men will leave me alone?"

"Yes, Anna," he said.

"What about all these gifts?"

"You keep. That how it works. Okay? We good?"

"Good," she said. "You know you could have come to me and asked. If you had told me this before, it would not have been like this."

"Anna," he said, tilting his head to one side, "yes, it would. You stubborn and hardheaded woman. You no understand."

"You are probably right. Thank you for being willing to keep me safe while I am here."

But Anna did not like the idea of someone looking after her. She had worked so hard to be out from under others and to prove herself. However, she did feel safe when he was around, and he was not bad to look at either. He had also promised not to touch her until she invited him to. She was not sure how long that would be. She would have to be strong and tell herself no. She could not take the chance of being tempted; she did not know if she could resist.

Mat took her by the hand and placed a bracelet on her left arm. It was made of shells and beads and had a beautiful crystal gem in the center. He had one exactly like it for his arm. Then he picked up a thin leather necklace with another crystal that was about two inches long. He placed it over her head, and she noticed that he was wearing one as well.

"I gave to you last night in front of tribe. You gave me mine. Exchanging gifts joined us. You mine, and I am yours. You accepted gifts in front of tribe of your own free will. I did no force you."

"I remember something to that affect, but it is all a fog to me now."

"These you wear everywhere. They tell all men you are taken. If you approached, even if just kiss, man will be put to death. You mine long as you wear them. I no protect you if you remove them. Without these, any man can have their way with you and claim you. I no protect you then. You understand?"

"Yes, I understand. So if I remove them, I am free to all other men and they can take me. Is that not rape?"

"No, Anna. If you no claimed, then man can claim you with or without your approval."

"What if they took it off me? This does not seem to be a sure thing."

"I could brand you as I would if you mine forever. But I no think you would approve. So this best I can do now. If man takes off, you best fight. If you no fight back, then no rape and you become his."

He continued, "Anna, this our way. Just because you here for short time no does mean you no be taken. Some men have many women. It not common, but is approved. You special with spirit. If mated with wrong man, could damage you, even send death upon you."

"Okay, I understand, and I will not take them off. But I do not like to share. So you will do the same."

"Anna, do you always have last word?"

"What's fair is fair. If I do this, I expect you to do the same."

Mat just smiled and shook his head as he turned to continue his work for the day. Mat knew he was in for it soon. She was too much of a busybody to keep things from her. If only he could make it be a few more days before she found out the truth about him. He would have to be careful and deal with it later. Right now he had to protect her from other men.

Anna went to visit with others in the tribe and was not afraid. She went to see the children and had the craftsman make more chairs. She showed the women how to make clothes to cover themselves and told them how to drive their husbands crazy with love by not giving themselves on demand. When a woman gave herself to a man, it was for both their pleasures, not just his, she told them.

The tribe always ate meals together. As she sat at the table with Mat that afternoon, she watched Teka running in the valley. She admired how much he looked like Mat and imagined Mat at that age. Teka was chasing a girl of about twelve years old around the valley.

"They look like they are in love," she told Mat.

"Yes, she is promised to him once she becomes a woman, which should be anytime."

Anna did not hear the part about becoming a woman because that vacant look had come over her face.

"Anna, Anna," Mat said. He waved his hand in front of her face, and she did not blink.

After a few minutes, Anna was herself again.

"Anna, where you go?"

Anna shook her head and said, "I saw him running in the valley with a white girl. They had no clothes on."

Mat just looked at her. "A white girl? Who do you see?"

"Teka and his girl, they are running around the field. They have no clothes on. She is a white girl."

"Teka's mother was white."

Anna looked straight through him and said, "No! Wait. It is you, Mat, with a white girl."

"She fell from the sky. The spirits sent her to me. Her name was Kati."

"My mother's name was Kati. What a coincidence," Anna said.

"Kati was two when she came and stayed with us until she died."

"So that is why Teka is so interested in me."

"Yes, you first white woman he see. It always been mystery to him. Anna, Mother tell me you have spirit no developed completely. If you could bring one back to life, would you?"

"Like your Kati? I do not know. I do not believe in spirits anyway. But if I could for your sake, I would try." She took his hands softly in hers and said, "You are so lost without her. I cannot imagine losing my soul mate. I really wish I could bring her back to you."

"Thank you, Anna. That means lot to me to hear you say that. I believe you would."

Anna got up, kissed him on the forehead, and went to check on the children.

Chapter 9

Mating

After dinner that night, Mat took Anna for a walk around the village while it was still light.

"Anna, remember when we were on trail and I said you be mine? I hope you believe me that when I made you mine, I did protect you. You special to our tribe. I also told you that you would hate me and love me."

"Yes, I remember."

"Anna, there are things we do and have been doing for thousands of years. I no expect you understand now. I hope one day you will learn to respect and understand our ways. I will teach you when time is right. Please respect our customs. I only want to protect you. When you are ready, I will share with you those customs. You still trying to adjust. I feel you need time to understand little at a time. Too much may shock you. Can you be patient in my teaching? I need you take your time. I know you want to know everything now, but it too much for you to take in all at once. I fear it would damage you."

"Mat, I understand your customs are much different than mine, and I need you to understand mine too. I have had a wonderful day with you."

"I too," Mat said.

They had spent most of the day together, sharing stories of their childhoods, or at least what Anna could remember of hers. She did not have much to share before the accident. It had been so traumatic that she had blocked most of it out. She was starting to remember some things, but it was not enough.

It was getting late, so he took her to their hut.

"Anna," he said, "I need you stay in tonight. Please, no wandering. Council sees you, be punished if you come. Promise me." He took her by the shoulders and looked her in the eye.

She did not say a word.

"Anna, please stay in. You be death of me. I no protect you when you no listen."

Still, she said nothing. Anna knew something big was about to happen. Why else would he demand that she stay in? *He should know better than to order me around. There is no way I am staying in tonight. No matter what he says or does to me, I will be there*, she thought.

Knowing Anna, Mat had arranged for guards to stand at the door to keep her in that night. Anna knew what he had done, so she formulated a plan; she would have to sneak out. Being the curious person she was, there was no way she would be kept from the council meeting.

She opened the door just enough to throw something around the corner. Both guards went to check out the noise, and she slipped out. The guards had no clue she had gone and returned to guard the empty hut.

Men—they are so clueless. Who do they think they are dealing with? she thought.

On the way to the stomping grounds where the council meeting would take place, she saw one of the children dressed in a beautiful robe made of soft fur. Her name was Mayi. Mayi had helped Anna with the babies that day. Anna liked her a lot. Mayi seemed to know what Anna said even though she did not speak much English.

"Hi, Mayi. Why are you out so late tonight?" Anna asked.

Mayi smiled. "I become woman tonight."

Anna was so busy admiring Mayi's cape that she didn't pay much attention to what the girl said. Anna told her to have a good time and that she would see her tomorrow.

Anna sat in the back row to keep from being seen. Soon the music started, and people started chanting and yelling. When Mayi walked out onto the stage, Anna was puzzled for a moment. Then out came a young man dressed in a bear fur robe, complete with claws. Anna could not see his face; it was painted black. The headdress the man wore had a full mane of feathers that reached the floor. Anna thought they were going to dance.

Instead, they took Mayi to the center pole, where there stood a table. Mayi removed her robe. She wore a ring of flowers on her head and additional rings around her wrists, ankles, and belly. Other than that, she was naked. They placed Mayi on the table and tied her hands above her head. They spread her bent legs as wide as they could go and tied them so she could not move.

Music was playing, and everyone chanted louder and louder. The man removed his robe; his body was decorated with paint, and on his hands he wore bear claw gloves. He too wore nothing else except the headdress. Then Anna remembered the mating. Mayi was going to become a woman tonight.

Oh no! she thought. *She is only ten.* Anna's heart started to race. *No they cannot do this to a child! She is so small and young!"* her mind screamed.

This man was not the chief. He was much too young to be the chief and much too firmly built. Then she remembered the headdress and the bear robe on the wall of Mat's hut. The headdress was the one he would not let her touch because it was of spirit.

It was Mat. She had seen most of that body before. This could not be happening. *This is why he did not want me to come tonight.*

She stood up and yelled, "Stop!"

No one could hear her over all the chanting and yelling, so she ran up to the front. Two guards stopped her before she reached the stage. Mat looked straight into her eyes and showed no emotion. He only shook his head. Mat knew he had to finish what he had started. It did not matter whether he wanted it to happen or not. It was the way it had been for generations. The ceremony must go on. Mat entered Mayi's body to open her. She didn't make a sound.

Anna, on the other hand, screamed in pain. Every time Mat moved inside Mayi, Anna would cry out as if she felt Mayi's pain. Anna was crying. "Stop, please you are killing her."

Mother came running to Anna and held her as she doubled over in pain. It was the most pain Anna had ever felt, even worse than the poison when she had thought she was dying.

"Can you not hear her screaming? She is in pain. Make him stop," Anna told Mother.

He entered Mayi again with several thrusts. Anna

screamed louder and louder. Then he released himself, and it was done.

Anna could see Mat standing beside Mayi's body. Anna was in so much pain, she could not focus on what was going on while he was still onstage. After a few minutes, Mat went to Anna. She was still screaming in pain, and then she began to bleed between her legs.

"Mother," he said, "what is wrong with her?"

"It is Mayi's pain, my son. Anna is taking her pain away."

"Mayi did not cry out in pain."

"No, son. Anna took it away from her. She is the only one who heard Mayi's screams."

Anna, who was still crying in pain, began to bleed from her nose. Then she went limp and passed out.

"Mother, why is this happening?"

Mother looked at Mat and said, "The girl is dying."

"Yes, Mother, but she never cried out. She was too weak."

"Anna took all her pain away, and she bleeds because Mayi is dying."

"Mother, can you make it stop? She hurts bad. I no stand it."

"No, son. This how spirit works. Anna chose to take pain away. Spirit decides when stop."

"Mother, you know I no go deep into the girl when in pain."

"Yes, but Anna knows not. No tell Anna. If she knew, no use spirit again. Rejecting spirit kills her soul."

A few minutes after Anna's nose bled, she woke up and looked at Mat with sadness and disappointment. "Mayi was my friend," she said.

Mat picked Anna up and took her to her bed in his hut. She was limp and tired. Mother cleaned her up and changed her clothes. Anna showed no emotion through all of it. It was as if she were numb. Sitting next to her on the bed, Mat gently rubbed her face until she fell asleep.

Once Anna was asleep, Mat went to his own bed. During the night, Mat woke up to see Anna sitting in a fetal position, rocking back and forth.

"Anna, you okay?" he asked softly.

She didn't say a word, only sniffled.

"You cry?" He went to her bed and sat by her side.

She lifted her hand to push him away.

"I—" he began.

"No!" she cut him off. "You killed her. She was a baby and my friend."

"Anna, it happens."

"No! It does not have to. What is wrong with you people? You killed her. Did you not hear her cry out? You kept on until you ripped her apart inside."

"This our way."

"No no no! You are a grown man. You are too big for her. She was just a baby."

"She bleeds."

She screamed at him, "She was a baby! You killed her! She was not ready. I hate you! Leave me now. You lied to me."

"Anna, I no lie."

"Yes, you said Mother was not your mother."

"She is not my mother. I no lie."

"You led me to believe the chief did the ceremony."

"No, I told you acting chief."

"Well, I guess I missed the part where you are the acting chief."

"Mother my grandmother."

"Your grandmother!" Anna said. "Leave now. I cannot stand to look at you anymore. Find me another place to stay."

Mat knew he had done her wrong by not preparing her in advance. He could feel her pain. He hung his head and left the hut. He could not bear to tell her what she had done was punishable by the whipping pole. No one interfered with the ceremony. Mat went to Father to ask for her forgiveness and to save her from being whipped.

Father did not forgive and set her punishment to three lashes.

"She is yours, my son," he said. "Teach her better. You are her protector and teacher. You allowed her to interfere."

"Please, Father. She know not."

Father told him again in a stern voice, "Three lashes."

Mat turned in sadness and left. What was he to do? Her saying she hated him had been like a knife to his heart. It was as if he had lost Kati all over again. Anna would be punished first thing in the morning. She had already suffered so much today, and in a few hours there would be more. If she would only listen and do as he said.

Early the next morning, the same two guards that had been outside the hut the night before came to get Anna. She knew she was in trouble, and she was determined to take it like a man. They were not going to say she was weak by any means. She held her head high.

Mat stood by the whipping pole with two more guards; one held a horsewhip. The guards took Anna to the pole.

Father announced punishment for interfering with the ceremony. "Three lashes. Agreed?"

Anna nodded. She knew it was going to hurt, but she did not care. They had killed a child for their selfish motives, and she was going to stop this behavior. She would take her punishment and then get down to business. There must be a way. She was determined not to stop until she succeeded. That was just the way she was. She had always gotten her way. This time would be no different.

Mat stepped into the circle and spoke to Father in his

language. Anna did not understand what was being said, but she knew he was serious. Mat turned to Anna and then to the crowd of people.

"We have deal."

Father nodded in acceptance. Mat had bought the right to whip Anna by receiving five lashes himself.

Mat said, "Three lashes by me."

"Yes," Father said.

Mat asked, "Can we leave dress on?"

Father said, "No!"

Anna looked at Mat with eyes full of disgust and hate. Mat stood face-to-face with Anna but didn't say a word. She held his gaze. For her sake, he didn't break eye contact with her so that he would not look at her exposed body. He reached behind her neck and untied the tie of her dress. It fell down.

He turned her around, unfastened her bra, and removed it. Then he slowly lifted her arms over her head and tied them to the pole. His heart was pounding, and he could feel hers pounding too. She could feel his pain and knew he did not want to do this, but it was their way, and his taking the guard's place meant he would be easier on her.

Anna was shaking, not for fear of being whipped but at being exposed in front of all the people. But she never once protested and held her head high. She would not give Mat or anyone else the satisfaction of knowing she was weak or in pain.

Mat struck her once, though not hard enough to break the skin. She tensed but did not cry out. Lash two was a little more painful, yet she did not cry out, though a tear fell down her cheek. Lash three was about as much as she could take. She let out a quiet grunt but still did not cry out. Mat had gone easy on her. The lashes left small welts on her back.

Mat cut her down from the pole, and she fell to her knees. He slowly stood her up and put her arms into her bra for her to slip it on, but he did not fasten it for fear of hurting her further. He slowly pulled her dress up and put her arms into sleeves, leaving her back exposed. Then he carried her home. She did not say a word.

Mother was waiting for them with cold towels to help with the swelling. Mat laid Anna facedown on her bed.

"I assume you no tell her," Mother said. "This your do-ing, son. You should have told her truth from the beginning and none of this would have happened."

"Mother, please let me handle it. She is mine."

"Yes, son, but she needs the truth, or she will not under-stand and will interfere again. You must be honest and not hide things. By not telling her, she cannot trust you. Your job in protecting her is to share what you know or else she will find out on her own, the hard way."

Mat stayed with her for a while. No one spoke. Mother rinsed the rags, and Mat gently pressed them onto Anna's back.

Mother said, "There should be no scarring. Anna, Mat was easy on you. It could be much worse."

It was not long before two guards came to escort Mat to the whipping pole. Mat reached for one of his white shirts before he left. He knew he had to hide his back from Anna. She could not find out what he had done.

They tied him to the pole, and he received five hard lashes across his back, which broke the skin and left him bleeding. When it was all over, he put on his shirt and went to see Anna.

When he got close to his hut, he could hear Anna screaming. He ran as fast as he could to her.

Mat took Mother to the other side of the hut and whispered, "Mother, what is wrong? She was not in this much pain when I left."

"Son, how is your back?"

"I am fine, Mother. It no hurt."

"Really?" she said. Mother raised her eyebrow and looked toward Anna.

Mat realized Anna had taken his pain away. "She did it, didn't she? How, Mother? She did not know what I did."

"Your bond. She feels your pain no matter where you are. Her spirit is getting stronger."

"Mother, she needs to leave."

"Yes, I agree, son, but I think it too late. Her spirit has a plan. It is not for us to understand. I am sure Anna will not know what it is until it happens. Just remember she is fighting with the spirit; she will not win. She may suffer more before the spirit reveals itself. We need to be there for her. I fear there is going to be an awaking for us all."

Anna, still in pain, looked at them as they stood in the corner. Mat's back faced her, and she saw blood seeping through his shirt. Anna stood up, her dress still open in the back, went to retrieve something from her personal things, and walked toward the door of the hut.

"Stop, Anna!" Mat yelled.

Anna did not look back or respond to his voice. Just as he started to go after her, Mother grabbed his arm.

"No, son. She is with spirit now. Let her be."

Anna stopped at the doorway, turned to both of them, and said, "Stay. I will return."

So they did.

Anna went straight to Father's hut. She burst through the doorway and told him that she wanted Mat sewn up and fixed if they ever wanted to see this land again.

Father said, "Are you threatening me?"

"It is what it is. I mean it. Do you understand? Fix him now or I tear up the contract immediately and all you believe in will be lost." She lifted the papers she was holding and shook them in his face.

Father knew Anna meant business. He sent word to Mother to fix Mat to Anna's satisfaction. Anna nodded at Father and went back to the hut to make sure they took good care of Mat. Mat could not understand how Anna had any power over Father, but somehow she did.

Anna made sure the stitches were close together to prevent scarring. She aided in Mat's care. Anna kept the wounds clean and softly wiped his skin. She was carefully wiping the blood off his back when he said, "I sorry. Anna, I never meant to hurt you, and I give anything to have you no see that."

Anna still did not speak.

"Anna, you have to understand, this our way of life. You no change."

She whispered, "We will see. I do not want to talk to you now." She looked at Mother and asked, "What will they do with her body?"

"They buried her."

"Already?"

"Yes, dear. We no keep body long. Must put into ground soon."

"What about the ceremony?"

"We no ceremony for dead, unless it the chief's family."

"May I see where they buried her?"

"Yes. I take you."

Anna walked away from Mat after Mother finished bandaging him up. She went outside, not once looking at him. She went to pick some flowers and knelt at Mayi's grave to pray. Mat followed her and watched from a distance. He had not seen anyone pray over the dead since his father died. The tribe only blessed the leaders and their families.

Anna had started to cry when he saw the white wolf come out from the woods and walk toward her. Mat started to run toward her, but something in his head told him to stop. The wolf went to her. Anna put her arm around the wolf as the wolf licked her tears away. Mat could not believe his eyes, a wild wolf coming up to a person as if they had been together their whole lives. What power did she have over the animals?

Anna dismissed the wolf, who returned to her pack.

Mat walked up to Anna. "Why pray for her? She weak."

Anna was silent for a little while and then looked him in the eye. "We are all God's creatures. He created us all. He knows what we are like and what we do. He is our protector. All people, no matter who they are, have God's grace. We are his children. Mayi deserves respect for who she was. Her life was taken too soon, but we are not to question why. It is how she died that bothered me the most. I do believe her time was up, and I am glad she did not suffer."

"If your God her protector, why she die?"

"It was her time to die. The *why* she died, I do not understand. Everything is done for a reason. We may not understand today, but we will when God wants us to. We do not question our maker. I bless the life she had and ask for forgiveness for the one who took her life in this way."

"Anna, I no tell you enough how sorry I am."

"I know. I asked my God to give you forgiveness and to help me understand the reason she died this way."

"She bleeds. Some die, some become with child, and most take on a mate."

"Yes, Mat, but that does not mean she is ready for a man to enter her. Her body is too small, and look at yourself. It would be like taking a knife and pushing it into a small bead like the ones on your clothing. The knife would cut through the bead and damage what is behind it. When a young girl bleeds, her body is just starting to get ready. It takes years before her body is ready for a man or to carry a child."

"Anna, you no stop this. I know you want to, but it not happening. My days being maker soon be over."

"How so?"

"When Teka turn fifteen in a few months, he have the honor."

"What about his girl?"

"She be opened by me if she bleeds before he ready."

Anna could not believe what he was telling her. How could he do that to his son's girl?

"Did your father open your Kati?"

"No. She my soul mate, and I was her first."

"Was she your first?"

"Yes."

"Did you tie her to the table?"

"No. We broke rules; we made love. There no lovemaking or touching allowed during the mating. The spirits got mad and took her from me."

"No, Mat. It was her time, and she blessed you with a child. That was her mission in life. What a good job you have done with Teka. Kati would be proud of him and of you."

"Do you see Kati?"

"No. But I know how she would feel. Quit putting yourself down," she said. "Everything happens for a reason. You cannot blame yourself."

"You blame me for Mayi dying."

"No. I blame your customs. How many have to die before you open your eyes and see how wrong this is? Was Kati not enough? I am not saying stop altogether, even though I feel that it is wrong at any age, but change the age limit. Why do you say boys have to be fifteen and not ten?"

"He no developed."

"But you believe a girl is at that young age? Think about it. Maybe change the age for girls to fifteen like you do for the boys. All I am asking is to make a few changes. You will save lives instead of taking them. Talk to your spirits, and I will keep praying to my God to let your spirits see the light."

"Why you say as if your God better than my spirits?"

"I believe in only one God. He is over all spirits, the creator of all."

"I no understand."

"Try, Mat. I will try to be more understanding of your spirits if you try to understand my God. We are all here to make this world a better place. Sometimes that means we have to make changes and sacrifices to make it happen. Mat, if you were my man at age fifteen, I would not want to share you with anyone. You would be mine forever, and you would only have me and I you. I do not like to share."

"I see that," he said.

Chapter 10

Stalking

Mat went to stay with Father for a few days to give Anna space. He knew he had hurt her very badly. He also knew she would fall apart if she knew he was the one who had opened all women for their men. She would not understand and have nothing to do with him. This is why he had not told her on the trail. She had strong feelings about being pure. It was Mat's duty as acting chief to follow all the customs of his tribe.

He could not look weak. His feelings did not matter. Kati was the first girl he had been with. She had lived with the tribe many years. She'd had no problem with him being the maker. But then again, that was how she had been raised; she had known no other life. Anna, on the other hand, had lived a different life, and the maker opening up women was unacceptable to her.

He knew she had spirit, but what kind? What hold did she have on Father? Staying with Father, he thought, would give him a chance to find out. Mat also knew he had to discuss with Father the dangers he felt were coming. Staying with him would give him that chance.

"Father," he said, "Anna has spirit. Mother believes it to be the great spirit."

"Yes, son, she told me."

"You know the other tribes will come soon to take her. I think we need to prepare to fight."

"I believe you are right. Call a meeting with all the warriors. If she has the great spirit as Mother believes, we must do all we can to not let her fall into evil hands."

That afternoon, Mat gathered all the warriors who were of age to fight to make a plan. One warrior told Mat that he had seen horse tracks around the lake.

"This is not good," Mat said. He assigned guards to posts around the village and sent scouts on the lookout. "Report any movement you see. Anna must be protected at all costs. She is of spirit, and the spirit chose us to protect her."

They all agreed.

Father was not feeling well that afternoon, so he sent Mat to make his rounds. Every day Father visited all the people of his tribe to see if they needed anything. While making Father's rounds, Mat walked past the sick hut and stopped. He stood in the distance and watched. He knew Anna was still not ready to see him, and he respected her wishes. He knew it would take some time, but she would come around. He was sure of it. She was rocking a baby in her chair. She was lovely. Mat knew she would be a great mother someday. Then he thought of Kati.

It made him sad to think about how he had missed that with Kati, watching her hold and feed their son. He loved her so much and had missed sharing the care of their child together. He thought how unfair it was that the spirits had taken her away from them both. Teka had not had a mother to nurture him; Mat had done the best he could.

There was something about Anna that kept him from staying away from her, and it was getting harder and harder. He watched her for a long time. She was so tender and caring. She looked as if she belonged there. The more he watched, the more he wanted her. What was he to do? He knew he needed to stay away, but he couldn't.

She wore her hair pulled back, twisted, and put up, exposing her neck. Many of the maidens were wearing their hair the same way. Their bare necks were driving all the men crazy, as it did him. He wanted to go to her and kiss her neck. She was so beautiful and intriguing. She was more irresistible each time he saw her.

What did she have over Father? He was sure it had something to do with the box she had brought with her. And then there were those papers she had asked him to give to Father if she died. Mat searched Father's hut and found the box. It was locked. Mat searched for some time but could not find the key or the papers.

After finishing for the day in the sick hut, Anna went back to her hut to rest for the night. Teka had not come home yet. She wondered where he could be. She looked around and saw that a lot of men were not around as well. She knew something was going on. It was not yet dark, so she decided to go see Mother. Mat was still watching her and wondered what she was doing. He followed her.

Anna and Mother talked about the mating ceremony and Anna taking the girl's pain away. Mother told her that they needed to work on controlling her powers and that sometimes it was not good to take pain away. Sometimes pain was good. Mother explained that during child birth, women needed pain to know when to push. Anna understood.

"Mother," Anna said, "I saw many horses riding around the village in a dream. What does that mean?"

"I know not, but we need to tell Father and let him deal with it," Mother told her. "Anna, are your powers getting stronger?"

"I think so. I feel that I have seen the future. Last night I dreamed that Mat and Father both died when their hearts stopped beating. Mother, it was so real, like it was going to happen soon."

"Anna, we all go to great spirit in the sky at some point."

Anna began to cry.

"Anna, you care for him?"

"Yes, very much. I do not know what to do. Mat seems to be glued to me. I feel his heart is broken, and I cannot help him. He is closed minded and will not let me in. I feel so bad for him. He asked me if I could bring life back, would I bring Kati back."

"Anna, one day he will see Kati. I sure of it."

"Mother, I do not know if I could carry on if he dies. He is part of me. I do not understand how or why I have these feelings."

"Yes, Anna, you two have a bond."

"How do we break it? I cannot be bonded to him. He has already had his love, and I am searching for mine. He cannot love me the way I want him to. I will always be second in his thoughts. I want someone who wants me first. I cannot ask him to forget her. She will always be between us. This is not fair to him or to me. What am I to do? I know he has strong feelings for me. How do I get him to understand that it will not work out if we come together?"

"Only spirit can break it. Anna, your power very important and must be used when needed. You must learn when it necessary to use the spirit. When Mayi died, your nose bled. This no good for your health. Taking pain no good for your health. This type of power drains you, and could cost you your life. Give it time and be patient with him. He has a lot to sort out, and one day it will come to him. He will understand. I know he cares for you. We have to trust spirits. They know what they are doing, and when it time, they will share with us."

"Mother, you know I would give my life for the ones I love."

"Yes, dear, I know."

When Anna returned to Mat's hut, it was just about dark. She noticed that the door of the hut was open. She thought Teka must be back, so she went inside without worry. But Teka was nowhere to be seen.

Where could he be? None of the men are back either. What are they all up to? she wondered.

She pulled down her blanket and screamed. Mat, in the distance, started to run to her, but he saw Mother and Teka coming. He stopped. They ran into the hut and saw Anna standing over her bed, staring at a dead snake that lay decapitated under her blanket. Written on the bed were words Anna did not understand.

Teka translated, "Go home or you die."

Chapter 11

The Run

Mat heard what had happened and became concerned. Who would do this to Anna? It could had been anyone, male or female. The men were not too happy since Anna had insisted they all wear clothing. They did not like for their women to cover themselves. As for the women, well he knew they all wanted him. Who wouldn't want to be the chief's wife one day?

He was going to have to protect her more closely. He spoke to his guards about round-the-clock protection. If someone could get into his hut without being seen, he was going to get more protection not just for Anna but for Teka as well.

Anna could not sleep, both because she couldn't stop thinking about what had happened and because of the love-making calls. Who would do that to her? Everyone had been so nice. She tossed and turned all night, calling out Mat's name. Teka could hear her struggling and decided to go find

his father. Anna needed him now more than ever. Teka knew
she had feelings for his father and that his father needed her
as much as she needed him.

Teka looked out the door and saw no one. It was brighter
outside than usual because there would be a full moon in a
few days. He felt it was safe to leave Anna for a little while.
When he got to Father's hut, Mat was not there. Where
could he be? Teka did not see anyone around, so he went
back to his own hut. On his way back, he met Mat, who was
standing near the hut door, looking concerned.

"Son, why have you left Anna alone?"

"I was searching for you. She is suffering with her
thoughts. She is very restless and keeps calling your name.
I went to get you. She needs your comfort tonight. Where
were you? I was surprised you were not in Father's hut."

"I sleep close. I heard her struggling and was not sure
if I would be welcome to come in. She still not too happy
with me."

"Father, you must go to her now. She needs you."

Mat went in with Teka. Teka went straight to his bed.
Anna was still tossing and turning, so Mat went to her,
crawled into her bed, and held her tightly. She embraced him.

"Where have you been? I thought you were my protector.
Did they tell you what happened? Someone here wants you
and is willing to kill me to get you," she said.

"I here, Anna. I never left you. I been everywhere you go. I watched you work with children. I saw how you were at peace rocking little ones. I with you when you talk to Mother. I sleep outside hut. I always been near. When you screamed, I came running, saw Mother and Teka run into hut, stayed back. I watch from door. I sorry that happened. It no happen again. I no come in to your aid in fear I no welcome. You told me leave and said you hated me. It like a knife stabbed me in my heart. I never want to hurt you."

"Mat, I was upset. Women say things they do not mean when they are upset. I for one speak before I think. I am glad you are here now. Will you stay all night? Just hold me and keep me safe."

"Yes, Anna. You safe with me."

He held her tightly and softly rubbed her arm until they both fell to sleep.

The next morning, Anna woke up alone. She looked for Mat, but he was nowhere to be found. She spotted more guards around and then she saw Teka. She ran to him to see if he knew where his father was.

"Hi, Teka. Sorry about keeping you awake last night. I did not realize I was making so much noise. It is very disturbing to me that someone here inside the village dislikes me so and is willing to kill me. Thank you for getting Mat. How did you know I needed him?"

"You no sleep, and I understand why. You kept calling his name."

Anna blushed a little and smiled at him.

"He really cares for you, and I know you care for him. Be gentle with him. He will need time. He is a lot of talk but still struggles with feelings, as you do," Teka said.

"I am beginning to understand. Losing your mother really did a number on him. He was so young. I am sorry you did not have a mother to nurture you as a baby. Someone did a great job, though. I am sorry it was not your mother."

"My father raised me. After my mother died, he kept me in his hut. He would no let anyone care for me except wet mother. She would come feed me every few hours. Father would no let me out of his sight. He was only man who carried a child on his back everywhere he went, except to train in fighting. He was both my mother and my father. The only person he ever left me with was Mother. As soon as he was free, he was back for me. He only left me with her when he was needed elsewhere and if unsafe for me. We always been together."

"Really? I am surprised. I did not expect that. I would have thought he sent you to the women's hut to be cared for like the other children."

"No. Those children belong to others in tribe. I am future chief. We no mix with the tribe. We not equal. Our family over all people. We no blend. My father raised me to respect all people. I have more training and more education than others. I one day be chief to my people. They look up to me and respect me. I will lead them, care for them, and show them the way through the spirits."

"I see. I had no clue your father could be that nurturing. He does make me feel better when he is near. Oh, by the way, I have been searching for him. Do you know where he is?"

"He went for run. He runs every day down by water. If you follow path"—Teka pointed to a small opening by Father's hut—"to water, you find him."

"Thank you."

Before Teka could explain further, she was off running. *Oh well,* Teka thought. *She will find out when she gets there that he runs in his bare skin. This will be interesting. She will be surprised. I hope he will survive, because everyone knows now not to be caught without clothing.*

The closer she got to the beach, the louder the sounds of girls' giggling became. When she reached the girls, she noticed that they were peeping through some branches, so she joined them.

"Girls, what is so amusing?"

Anna moved aside a branch that the girls had dropped upon her approach. They stood there frozen with their mouths wide open, not knowing whether to flee or stay.

This was Anna they were dealing with, and no one messed with the maker's woman.

Anna looked out and saw the bluest, clearest ocean she had ever seen. All the beaches she had seen were murky and dull. It was a sight to see. The beach was white as snow as far as she could see in either direction. She could even see the bottom of the ocean floor; it was as if she were looking through a clean glass of water. She was speechless. She did not see Mat running anywhere. Then Anna spotted something floating farther out in the ocean. It was Mat. He was floating in the water buck naked.

The girls started to sneak away, but Anna called them back.

"Where do you think you are going?"

Anna looked around and saw a log next to the path. She cleaned it off and had the girls sit. The girls were between ages eight and ten. Anna turned and saw the rock that Mat had left his clothes on. She sat on the rock and spoke to the girls.

"I see you girls were having a good time. Did you enjoy watching a man run and swim with nothing on?"

The girls nodded. Anna tried to talk so that they could understand her using hand motions. By then, Mat stood behind the branches, where Anna could not see him, watching her express herself as she spoke to the girls. He admired how she adapted her motions to communicate with them. He decided to let her finish and see what happened. He knew he was in hot water, but it was too late now. He would have to swindle his way out again. He knew she would be mad at him, and it wouldn't be the last time.

"Is he yours?" Anna asked.

The girls shook their heads.

"No is right. He is mine." She pointed to herself. "And I no like you looking"—she pointed to her eyes—"at my man. No look." She waggled her finger back and forth, pointing to her eyes. "Shame on you," she said, pointing to each girl. "He is a man of honor, power, and respect"—she bent her arms at her elbows to indicate muscles—"and you no laugh at him. You keep your eyes"—she pointed again to her eyes—"on yourselves"—she pointed at the girls—"and not on my man or any other man. Are you promised to anyone?"

One girl raised her hand.

"Good. Then you keep your eyes on him and no other man. You love him?"

The girl nodded.

"Does he love"—Anna pointed to her heart—"you?"

The girl nodded again.

"Then he looks at no other. He will be yours and only yours and you his. No girls should look at man until they are united."

One girl spoke up. "The maker."

Mat signaled to the girl to be silent by putting his finger over his lips. He did not want her to give him away. He wanted to hear what Anna had to say. It was funny to him, and he knew she did not like that they had seen him naked.

"Yes, there is the maker." Anna got serious when speaking to the girls about mating. "Your body is yours and only yours. It is sacred. You only give it to the one you love. You will become a woman with or without the maker. He has no right to take you that way. You save yourself for your man only."

Mat was not happy at that point and had to put a stop to Anna before she put ideas into the young girls' heads. He stepped out and stood beside her. Anna did not move. She would not turn to look at him, as his waist was eye level. She was so mad at that point, she could not speak. He could see her face and ears turning red.

"You girls done here. No harm done. Go on your way now," he said.

After the girls left, Anna grabbed Mat's clothes and slammed them as hard as she could where it hurt the most. "Here, you forgot these when you went for your morning run."

"Woman, you try damage me?" he said as he doubled over in pain.

"Someone needs to," she said as she stomped away.

Mat hopped around and stumbled, trying to get his pants on quickly. Then he had to run to catch up with her.

"Anna, wait. We talk."

"I have nothing to say to you."

"Oh yes, you do. When you no have something to say? Now or later, you do have something to say. Say it now."

Anna kept silent and stomped off. Mat stayed back to watch her hips sway. *She is so cute when she is mad. Just need make up time*, he thought.

"I heard that!" she shouted.

"What? I say nothing." Mat was stunned. Could she hear his thoughts? He would not have let his guard down so easily if he had known she could hear his thoughts. He only knew of one other person who had that gift, and she was dead. However, Anna had spoken in her mind to the savages. So he guessed she could do the same to him.

"Anna, wait. We talk. Anna, please, let us talk," he called and started after her again.

"What more can I say? We have gone over this before. You have not heard a word I've said. You choose not to understand me. I have nothing to say, Mat," she said.

When he was close enough, he reached out and grabbed her by the arm. "You no tell girls they no mate. This no happen. They will mate when it their time."

"No, Mat. I am a jealous woman, and I will not allow it if there is anything I can do about it."

"There nothing you can do. You have to deal with mating. It is not in your hands."

"Mat, you underestimate me. You will see."

Mat was now getting upset with her, and before he could stick his foot in his mouth, as she always seemed to make him do, he walked away. He knew he could not talk with her until she had cooled off and was ready. *I am a patient man. I can wait*, he thought.

"You patient? Ha! I think I have made myself very clear on how I feel about going around in your birthday suit, bare skin, whatever you call it. I do not like it, and I want you to stop. Do you not have any pride or modesty?"

Mat turned to her and said, "I proud man. Have much pride. I know not of this modesty."

"That's for sure. Modesty means one takes pride in his or her body. No showing it off. You keep some things to yourself. You are self-reserved."

"I no care if see me. I proud how I look."

"That's what I mean, Mat. You like the girls making googly eyes at you. You think you are hot stuff. This gives them the wrong impression and makes them feel that you want them as they want you. It is one thing to look good and being proud of it. It is another to show it off to a degree that you are boasting. My God tells us to not boast. Take pride in yourself and only share your body with your lover. It is not for all to see. If you are mine, then keep it covered. I've said that before. Mat, you say I no listen to you. Well it seems you no listen to me. Enough! I am not speaking to you now."

She walked off.

Mat headed toward Father's hut to cool off and give her space. He looked back at her one last time before entering the hut and saw her slap at her shoulder and fall to the ground. He ran to her aid, and he saw it—a poison dart. He jerked it out of her shoulder and carried Anna to Mother. Once Mother took over, Mat went looking for evidence of who had fired the dart. It was one of their own darts, so the culprit had to be one of his people. Luckily, the dart did not contain poison, only a sedative that would put her out for hours. Anna could have hurt herself when she fell, so Mother kept an eye on her until she woke.

Whoever had fired the dart knew to cover his or her tracks, which meant it was an adult. Mat was sure it was a woman because the dart had not been dipped in poison. Only men handled the poison. Women just put on the sedative solution. Women were not allowed to handle the poison.

It could be anyone. They all have reason to get rid of her so they can have me. Anna was right all along. I can't tell her. It will give her a bigger head than she already has. I would not hear the end of it. I can hear it now. I told you so, he thought.

Mat searched the grounds but could not find anything that would lead him to the perpetrator. It had to be the same person who had left the snake in Anna's bed. He had to make Anna understand the danger she was facing. From now on, she was never to be left alone. He knew she would not agree. She did not like to be followed around. For some reason, she thought she could take care of herself. But this was a different world than she was used to.

She might have been able to care for herself where she came from, but this place had many dangers that she knew nothing about. A simple flower could take a person's life. The savages all wanted her and would do anything to get their hands on her. And now someone within the village wanted to harm her.

The people here did not value life as she did. It was nothing for a man to take an unclaimed woman for himself without the woman's consent and have his way with her whenever and wherever he chose. Women had no rights as they did in the white world. The world she came from had consequences for one's actions.

In his world, they had rules to follow, and if they broke them, there would be punishment. In her world, a man who defended himself from one who would harm him was as much or even more in trouble than the one who had done the bad deed. He had learned that the hard way while living with the whites.

Somehow he was going to have to get Anna involved with the tribal women so that she could have people around her at all times. It would have to be on her terms. He would have to suggest some things she could do. He knew she wanted to learn to make things like beadwork, pottery, and baskets. That was what he would do. He would help introduce her to the activities that happened on a daily basis. That way she would always be around people. This would help keep her safe.

Now that they were looking for someone within the village, he needed as much help as he could get. There was no way he could fulfill his duties, train the men, and stay with her all the time.

That night, before they went to sleep, Mat said to Anna, "Women making baskets tomorrow. Would you like to join them?"

"You know, Mat, I think I would like to. It is time for me to be more involved with the women's work. There is so much I would love to learn. Thanks for asking me."

"Then it set. Tomorrow afternoon, they be down by the river. I think you enjoy it."

"Mat, I know your ways are different, and I am trying. Thank you for being so thoughtful."

They fell silent as they listened to the lovemaking calls and the howling of the wolves far in the distance. It was a peaceful sound to their ears, and before long, they were both asleep.

Chapter 12

Self-Defense

Anna wanted to be part of the tribe, so she could help with the duties the other women were performing. The next day, Anna was at the river with the others, learning to weave baskets. She took a reed and soaked it in the water to make it bendable so she could work with it. She had never had much experience with crafts, but she really liked working with the reeds.

She had already made three baskets and was working on her forth when it started to get dark. She wanted to finish her basket before she went back. All the other women were finished and were going back to the village for dinner. Anna did not care if she was last. She was not going until her basket was done. She knew she should not be left alone; Mat had told her many times to always be with someone. But she did not care.

I can hear him now, getting on me for not going back with the others. I want to finish this basket first. I am pretty sure he has his spies watching me anyway. What could possibly happen? I feel like I am in Fort Knox, she thought.

When the women returned to the village for dinner, Mat noticed Anna was not with them. He went to see why. They explained that she had wanted to finish her last basket and would be on her way soon. Mat scolded them for not staying with her. At least one of them could have stayed to walk Anna back safely. He was not happy with them at all and sent them on their way.

What was he to do with Anna? It did not matter what he told her; she was always going to do what she wanted. He was just going to have to teach her a lesson.

He sent out a bird call to check with his guards to see if they had eyes on her. They sent word back that they did see her still by the riverside working on her basket. He sent word back to them to not interfere. He had a plan to sneak up on her and scare her enough that she would not stay alone again. They agreed but stayed close.

Mat followed the trail to the riverbank and hid in the woods. He threw a stick past her to make her turn the other way. Anna looked up and listened. She did not feel any danger and thought it must have been a branch that had broken off a tree and fallen. When she heard another sound, she began to get concerned. She knew someone was out to get her, and they were from within the tribe. She was not going to let this person get the best of her. She knew she should have gone back with the others, but it was too late now. She would have to deal with it on her own.

Mat could walk around without making a sound, so he continued to move around in different places. Anna could not pinpoint exactly where the noise was coming from. She turned her head each time he made a sound to scare her. He even made a growling sound. Now Anna was on her guard. She could feel that it was not an animal. If it was, she would have sensed it and talked to it. But it was not like that.

She searched the spirit world and did not find any animals stalking her. When she tried to talk to the animals, she got no response.

"Who is out there?" she shouted. "Show yourself!"

Then she heard a funny bird call. She knew it had to be a person. Someone was out there watching her.

"I know you are out there. Show yourself or be sorry!"

Mat was about to bust out laughing. There she was, out there all by herself, threatening someone she did not know. What did she think she could do?

Anna stood up and shouted again. "Show yourself now! Do you hear me? Do you know who you are dealing with? I am a great woman warrior, and I am not afraid to shed your blood. You mess with me, and I will tear you apart."

Mat could hardly keep quiet.

When she still received no response, she became greatly concerned. What was she to do? She knew she did not have half a chance in a fight. Where were the guards, and why had Mat not felt her fear and come to her rescue? She knew that, whoever it was, they were moving around. *Why can I not feel them?* she wondered.

"If you do not show yourself, I will send for my man to come and get you. I spoke to him through his mind, and he is already on his way. He will fight you to your death if there is anything left of you once I am through with you. Don't make me come find you. Save yourself now. My man is a big, strong, great warrior, and even he is afraid of me. If we are going to do this, let's do it now."

Mat could not stand it anymore. *She could scare off a grizzly bear,* he thought. All the guards were watching from a distance, laughing among themselves as Mat teased his woman. Anna was really on her guard now.

Mat snuck up behind her and gave her a gentle tap on the shoulder. But all of a sudden, Mat was taken by surprise. She grabbed his arm, flipped him over her shoulder, twisted his arm back, kicked him between the legs, and hit him across the forehead with a rock.

Mat lay flat on the ground, unable to move. A little dazed, he whispered, "Anna."

"Mat? What are you doing out here?" Anna said softly. "Where did you come from? There is someone in the woods."

"No, Anna. It me."

"You? Why would you do that?" In the moonlight, she could tell he was hurt and bleeding. "Mat, you should never sneak up on someone like that. I believe you were trying to scare me or something. That was mean."

"Anna, I told you no go out alone."

"I know your guards are always watching me. Don't sneak up on me like that again. It's a good thing I did not have a weapon."

"That is good thing."

Mat still could not get up, so Anna held his head in her lap and stopped the bleeding.

"Where you learn to fight like that?" he asked.

"I am from New York City. It is a jungle out there. Women are attacked all the time. I took self-defense classes. I can take care of myself. How many times do I have to tell you?"

"Well, I guess you being a strong warrior and all, I should be scared of you."

"I am sorry I hit you. Are you still in pain?"

"No much now that you holding me."

"Let's see if you can get up so we can go to dinner."

When they reached the dinner table, the guards came in, snickering at Mat.

"Ha, big strong warrior man got taken down by his woman. We know who in charge of that hut."

Mat just glared at them as they walked past. Then he looked at Anna and shook his head.

When Mat was finished eating, he went to the guards and said, "Maybe you need to go to New York City to be trained. She can outdo all of you. That's my woman, so you don't mess with her if you want to stay in one piece." Then he smiled at them. He was not ashamed of getting beat by a woman; instead, he was proud of her for standing up for herself.

Chapter 13

Full Moon

A few days later, Mat went to Anna to tell her that they would be celebrating the great spirits that night. It was the full moon.

"Anna, you dance with me tonight without spirit water?"

"Are you asking me out on a date?"

"What you mean date?"

"When a man asks a lady to go out with him, to have fun and get to know each other better, it is called a date."

Anna was surprised that he would ask her instead of demand that she go. This was an improvement in his attitude. There may be some hope for him yet. If only she could get him to open up more. He was too set in his ways and would not even think of any change, even if it was for the better. She needed him to try to understand her more and be more open-minded.

"Yes, I guess so. Will you go with me without spirit water? We both know how that turned out last time."

"Mat, I will only drink water, but I am not sure I can dance without the spirit water."

"It okay. I know you were no yourself last time. I teach you, I know you can dance."

"I do not know if I can. I think I was pretty lit last time."

"You full of spirit water," he said.

"Well, that was not my fault," she said.

"Anna, if you no be stubborn, you have no trouble. I tried stopping you, and you no hear it."

"Yes, yes, you told me. Trust me, Mat—I will do my best not to embarrass you."

"You no embarrass me. In fact, I enjoy you dancing."

"Did it turn you on?" she asked.

"I no understand, turn on."

"Did it please you?"

"That dancing you do pleased all men."

"Was I that bad?"

"Anna, after you danced, many children made."

"That bad? Huh."

"Yes, in good way."

"Mat," she said, "you have not been around much."

"I wanted to give you more space. The men and I have been preparing for war."

"War! Why?"

"Anna, I no want to hurt you. I do anything to spare you

sorrow. You being here put us all in danger. You have a spirit. Everyone wants it. Some will fight to get it. We be ready to defend and protect you when they come. It no matter of if but when. Anna, you mate with another great spirit, you create a grand spirit. You very important to our world."

He continued to explain, "The tribe with grand spirit has all spirits on their side. It be used for good or evil. The grand spirit heals and brings life back. It sees future and into soul. It even get into head, change you forever. Spirit in wrong hands cause great destruction. Our tribe protects you. This why you must leave."

"Mat, do you want to see me leave?"

"Anna, it no that easy. I be chief one day. My people in danger with you here. Being chief comes with many responsibilities. I protect tribe first before myself. I no force you to go. Attack on you proved we must ready ourselves and protect you. It been years since there was a great spirit, thousands for grand spirit.

"Now other tribes know, they will try again take you. They will breed you until you with child. Your offspring rule our world. I fear for you and my people long as you stay. I see no future for us; you made very clear, and I promised to take no other. If I could, Anna, I would take you right here, right now. I promised protect you, a promise I keep. If not for my loyalty to Kati and you having spirit, I would like nothing more than to have you my wife. But it is what it is, Anna. You too important to us and to me. We here for you. So dance with me?"

"Yes," she said. "I will do my best to behave tonight."

"Well, no too much behaving. We do want some fun."

"You are full of it."

"Full of it? How so? I no understand."

"Just get out, and I will be there. Look for the girl drinking water."

"Anna, what am I to do with you?"

"I am sure you will find something."

Mat was excited that Anna had agreed to dance with him. He wanted to know if she would know the songs he had written without spirit water. He had asked around, and no one said they had taught her the songs. He could not understand how she knew them, word for word and their tunes. Mother knew something about it; he was sure of that. Why else would she beg him not to play them? Mother had told him that Anna knew the words because Kati's spirit had sent them to her.

He had to know for sure. Did Kati send them to Anna? Could Anna speak to Kati? He just had to find out. He and Kati had written the songs together, yet Anna knew all the moves to them. Kati had been a lively person, so full of spirit. She had been the life of the party and his life.

Mat remembered what Mother had said: if Kati did not have spirit and he did, he would die. He could feel it. His heart died the day Kati died, and he knew it would not be long before his spirit died along with his body. There was nothing he could do about it. He would just have to accept it and not get involved with another; he didn't want for her to see him die.

Tonight, he would play the songs for Anna to see if Kati's spirit would come out again in hopes of speaking to Kati. He wanted Anna to be sober. Did she need spirit water to bring out the spirit? He was going to wait and see what happened.

Mat did not leave Anna alone again after the last attack. She always had someone with her; he made sure of that. Mother, Teka, his guards, or himself always had eyes on her to protect her. She was not too happy about that and of course tried to sneak off.

Today, Teka and Anna were to pick berries for that night's meal. When they came back with the berries, Anna sent Teka to the cook so they could begin preparing them.

Anna went back to her hut. When she arrived, she went inside alone. Lying on her bed was another beautiful dress. She knew Mat had put it there for her to wear to the dance.

I know he is trying hard to please me. Could I please him? she thought.

As she got closer to the dress, she noticed something was

wrong. It had been sliced up. *Who would do this?* She could not believe it. *Everyone seems so nice and welcoming.* There was no way she could fix the dress before the party tonight; she would have to wear the dress she wore last time.

Anna went to check on the children one more time before she had to get ready for the party. A young girl was walking around the hut in hopes of starting her labor. She seemed uneasy. Anna tried to calm her, but it did not seem to work. The girl was upset about something and seemed a little disturbed. Anna knew she could not help the girl, for there was something not quite right with her. Anna was kind to her, but the girl seemed standoffish.

Mat came into the hut, and the girl ran out. "What her problem?" he asked.

"I do not know, but she is not right."

"We know. She be problem," he said.

"I am afraid so," Anna agreed. "Is it your baby, Mat?"

Mat did not answer. "Let's go. Party about to start. Did you like dress?"

"Yes."

He saw the expression on her face. "What wrong with dress?"

"Mat, it was all sliced up."

Mat looked confused. "What you mean?"

"Someone took a knife to it. Why would they do that?"

"I no know, but find out. They be punished."

"No, Mat. Just leave it alone. I will wear the other dress tonight."

"Go, hurry. Get dressed for party."

Anna went back to her hut and dressed. This time she put some of his war paint on her face. She had no clue what the colors she used meant; she just used whatever she wanted. When Anna arrived, Mat had already started to play. She smiled at him and went to sit in the front row where he motioned for her to go.

He could not keep his eyes off her. He smiled and shook his head. Everyone else was looking at her as well. She thought she had done well with her makeup and held her head high. She sat down beside Mother. Mother looked at her and raised her eyebrows.

"You look nice tonight, Anna," she said.

"Thank you. Do you think he likes?"

"Oh yes, Anna, I sure he does."

"Good. That is what I was going for."

Anna was enjoying how beautifully Mat was playing. She did not go dance to the first song, but when the second song began, he motioned for her to join him. She held up her cup and mouthed, *Water,* and placed her cup on the edge of the stage.

He smiled and, making a circle around his face with his finger, he asked wordlessly, *You sure?*

Water, she mouthed back. *Yes.*

He smiled and rolled his eyes.

She mouthed back, as she motioned a circle around her face, *You like?*

Mat knew she did not know what her face told everyone, so he just grinned and nodded. *Oh yes!* Mat thought to himself. *What will this girl do next? She is so unpredictable. There is never a dull moment when she is around. The tribe will never be the same when she leaves. I hate for that day to come, but I know it has to for the sake of my world.*

Anna was not sure how to dance. Last time she had lots of help to get loose. Mat put his arms around her waist and pulled her close. They danced so close together an observer could not tell where one ended and the other began.

Anna looked out and saw how unhappy the pregnant girl looked. But she dismissed it and said to herself, *No one is going to spoil my fun tonight.*

"You beautiful tonight, I like your face paint," Mat said.

"You pleased?" she asked.

"Yes, Anna."

They danced to a few more songs before he said, "Anna, you mean it?"

"Mean what?"

"The face paint."

"Yes. I meant to put on the face paint to impress you. Is it not pretty? Do you like it?"

"Oh yes, Anna, but do you mean it?"

"Mean what?"

"What your face tells me. Remember—when I first showed you the war paint, I told you what it meant to others."

"And what does mine tell you?" she smiled.

He giggled. "Anna, you tell everyone you want to sleep with all tonight. We have orgy."

"*What!*" Anna screamed. She reached for her cup of water, splashed her face, and started rubbing off the paint. "Mat! Why did you not tell me when I came in?"

"Anna, remember you are your own woman. No man tell you what to do."

"Oh, shut up. Help me get it off. I cannot believe you let me go all this time. I should slap you for letting me make a fool out of myself."

Mat just laughed at her and pulled her even closer; she could feel his heart beat as they grinded to the music. He was really getting into it. He put his hands on her hips, and they moved together.

She thought this was a bit too close. Had she done this last time? *Oh my*, she thought. She had gone all out. What must they think of her? She was starting to get turned on, and she could feel that he was already. How was she to end this night in her own bed? She had to stop. After a few more dances, Anna became thirsty, so she went to get some water.

As she was returning to Mat, the pregnant girl jumped in front of her.

"You think you someone special," the girl said. "You think he yours. I have his baby inside me. He never be yours. He mine."

Anna just pushed the girl away and said, "Leave me alone."

"He mine always, and I have him. Stay away from him, or you die."

Anna brushed it off again and went back to Mat.

"What took you so long?" he asked.

"That girl stopped me. Mat, she carries your child?"

"Anna, please no ruin the night."

She smiled gently at him and nodded.

Mat started playing the songs he and Kati had written. Mother looked straight at him and shook her head, but he continued. Anna froze. She looked at him and joined in each song just as she had done before. This time, she sang and moved with even more passion and sensitivity. She was so smooth and calm. She looked at him with so much love in her eyes. It was the most loving feeling he'd experienced in nearly fifteen years.

How could she know these songs? It must be Kati's spirit, he thought.

Screaming suddenly came from across the room.

"No! He mine!"

Anna looked over and saw the pregnant girl running at her with a knife in her hand. She attacked Anna, grabbing her by the hair as if she was going to scalp her. Mat and a guard grabbed the girl. Mat threw her down to the ground. She fell on her own knife and died.

"Anna, you okay?" Mat asked.

"Yes. I am fine. Is she dead?"

Mat motioned for the guard to take the girl's body away.

Anna screamed, "No! The baby!"

Mother said, "Mother dead, baby dead."

"No! Baby still alive," Anna said.

Anna grabbed the knife from out of the girl and cut the dress from the girl's body. Mat stepped in to stop Anna so they could take the body away.

"No, no, let her be," Mother told them. "She knows what she is doing."

Anna looked for Mother to come help. Anna showed Mother where to cut. She showed her how far and deep to go. Then Anna reached inside and pulled out the baby. It was a girl, a healthy little girl who looked like Mat.

Mat was surprised when Anna looked at him, smiled, and handed him the baby. "This is your daughter."

Mat looked at the guard and said, "Take away."

Anna was stunned. "Mat, she is yours."

"No, Anna. She no belong to me. Belong to tribe." Mat instructed the guard to take the baby away and brand it. "Anna, you stay away. No get attached."

Anna bowed her head as tears streamed down her face. Her hands were covered in blood.

Mother went to Anna and said, "Come—let me take you back to your hut to clean up. Anna, you saved a life tonight. How did you know to save the baby?"

"At my job I had watched doctors do the procedure many times. We saved many babies but only when they are this far along. Mother, will Mat not have anything to do with her?"

"No, Anna. The only child he attach himself to is his own, with his wife. These children mistake, no made from love. Only children entitled to him are ones made from love."

"How sad," Anna said. "No child is a mistake. Your spirit and my God do not make mistakes. All children deserve to be loved and are put here on earth for a reason. Mat is missing so much love."

"He is, Anna. He needs you. You are our last hope to bring him back before spirit dies."

"Mother, I do not know if I can. He is so closed. I feel his pain, and I am not sure I can do any good."

"Please no give up on him. The spirit has sent you for reason, and here you saved a life. Mat needs you teach him how to love again. Anna, I am sure you can do this. It going to take some time. Please no give up. I watched him suffer for so long. It time for him live again. Anna, do all you can. You are his last chance to continue with life. He needs you."

Chapter 14

The Child

Anna was disturbed by what Mother had told her about Mat not taking part in his children's lives. How many did he have? She knew the one from the C-section was his. He had not denied it. The look on his face had told all. But how could he dismiss the baby like it was nothing? Then there was Mat telling her not to get attached. How dare he tell her what to do.

He had been the maker for almost fifteen years. Some of these girls could be his daughters. *Oh my God*, she thought. Mayi could have been his daughter. But she had not had a brand. What if the girl who attacked her was his daughter? What if? What if? *Stop, Anna*, she said to herself. *Surely, they have a plan for that. Mat said he mated all, but surely not his own.*

She could not stand it any longer. She needed answers. She knew Mat would not tell her; it was a subject that he had no plans to share with her. The only person she could go to was Mother.

Anna took the baby to Mother to make sure she was okay. Mother checked the baby, and she was fine. Then Mother took the baby, placed her on the table, undressed her, and was going to cut her in her female area.

"Mother! What you are doing?"

Mother looked at Anna. "I know why you here. You need answers. This baby girl Mat's. All females that belong to the maker are opened as babies. Therefore, they no go to the mating ceremony. When she becomes of age and Teka is maker, she would be his sister. This wrong. Things no turn out well when a child created from family."

"Mother, this is so unnecessary. Just stop the mating. It will all work itself out."

"Anna, this our way of life. Honey, you need trust us and learn our ways."

"No, Mother. I feel I was sent here to make it a better place, and this is where I am going to start. Before I go home, back to the white people, as you call them, I will stop the mating or die trying."

"Anna, be smart. You lose this battle. I fear maker and all makers like it. I no see how you change that."

"Mother, this is Anna you are speaking to. You know I will not stop trying until I get what I want."

"Anna, I fear you going to live a short life if you no stop."

"Mother, the girl that attacked me. She was not right."

"Yes, she was disturbed. She Father's child, and Father mated her mother as well."

"Her mother!"

"This no happen often, but somehow she no get opened or branded as baby. There no way Mat could have known she of same blood. He never meets girls before ceremony. For the last hundred years, we have been opening maker's girls when are babies. They free to choose their men when they ready. No ceremony."

"Mother, I think I am going to be sick. This baby is Mat's daughter and a part of him. I don't know why this happened, but it is not right. Do you think she will be okay?"

"We not know. For now, we just wait to see."

"Mother, are there many children fathered by Mat?"

"Not many. We mate during bleeding. It safer that way. But a few times a child is created."

"So there are children old enough to be mated by Mat that are his children."

"If they are girls, they already been opened and branded. The skin removed from all the boys in tribe, and they too branded."

"Mother, this baby has been branded. Do you have to cut her too?"

"Yes, to ensure she no mated."

Anna could not stand to see them cut this baby. She felt that it was wrong. The baby was so small and innocent. How could they do this? It made no sense to her.

Anna picked the baby up. "I do not care who the mother was, only that it is Mat's baby." Anna could feel love for the baby; it was part of Mat. "Can the brand be enough?" She told Mother, "This child will not be cut today."

"Anna, no wait too long. It easier at this age, and will be done."

"No. It is not easier at any age."

Mat walked passed Mother's hut and saw Anna. She had the baby with her. He knew she was not going to allow what needed to be done.

He came in and said, "Anna, I told you no get involved with child."

She looked at him, smiling, and held the baby girl up to show him. "See, she has your eyes."

Mat did not look at the child. He looked at Anna with a serious expression. He was not happy.

"Mat, look how beautiful she is. How can you not have a relationship with a child that belongs to you? I do not understand how you can turn your back on her. She is so small and has your eyes. Mat, she is part of you. Please, Mat, just hold her and see for yourself. You will see."

"Anna, I told you no get attached. Her mother not right. Chances are good she no be either."

"Mat, you do not know for sure!"

Mat looked at Mother. "Has it been done?"

Mother looked at Anna, hung her head, and shook it.

"Anna," Mat said. "It has to be done. Give Mother baby."

"No!" Anna said and ran out of Mother's hut with the baby. She ran as fast as she could to find a safe place.

Mat knew he would have a hard time getting the baby away from her, so he did not run after her. He instructed his guards to follow her and come get him when they found her but to not approach her. He would be the one to retrieve the baby. He had to help her understand. She would need him.

Mat gave her some time to calm down and put herself together. About an hour passed before he went to her. He knew he would have to be gentle with her, for this was way over her understanding. Women always had a hard time when it came to babies, and Anna was no different. In fact, it could be a little worse because she was with spirit.

A guard led him to where she was hiding. Mat slowly went to her. He was very calm and sympathetic. He was going to have to handle this with care.

"Anna, please. I need you with me on this. We do this to protect them. I know you never understand, but it has to be done." He walked over to her and put his arms around her.

"I know this no easy. I here for you. It no hurt her. It only make better. Anna, please let me have baby."

"No!" she said. "This is wrong. Get away from me."

"Anna, you only one who sees it that way. This happen today or another day, but will happen."

With tears in her eyes, she said, "Please, Mat, do not do this. She is so small."

"Anna, there things we do you have to accept."

"No! I will not! Do not touch me!" she shouted.

He did not let go. She started to cry harder.

"It okay. Cry if you need, Anna. I need you hear and trust me. I no going to take baby away from you. You have to give her to me when ready. Take much time as you need. I stay with you as long it takes."

"I need forever," Anna cried.

Mat motioned the guards to stand next to her so she could not run.

"What is this, an ambush? You are going to overpower me and take the baby."

"No, Anna. I said I no take baby until you ready."

"Well, I will never be ready for this. Mat, please. You cannot do this. It is so wrong and does not have to be done. There has to be another way without cutting her."

"Think, Anna. It be done."

"Please, Mat. Do not make me do this," she begged. "I

will leave and take her with me. Then there will be no problem of her mating with Teka and I will no longer cause you or your tribe anymore grief. Please, please, Mat."

"I no make you do anything. You do on your own. You must accept it. You know it happen now or later. Now better for child. Anna, look at me."

Mat looked into her eyes. He could feel how much she was hurting. He was very gentle with her. He had one arm around her waist, and he placed his other hand gently on her cheek.

"I know how you feel. It very hard for you let go. Anna, it has to happen. She be fine. Trust me. I know how painful is for you. I feel it. I help you get through this."

She whispered, "No, Mat. Please do not make me. I will do anything you want."

"I no make you. Just let go and hand me baby when you ready. It going to be okay. You see."

Anna knew she was outnumbered and that he was right; it would be done at some point. She knew she had no place to run to. They would catch her and take the baby if she ran.

With a heavy heart, she looked at him and then kissed the baby's forehead. Then she slowly handed him the baby. Mat passed the baby to the guard and held Anna tightly.

"You did good, Anna. It for the best. I no leave you."

She made up her mind then and there that this practice

was going to stop if it was the last thing she did on this earth. There would never be another child cut like that again.

Mat held her for hours. Neither spoke. Then she got up and walked away, leaving Mat behind.

Chapter 15

The Chase

Anna could not understand how Mat could father a child and not have anything to do with it. This child was not an orphan; she had a father. Anna thought long and hard all day about how she could stop the mating ceremony. She knew she could postpone it for a while, but it would not be forever. She did not have enough collateral. There was the land, but she would only use it as a last resort.

That night before bed, she asked Mat, "Why do you think it is necessary to mate with these young girls instead of letting their man open them when they come together their first time?"

"Anna, it our custom. It has been done that way since beginning of time."

"But why? Mat, my question is, Why is it necessary?"

"Anna, we do to provide an easier path for her man to enter her once they united. Once she has healed, they are ready to mate."

"No, Mat! Why can't her man open her? Does it matter that she has healed? He has to wait until after the maker enters her. Why can't he wait after he enters her?"

"It no up for discussion."

"Mat, do you want me?"

"Anna, you need not ask me that. You are mine. I have right to have you whenever and wherever I chose, and it would no be wrong. I promised you I would not until you were ready."

"What if I said I was ready now?"

"Anna, don't play with me on this matter. If you told me that, I no waste any time. I take you right now before changed mind."

"Mat, I am ready the day you stop the mating ceremony forever."

"You know I no do that."

"You have the power to make changes within your tribe. You just choose not to, and I believe it is because you enjoy being the maker. It gives you power."

"Stop talk now. No ruin our night. Please understand our ways. But I no sure you ever will."

"I do understand the reason for the mating, but it is not necessary to have the maker do it. Her man can do the job better. It would mean more to their relationship."

"No more talk. Go sleep now."

Anna knew he was done talking. She turned over in her bed so she would not have to face him and went to sleep.

Mat lay in the bed facing her. She even looked beautiful from behind. He admired her curves. If only he could have her all the way. He knew not to push it even though he wanted her. He did not know if he could go through with it, taking Anna and having his way with her with Kati in the back of his mind. He knew everyone was right about moving on, but he was the one who was not ready. His body was, but his heart was not.

The next morning, Teka got up early. He was to become man soon, and he was going to go hunting to prove himself to the tribe by bringing home food. He spotted a deer in the clearing and thought it would be a fine catch. He started to sneak up on the deer, but the deer turned and ran into the woods. The deer ran fast, but Teka was fast too. He did not pay attention to how far the deer had traveled.

Before he realized it, he was no longer on his land. But he was determined to get that deer, regardless. The deer crossed a river and went over a mountain. Against his better judgment, he followed, even knowing the danger of being on the other tribe's territory. He was no longer safe if he was caught. He followed the deer around a bend, and out jumped two savage boys who were not much older than him.

Teka knew he was in trouble.

"I come in peace. Chase deer. Traveled too far. I mean you no harm," he said.

The savages did not care. They knew who he was, the great grandson of the chief. He was worth a lot to them. They needed him to get what they wanted. They decided to capture him and trade him for Anna. Teka knew this, and he was determined not to let them catch him. He knew he was outnumbered, but he had been training extra hard to fight. One day he would be chief, and he had to prepare himself. This would be a challenging fight, but there was no way they were going to get their hands on Anna. He would give his life if it came to that. He fought with all he had, but they too were well trained, so he ran.

That afternoon, Anna was working with the children, teaching them English. She had already seen a big difference in their speech. They were fast learners. She could not believe how quickly they caught on. Mat came in, as he did every day. Father or Mat always made rounds to see if all the tribe members were doing well and if they needed anything. They really looked after the people like they were family.

About four times a year, Mat made a trip to town for supplies. Anna had a list of things she needed the next time he made the trip.

"Mat, I have a list for the next time you go town," she told him.

"When do you no have a list?" he said.

She just smiled at him. "Here are the items I need: I need baby bottles, soap, shampoo, toothbrushes, toothpaste, crayons, paper, pencils, tampons, and condoms."

He looked at the list, confused.

"What is it?" she asked him.

"I no see why you need anything on this list. Babies need bottles, yes. I understand that. But why the rest? What wrong with our soap? We have soap."

"Yes, but this soap smells better. I noticed how you like the smell I have after my shower."

"What wrong with the way we brush our teeth?"

"Nothing, but toothpaste and brushes would work better than chewing on sticks. You will see."

"What are crayons?"

"Children draw and color with them on paper."

"We have paint that they use. No need for them. I no understand tampons."

"This is for women to keep clean when they bleed."

"No need. We have women's hut for that," he said. "What is this condums?"

"Mat, they are called condoms."

"Condums or condoms, I not know what they are."

"I thought you said you went to white school. You were never told about condoms?"

"No," he said.

"Condoms protect women during the mating ceremony to keep them from getting with child."

"How that work?"

"The man wears it before entering a woman."

Mat made a funny face and asked, "How so?"

"The maker would wear it to protect the woman by placing it on his ..." She hesitated and whispered the rest of the answer in his ear.

"No! I no need that. No, Anna. Baby bottles it is. No need for all the others."

Anna just looked at him. "Mat, someday you are going to have to make changes. Change is good at times. Mat, please at least get me the tampons, or maybe I just need to travel with you to town.

"Woman, you take too long, and you will have to ride your own horse. No ride with me again."

Later that day, Anna was reading a story she had written for the children. Mat sat back and admired her. He could see how she enjoyed being with them. She was so happy. When the story was over, she sent the children out to play.

"Mat, when did you go to white school?" she asked him.

Mat hesitated for a second and said, "When I became the maker, I refused and ran away. Kati was not ready to mate, and I had promised her she would be my first. I was a few years older than her, so I was gone for two years. I lived in barn on the trail and off the land. I got job, and went to school. I went against our customs, and spirits turned their backs on me. My father had already left this world, so Father took my place as Maker until I returned. Kati and I had a very special bond; we could talk to each other in our minds."

He continued, "When it was Kati's time, I came back home. Kati could see the future and knew when to call me home just in time before she mated with Father. When I got back, I became the maker with Kati. During the two years I went to school, I learned to drive that piece of junk, as you called it."

"It did do a good job. It was just not what I was expecting," she said.

When Mat started to leave, he glanced back at Anna. She had that stare. She was having a vision. He went back to her.

"Anna, what is wrong? I know you see something. Tell me."

"Teka, where is he?" she asked.

"He went hunting on the far side. Should be home soon."

"No. He has passed the river and the mountain."

"He knows not to go there. Are you sure?"

"I see him bleeding, cuts, and men chasing him. Mat, you need to go get him. Take many warriors with you. He is in danger."

Mat got some men together, and they went to find Teka. Mat was a great tracker, and Teka was not good at covering his tracks yet. Mat intended to teach Teka how to hide his tracks better but was glad today that his son did not know how.

Teka had crossed over into the enemy's territory, and Mat needed to catch up with him soon.

What is wrong with this boy? He knows better. You never go outside our territory alone. I am going to have a heart-to-heart talk with him when we get home. He could be killed. No one goes alone, Mat thought.

Teka was running fast through the woods, through the briars and branches, scratching himself all up. He knew he had to get back, fast. They were catching up with him. Suddenly, he tripped and fell down the rocky mountainside. He landed on a cliff. His arms and back were bleeding where he had cut and scraped himself on the rocks. He had no time to stop the bleeding. He just had to get out of there. He could hardly stand. He stood up and fell back down. He tried again, and a hand reached out to help him up.

There stood an old wretched-looking woman who reeked of death. He almost stumbled off the cliff at the sight of her. *Where did she come from?*

"Here, my son, take my hand. I am not here to harm you."

Teka looked at her and was afraid.

"Don't be 'fraid. Hurry. They are coming. You must get up and out of here. Here is the way. I show you."

"Who are you?"

"It no matter. I am here to help you."

"I do not know you."

"Our spirits knew each other, and the spirits have sent me to help you. Hurry. Take my hand. They are quickly approaching. Trust me, son. Take my hand."

Teka cautiously took her by the hand and let her help him stand. For some reason, he could not let go. He could see her past. She had been a lovely, beautiful woman. She'd had a family and a good life. Then one day, it had all been taken away from her. She was left for dead and lost her family. She had spirit but did not use it. When the savages took her, she'd had to use spirit to survive. They knew she had spirit and used her. She had a sad heart.

When he finally let go of her hand, he told her how sorry he was about the things that had happened to her many years ago. He told her in her mind that she was loved.

Then he spoke aloud to her. "Thank you for your help. You are a good person. Never forget it, no matter what they do to you. Keep your spirit alive."

Teka had turned to leave when she asked, "How is Matete doing? Is he happy?"

"Matete?" he said. "You know him? He is well." He

looked back and saw the savage boys coming and asked her, "How do you know my father?"

But when he turned to look at her again, she was gone. He was puzzled. How did she know Mat? No one had called him by his full name since Teka's mother died. *What was that all about? That was strange*, Teka thought.

Teka escaped and found his way back to his territory. Mat was there to greet him. He saw the disturbed expression on his son's face.

"Son, are you okay?"

"Yes," Teka answered as if it had been an average day with no complications.

"Are you sure, son? You do not look it."

"Father, I am okay. I was hunting a deer and lost my way."

"It looks like the deer was smarter than you and won."

"I slipped and fell down the mountain. I will be fine."

"Let's get you back to Mother; she will dress your wounds."

"Father, how did you know where I was?

"Anna," they both said at the same time.

Chapter 16

The Cave

The next day, Anna went outside before breakfast. She heard peaceful music playing in the distance and needed to see who was playing. She walked down the river path, knowing she was not to leave the village, but she just had to go see. It was like the music was calling her.

She saw him down by the river. Mat was playing. She decided to hang back and listen. He played for a long time, but she did not mind. The music put peace in her heart. She sat back on a log, closed her eyes, and relaxed.

Mat looked up and saw her sitting there. "Anna, why you here?"

"I am sorry, but it was so beautiful I could not help myself. Mat, you do not understand how your music makes people feel."

"I have told you no leave the village by yourself. It is not safe. I cannot protect you if you do not do as I say."

"I cannot live in fear all my life. I cannot be smothered

either. I am sure you have people watching me all the time anyway."

"I see you are getting to know me. So you enjoy the music?"

"Yes, very much. You are very good, and you put your whole self into it."

"Anna, I would like to show you something. We will have to travel a long way on horseback. I think you would like it. It is a sacred place and only my family allowed to visit. I have never taken anyone other than my family there before, but I feel you will understand how special this place is once we get there. I know Teka has been teaching you how to ride. Will you go?"

"Yes, I think I would like that, to take an adventure, and it is a beautiful day to get out."

"Anna, every day with you is an adventure. Trust me."

She looked at him with a funny grin and said, "You think? Someone has to keep you busy."

"I will get horses ready and come get you. You put on riding clothes."

He walked her back to their hut and went to get the horses ready. He packed a few things and met Anna outside the hut. Anna wore her blue jeans, boots, and a blouse. Mat had on his brown leather pants with an orange and white feathered headpiece. He wore a breastplate decorated with teeth and a bone choker. His arm- and wristbands matched his headdress. She could not believe how handsome he looked when he was all dressed up. It made her melt.

"Wow," she said. "This place must be really special. I believe I am underdressed."

"No. You look nice."

"Nice. Not like you. You look like a chief."

"I will be one day. I wear this headdress because it is sacred. Only used when with the spirits."

"Chief, and a good one at that," she said.

Mat lifted her onto her horse and got on his. Anna was so impressed at the way he was dressed that she could not keep her eyes on the path. She was looking at him as he rode behind her when he yelled.

"Anna, look out!"

She turned her head and hit a branch just above her forehead. He laughed at her until he noticed blood running down her face. He went to her, pulled the horses together, and took a cloth out of his bag to clean her up. He applied pressure to the cut until it stopped bleeding.

"There, you better now. It stop bleeding. Anna, you do need to watch where you go."

"Then you need to be in front of me. How else am I to see you? And besides, I do not know where you are taking me."

"Anna, you stay close. We be traveling long way today. I want show you something. I think you will like."

She did not leave his side for the rest of the journey.

"Mat, are you sad that I came here?" she asked him once they were on their way again.

"No, Anna. I enjoy your company."

"Why is it hard for you to be near me?"

"I do not know. Mother tells me that it has something to do with our spirits."

"Our spirits? Do you have spirit too?"

"Mother thinks our spirits knew each other in another life. She said we are both fighting the spirits. I did not know I had spirit until you came. They did not tell me. You seem to have many spirits. I thought if we were out alone, we could see where the spirits take us. Look. We are here."

He helped her off her horse, took her by the hand, and led her through the woods to a clearing.

Anna stopped and looked. "Oh. Look how beautiful," she said. She was looking at the base of a mountain. The mountain's peaks were covered with snow. "Mat, this land needs to be protected. Look! There are some goats climbing on the rocks, and over there is Missy. I think she is following me. I have never seen anything like this before."

He led her closer, and she saw an opening in the rocks behind some vines. It was a cave. Mat had brought two woven capes to cover them while they were in the cave; it was chilly underground. He put one on her and the other on himself.

"Thank you," she said.

Mat made a torch for light, lit it, and they went inside. Anna knew the cave was special. Inside she could see writing on the walls with pictures.

"Who did all this?" she asked.

"My people. Thousands of years of history from the beginning of time on these walls. We keep it safe from all others. There is always someone on guard to protect this secret place. No one allowed to come inside without spirit."

"Are they out there now?"

"Yes. I told them we were coming, so they let us be. They watch closely and will fight to the death to protect this place."

"Mat, this is unbelievable. Look. These markings look like spirits."

"Yes. This place has lot of spirits. When one is uneasy with the spirit, they come here to get back in touch. I come here often, but the spirits have turned on me. They no more speak to me."

"But you still come?"

"Yes. It gives me peace. Look. Here marks the spirit of light. Over here is the spirit of darkness." He pointed out each to her. "The spirit of peace is there, and here is love. All spirits are carved into the rock. Some say when called upon, the spirits will present themselves and talk to you. I have never seen this. Maybe one day."

"Mat, there are so many."

"Yes. We have a spirit for everything. If we need rain, we call on the spirit of water."

"When do you come here?"

"When I feel down."

"Do you feel down now?"

"Anna, you being here has done something to me. I am torn between the love I lost and the love to come. I have deep feelings for you, and I do not know why. I have only known you for a few weeks. Mother tells me the spirits want me to watch over you and keep you safe. I feel you are here to save me."

"How so?" she asked.

"I do not know. I was hoping the spirits would tell me. Here we are as close to the spirits as you can get. This is why I brought you here. You see things differently than I do. I was hoping they would speak to you."

"I do not know why we have these feelings, Mat. It is not for us to understand. My God is only one, not hundreds as you have. My God takes care of all my needs. I will ask my God to help you. I believe my God is over all of the spirits, and when it is time, God will let you know what you are here for through your spirits. I believe we are all here for a purpose, and your job here on earth is not finished. Your spirits need you for something. You will understand what it is in time."

"Anna, you always know what to say to me. Mother told me you have the spirit to calm. It works all the time when I am with you. I saw you when you calmed the little ones. I have seen you get into the savages' minds. Then you have visions. What spirits do you have? You have many spirits, but we do not know which ones yet. I thought if you came here, the spirits would come to you. You are important to our world. We no had anyone with many spirits before. Most of time there is only one or two, but not you. Having many spirits gives you great power. You must learn to use them."

"I do not know if I want to use them."

"You must or your spirit will die and then your soul will die. My mother died because she no use her spirit. She refused, and they took her life. Having spirit is a great honor. Makes you special, above all. Use the spirits you have to do good, and use them wisely."

"Mat what spirit do you have?"

"I not know. Mother has the spirit of healing. We did not know the spirit my mother had, for she did no use it. It cost her life."

"What about your power, Mat?"

"Men no have power like women. Men carry the spirit to pass to his children, but I do have strong feelings when danger is near, and wisdom."

"Like when you knew the savages were watching us?"

"Yes. And at times I can feel danger coming."

"Mat, you do have a lot of wisdom. That impresses me. And the way you play your music, it is from your soul. You put your whole self into everything you do."

"I feel that we should be the best we can be," he said.

"Mat, you put in more than your best. You put your whole body, soul, and mind into your work. This cave is a special place. I can feel it. I am glad you brought me here. I do feel the spirits are here, and they are with you. I am sure in time it will become clear to you what your purpose is. Do not think the spirits have left you. I feel that they are with you always."

"Thanks, Anna. I feel much better, but I always do when I am with you."

Mat took Anna's hand and pulled her close. He looked into her eyes and smiled and then kissed her on the cheek. She smiled back at him. Then they started to walk out of the cave.

When they got to the horses, Mat put the capes back into his saddlebag.

"Anna, you really do care for my people?" he asked.

"Yes, I do." Anna looked around and sniffed. "Do you smell that?"

"Yes."

Anna heard a strange bird sound, and Mat returned the call. It was one of his guards calling, warning him that danger was near.

"Anna, you must leave now. My guards will be near you until you reach the village. They are close. I need you ride fast and stay on the trail. Do you hear me?"

He picked her up and placed her on her horse.

"What is it, Mat?"

"I do not know, but it does not feel right. Just do as you are told."

"I am not leaving you. I am going to stay and help you."

"You will be in my way. Stay on the path. Do not look back. No stop until you get to the village."

"Mat."

"No, Anna!"

Mat flanked the horse, and off she went.

Mat did not ride; he ran. He knew someone was close, and he wanted to surprise them. He ran through the woods until he came face-to-face with four savages. He knew he was outnumbered; he was going to have to fight them to save Anna. He knew some of the guards would follow Anna and some would come to him. They would be here soon.

The savages surrounded him, brandishing their knives. A savage kicked Mat in the back as he went after another savage with a knife. Mat fell to the ground, and they began kicking him. All he could do was pray. He reached out, caught one by the leg, and pulled him down. Mat swiped at the rest of them with a knife, trying to defend himself.

Anna could feel Mat's fear as she rode, and she felt the blows he received. She turned her horse around and went back to where she had left him. His horse was still there, but he was not.

Why was he on foot and where had he gone, she wondered. She knew she had to get to him quickly. But which way had he gone? Anna slid off her horse and stood with her eyes closed and asked the spirits to help her. Before she knew it, she was in Mat's head.

Mat heard a voice call his name. He looked around and saw no one. Who was speaking to him? Then he heard it again. It was Anna. She had gotten into his mind and was speaking to him.

"Mat, I am with you. Listen and do as I say. Look into their eyes."

Mat looked into one of the savage's eyes. The savage fell to the ground. Then he looked into another's eyes and another's until they all fell.

"Now run. Run to your horse. They will not sleep long. Come and you will get out alive. Come, Mat."

Mat did as she told him. When he reached his horse, Anna was there.

"Hurry, Mat. We must go. They will wake soon."

He put her back on her horse and mounted on his. As they were leaving, Anna thought she saw an old woman standing by the cave. When she looked back again, the woman was gone. They did not stop riding until they reached the village.

"Anna, you save my life. How you do that?" Mat asked her.

"I do not know. I asked the spirits to help me, and then it happened. They led me to you and connected my spirit to yours. The spirits let me communicate with you."

"Yes, Anna, but how you get them to fall asleep?"

"I do not know, Mat. We are safe. That is all that matters," she said. "Thank you for taking me to the cave. I did enjoy myself today. Are you okay? They were fighting hard, and you were hit several times."

"I am fine. Thanks for no listening to me this time. You saved me."

She smiled at him and said, "It was the least I could do since you have saved me so many times."

Chapter 17

No Blood

Anna spent a lot of time with Teka while Mat was away hunting. She even met Teka's girl, Lilly. Lilly was a pretty girl and around twelve years old. Anna knew there was no way Lilly was going to the mating ceremony. But how could she stop the mating? What could she do?

Anna knew Teka loved Lilly very much, so she talked to him about marriage. Teka said he would love for Lilly to be the first girl he mated, but if his father had to do it, he would not protest. Anna told him that she believed in only having one mate. Lilly should be his when she was ready, she said.

"If I could stop the mating, Teka, could you withhold yourself until Lilly is ready and only have her for life?" Anna asked.

"Anna," Teka began, "this is impossible. Father will not allow that. But if I could have one love for a lifetime, I would."

"Done," she said.

"Anna, how do you plan to change our customs?"

"I have my ways, Teka."

Next, Anna went to find Lilly.

"Lilly," she said, "would you like to mate with Teka when it is your time?"

"Yes, Anna. I would like that much."

"If you had a choice, would you allow Teka to continue the mating ceremony after you mate, even if there were a way to stop it?"

"I would only want him to be with me, but that is not how it works," Lilly said.

"Lilly, I can protect you from the mating for a few months until Teka becomes a man."

"How?"

"I have a way, but I need to know this is what you want."

"Oh, yes. Please. I do not want another man to touch me."

"I know how you feel," Anna said. "Lilly, it must be our secret. You must tell no one. Can you bring me all the girls who are about the age to mate? I need them to come to me once they start to bleed. Have them tell no one of their bleeding and bring them straight to me."

"I will."

"It must be a secret. If Father or Mat found out, who knows what they would do. Promise me you will not tell, not even your mother. She will tell, and my plan will not work."

"You can hold off my mating for Teka?" Lilly asked.

"I can hold off your mating so you and Teka can mate together in your home, not out in front of the tribe. Your first time will be special for the both of you."

"Thank you," said Lilly.

When Mat returned from the hunt, he could not wait to see Anna. But there was something different about her. She seemed more at ease when he got close to her.

"Anna, are you okay?"

"Yes," she said.

Mat was on edge. It had been a while since his last mating, and he knew it would not be long before the next. He wondered how she would react the next time. Would she take the girl's pain away again? He was a man with needs. He refused to take another as his lover, so he felt justified in only releasing himself during the mating ceremony. There was no commitment to the girls he mated. It was his job, and he had no other woman to fulfill his manly needs.

It would only be a few months before his son took over the role of Maker. Mat did not know what he would do then. Every day he prayed to the spirits to tell him what to do. His heart was dying; he knew it.

He was still a young man and had desires. Anna's aroma was getting stronger. He did not know if he would be able to control his desires for her much longer. Would she meet his needs? He did not want a relationship with anyone. As long as she was in the village, he did not know if he could stay.

The next day, Mat got up, got dressed, and then it hit him. "Wake up. You bleed," he said to Anna.

"What?" she said.

"Is your time to bleed?"

"Yes. Why?"

"Women go to women's hut during that time."

"Why?"

"To keep clean."

"I can keep myself clean. I do not need to stay at the women's hut."

"Anna, please, you do not understand. I cannot be with you as long as you bleed."

"You can open a child who bleeds, but you cannot stay in a room with a woman who bleeds?"

"It is not that, Anna. I do not know if I can stay away from you."

"Are you saying you have desire for me because I bleed?"

"You already know that."

"So you just want to be with me for your pleasure. Do you really think women do not have desires too?"

"What you mean?"

"Women have desires too. I see how some of the girls

look at you. You open them and they have dreams of what it would be like to be with you all the time."

"That will never happen," he said.

"Do they know that? These girls look at you as their hero. You just made them women. It is the most important day of their lives, and then you have nothing to do with them. Do you not know what that does to a young girl?"

"Anna, I cannot stay here tonight while you bleed."

"What if I tell you, you can stay?"

"In what way?" he asked.

"Would you stay?"

"No, Anna. If I stay with you, I no be able to stop. I cannot do you that way. I will stay with Father until you stop bleed."

A week later, when Lilly started to bleed, she did as Anna had asked. She went straight to her and did not let anyone know where she was going. Anna pulled out a box of tampons.

"Here, Lilly. This will stop your bleed." Anna showed her how to insert the tampons into her body. "Now go. Come back tonight to shower and we will change it."

Before long, other girls came for help. Anna helped them as well.

Mat was becoming impatient that there had been no

mating ceremonies. *What has happened? Why are none of the girls bleeding? It is if they stopped,* he thought.

Mat was at his wit's end not being able to release himself. He did not believe in doing it himself. He went to Mother for advice.

Mother told him, "Man needs to learn to control himself."

"Mother, I do. I no use women for my needs, only the mating."

"Son, sometime you are going to have to forgive yourself and open your heart to another. It is not meant for man to be alone. He needs woman. Go to Anna. You already have a bond."

"I no do that."

"Why? I am sure her desire for you is as strong as yours for her."

"Mother, if I go to her, I am doomed. I will not have the strength to stop. You know I cannot love another."

"How are you doomed? Anna is there for you. You are the one that is holding back."

"I do not know, but there is something about her. If I start, I no stop. You know how I feel about Kati."

"Kati is gone, son. It is time to move on."

There were many girls who would love to lay with him. In his condition, he felt like he would have to go to one. He knew that would be wrong. He was a man of honor. He would not disgrace his family that way. Since Anna was his, he did have the right, but he had promised not to. What was he to do? He had no choice but to go to her. Besides, he had already tasted her, so it would not be wrong. It was his right; she was his.

That night after prayers, he went to her.

"Anna," he said in a serious tone, "I need you. I have needs, and I have no one to go to."

"What kind of needs do you have that you need me to help you?"

"I have manly need. There has not been a mating in a while. I have not gone this long before. I am in pain."

"With all the women in this village, you could not find someone or do it yourself?"

"Anna, please. I am no like that. But no one ready for the mating, and I no understand."

"You mean that the mating ceremony is the only time you …"

He stopped her and said, "Yes. I have no one. Those girls want the power that comes with being with me. If I go to them, then they are mine. You are the only one who has ever had that honor since Kati."

"So you want me to relieve you?"

"Yes, Anna. I am in pain. Will you help me?"

"Okay."

Mat looked at her, surprised. "You will help me, just like that? After all this time saving yourself for your true love?"

"Sure."

"Thank you," he said and went to undress.

But she said, "Stop! You do not need to undress."

"What you mean? Why?"

Anna went to him and brushed herself against his bare back. It sent chills all over him. Then she stood in front of him and removed his breastplate and necklaces. She gently rubbed her hands across his hairless chest. She kissed his chest, neck, and cheek. She ran her hands through his long black hair and down the outside of his pants.

He was getting aroused. Her hands were so soft and gentle. It had been so long since he had felt the gentleness of a woman's hands. She pretended to breathe heavily to arouse him even more. He was ready to take her now.

"Do you feel that?" she said in a sexy voice.

He was breathing harder. "Yes. Anna, please. I can no go much longer."

Anna walked around to his back and felt his strong muscles. She walked back around to his front, placed her hands on his face, pulled his face to her dress, and pressed him gently to her breast.

"I need you, Anna. Now!"

"I am here," she said. She pretended to breathe heavier and faster. "You want me, don't you?"

"Yes!"

"How much?"

"With all my being."

"I want you too," she said in a husky whisper.

"Anna, come on. I must have you now."

"Oh, you don't need me, Mat."

"Yes, I do." He tried to touch her breast, but she stopped him and pushed his hands down.

"You no touch. You came to me for help. Let me help you." She kissed his neck and then bit his ear.

He was ready. She pushed him up against the wall, caressed his chest, and then moved her hand down below his belt, just far enough to feel his hair and nothing else.

He gasped. "Anna, you killing me. I must have you now."

"Now?" she whispered in his ear.

"Yes, now." He could hardly talk.

She rubbed her hands down the outside of his pants and licked his lip but didn't let him kiss her. She reached between his legs and gently squeezed. He started to let out a yell, but Anna placed three fingers over his lips to keep him quiet. Then it was over. Mat looked down and then back up into her eyes. He was speechless.

"There. Are you better now?" Anna asked. "That should last you for a while. Is there anything else I could do for you?"

He could not say a word. He got another pair of pants and left to clean himself up in the river. When he came back to go to bed, he did not know what to say except "That not fair."

Anna thought about how unfair she had been to him. He had expected something different, but she was not ready for that. She did not want to be used to satisfy a need. She needed to be loved to give herself to him. But he had to be willing to give himself back to her. She was falling for him, and she knew it, but was he her true love? No. A person could only have one true love, and he had already had his. So in her mind he could not love her back the way she wanted him to.

"Good night, Mat. I hope you are feeling better."

"Anna, one day, yes, one day I will have my way with you. That, I promise."

"Sweet dreams, Mat."

Anna knew if she stayed much longer, it would not be long before she gave in and gave herself to him. She wanted him as much as he wanted her, but it was not in her plan.

A few days later Mat noticed a lot of young girls going to see Anna. *What is she up to now?* he wondered. Lilly was the last one in the hut with Anna that night. Mat decided he needed to see what she was up to. When he came into the hut, he could smell blood.

"Anna, she bleeds?"

Anna was hiding something behind her back.

"Anna, what have you done?"

"This is girl business. You should leave," Anna said with a stern face.

Mat walked over to her, pulled her hand from behind her back, and opened it. Inside was a tampon.

"What is this?" He looked at Lilly. "You bleed?"

Lilly started to tear up.

"Leave her be," Anna said.

"Anna, you cannot interfere. How long has this been going on? This why no one bleeds? You hide it from me. We mate tonight."

"Mat, no," Anna said. "This is Teka's girl. Teka will be of age soon. Please let him mate with her."

"No, I said. You should have never done this. You let me suffer all this time. How many others are there?"

Anna would not speak.

"Ceremony tonight, and you will not interfere. Do you hear me? You no take her pain."

Anna begged, "Please. I will do anything if you would just let her have more time."

"No, Anna. I will deal with you tomorrow. Now we prepare for the ceremony."

Mat took Lilly for the preparation.

Anna ran to Mother for advice. "Mother, please tell me how the mating ceremony works. Please help me?"

Mother told her, "The girl must agree. If she does not agree, then she is put in the women's hut, where she is guarded until she bleeds again. She will stay there until the ceremony is done.

"What if she never agrees?"

"After she refuses three times, she will go to the whipping pole. If she does not go to mate, she will go to her death."

"They kill them if they choose not to mate?"

"All women belong to men, and all men belong to women."

"Three times, huh?" Anna said. "If the girl refuses, someone can take her place to buy her extra time? So you are saying if someone else took her place, she would have up to three times to refuse?"

"Yes, dear."

"Thank you, Mother."

"Anna! Anna!" Mother yelled. "Think what you do. Think!"

Anna met with Lilly and asked her, "Do you agree to do this?

"What choice do I have?"

"You do have a choice. Tell them no you do not want to be opened tonight."

"They will whip me."

"Trust me. They will not. I have the answer, and you will not go to the whipping pole."

"Anna, I do not want to make him mad."

"He will not be mad at you. He will be mad at me. Think of Teka. If I can buy you time, is it worth having your first time be with him and no one else, forever? He would be yours and you would be his."

"Oh yes. Can you do that?"

"I am sure of it. Just follow my lead. Say nothing except that you do not choose to mate now."

It was time for Lilly to walk out. Anna walked with her.

"Hold your head up high," she told Lilly. "Do not let them know you are afraid. We mean business, and they will listen."

Out came Mat. He walked up to them and said, "Why are you here, Anna? You must leave. We will talk tomorrow. You are dismissed."

"Dismissed?" she said to him. "You do not own me, so you cannot dismiss me."

"Anna, you need to leave."

"No!" Anna turned to the crowd. "This girl has something

to say." Anna held Lilly's shoulders as the girl stood in front of her.

Lilly said, "I chose not to be mated tonight."

Mat looked into Anna's eyes with deep concern. "Anna, what are you doing?"

"I will do anything I can to protect these girls, even if it means you taking me instead."

"What are you talking about?"

Anna turned to the crowd and said, "I understand that if one does not agree to be mated, someone else can take her place."

"No, Anna! What are you doing? You cannot do this. No!" Mat yelled.

Anna, still looking at the crowd, said, "I choose of my own free will and agree to be mated in the place of this child, Lilly."

Mat hung his head and shook it from side to side.

"Anna," he whispered. He closed his eyes tightly, pulled himself together, and looked at her. "Let it be as she has stated. Prepare her now."

Anna did not resist. They undressed her, placed her on the table, tied her arms above her head, spread her legs apart, and tied them so she could not move. Mat was sick to his stomach. He did not want to do this to her. He knew how she felt, and he had promised not to take advantage of her.

This was her choice, though, and he could not do anything about it now.

Anna was shaking all over. This was harder than being on the whipping pole. Being undressed completely in front of the tribe was deeply embarrassing. She felt like nothing but an animal. The most intimate part of her life was being exposed for all to see. How could these women allow this to happen? She would stop this if it meant she would take every girl's place.

Mat walked over to her, bent down, and said into her ear, "Why you do this?"

Anna said nothing.

"Stop this now Anna."

Again she said nothing.

"Anna, I no want to do this."

A tear rolled down her face, but she still said nothing.

"Anna, you not bleed. You know what can happen."

She looked in the eye and said, "You know what to do. Just get it over with. You are a great man of power. Do your duty. You heard me. Just get it over with."

Her words were cold. Mat could feel it. He knew this was wrong, but like she said, it was his duty.

Anna, still shaking, told herself, *Be strong! I will not cry out.*

He entered her body. She arched her back and held her

breath with each thrust. He started slow and got faster. She could feel him inside her much like what had happened on the trail. She breathed heavily, gasping for breath.

She was lost, as was he. He became more forceful as time went on. Both were sweating and breathing hard. This was more than mating; he knew it, but he could not stop. He had been wanting to be with her for some time, and he got lost in the moment. He watched her every move.

She was pulling so hard with her arms to touch him that her wrists began to bleed. He wanted to hold and touch every part of her body and drink from her, but it was forbidden during the ceremony. He knew he could not make her with child, so just before he released, he removed himself from her without anyone seeing and sang his lovemaking call. Anna knew, and that was all that mattered to him. He was her protector, and that was what he was doing, protecting her from becoming with child.

Once he had finished, Mat waved for the guards to leave her tied. Father, dressed in a similar headdress, but one with more feathers than Mat's, along with the elders, danced and chanted around Mat in front of the tribe. Mat went to his knees. Father held a feather and brushed it over Mat's body. Then, holding the feather with both hands, he lifted it into the air to bless it. He slowly handed the feather to Mat, who also held the feather gently, flat in both hands, lifted it above his head, and chanted as if he too were blessing it.

Mat stood up to address the tribe. Then he put on his robe, went over to Anna, and said, "You are in my world now, and you are mine."

He cut her arms down. She covered her breasts. Then he cut her legs loose so she could bring them together. She turned away from him. He picked her up and carried her all the way to his bed.

He wrapped her wrists to stop the bleeding and said, "You sleep here." Then he left to clean himself up.

Anna lay there in shock. She did not know what to do. What had just happened? She had been told that the mating was fast and without emotion. But she did have emotion, a lot of it. Other than the fact that they had tied her up and he hadn't touched her, it had been wonderful. What had she done? How was she to stay away from him now that they had shared themselves with each other? They had united. Her spirit wanted more, but her mind told her she was dirty. Anna got off the bed and walked outside without any clothing on.

When Mat returned, she was not there. *Where would she go?* he wondered. *She is not dressed. Her clothes are still on the bed.* Mat's heart began to race. Had the savages come back to take her? He was in a panic. He ran out of the hut and saw her sitting in a fetal position in her shower.

Anna was numb and in a daze. She made no effort to move. He joined her, fully dressed, helped her stand, and gently washed her off in the dark. First he washed her tears away. Then, slowly moving downward, he washed her arms, breasts, back, and legs. He then put the cloth into her hand for her to wash between her legs. He would let her do that herself.

Mother met him outside the shower with a blanket to wrap Anna up in. With one arm around Anna and holding her hand with his other hand, he gently led her safely out of the shower to Mother to be covered.

"Mother, I can do this. She needs me now."

"I know, son. Anna is in shock. She feels she is no longer pure. She has sacrificed herself in order to save Lilly from having to go through the mating. Her spirit is telling her something different. The spirits are helping her cope, but she is resisting. She knows what she has been taught and feels she has done wrong. We must handle her with care to not damage her mind. She will need time to accept what has happened so she can move on."

"Mother, I feel her pain, and I am not going to leave her here to handle this herself. I did not want this to happen. I had no other choice, did I? If I had refused, Father would have taken over. Then where would we be tonight? I had to finish what was started. I feel you had something to do with her trading places with Lilly. I heard you talking with her about the mating ceremony. You put ideas into her head. I blame you this time for what happened. She did not know about taking Lilly's place until she spoke to you. I will take care of her now. You may leave."

"Son, do you remember the sacrifice you made when it was your turn to be the maker? Anna is doing the same. She has strong feelings about Teka and Lilly starting their lives together, being pure. She will not stop until she gets what she wants."

Mother turned and patted Mat's shoulder before returning to her own hut.

Inside their hut, Mat laid Anna, who was still wrapped in the blanket, on his bed. She was still in shock. Mat went to the other end of the hut to put his sleeping clothes on. When he returned to dress her in her gown, Anna would not let go of the blanket. He was not going to force her, so he lay with her and held her close.

"Anna, I know you no want me here right now, but you need me. I am so sorry. My heart is breaking. I feel your pain." Tears came from his eyes. "Please, Anna, understand I would have never forced myself on you. I do want you, but not like this. There will be a time, and it will be for the right reason."

She did not resist lying in his bed. She remained motionless for a few minutes. Then she started to shake. He brushed her hair away from her face and gently rubbed her face and arms. Then he held her tightly. When Anna had calmed down, he felt a power come over her.

"Mat, I need you now more than ever."

She removed the blanket to expose her naked body to him. She rolled over and placed her head on his chest. Mat knew what was happening and had to think fast. He knew the spirit had won this battle. He was not dealing just with Anna, but with the spirit as well.

"Mat, take me now. I feel so close to you, and I want you as you want me. Please, take me now."

Anna reached up to kiss him, but he pulled away.

"Anna, this is not the right time. I do want you. I want you so bad I cannot stand it. If we go together tonight, you will regret it tomorrow. You are not yourself at the moment. You are with Spirit. I promised I would not take advantage of you, so I cannot take you tonight."

Mat could feel her body wrap around him as she climbed on top of him. He placed a finger over her lips. "No, Anna. We need to sleep."

"Please, Mat. I cannot stand not having you all the way. I need you. I love you."

Anna was getting excited. She tried to kiss him again.

"No, Anna. We must sleep now. There will be a time when I will have you, and it will be soon, but not tonight. Please understand this is not the right time. I want our first time together to be special, something we both will remember the rest of our lives."

Mat wanted her just as badly as she wanted him. It took all his strength to resist her. He had been waiting for her to give herself to him of her own free will. Here was his chance. But he knew it would be wrong; he had to withhold himself from her.

"Then hold me close," she said.

He covered her body and held her all night as they listened to the lovemaking calls from throughout the village.

Chapter 18

True Love

When Anna woke the next morning, Mat had already gotten up. She saw the headdress hanging on the wall. She remembered that during the ceremony Mat had received another feather to add to his collection. Anna then realized that each feather represented a time he had mated. There were so many, hundreds. She felt sick.

Father had one too, with even more feathers than Mat's. Father was on his third row; Mat was on his second. It had to be because he had performed more mating ceremonies than Mat. Father had had to take Mat's place when he ran away and Mat's father's place when he died before Mat could take over.

There were so many feathers. She started to count but then decided she did not need to know. She went to breakfast looking for Mat, but he was not there. She knew how he must feel after being with her, and she was sure he had regrets. Anna went to look for him at Kati's grave. There he was, praying. She stood back and watched him as he was in deep thought.

She wondered what he was thinking about, so she decided to get into his head to find out for herself. She knew it was wrong, but they did have a bond. She so desperately wanted to help him and find out what this girl had had that she did not to have such a hold on him. If she could find out, then maybe she could help him. Anna knew she was falling in love with him, but she was not sure if he had the feelings that she wanted from a man, and this Kati was in her way.

Anna entered into his mind with no trouble and could hear his thoughts:

Kati, I miss you so much. I remember the first time we met. I was eight, out trying to track a deer. I had just learned to walk without making a sound. As I crossed the river, the deer took off toward the mountain. It was an overcast that day. There were many clouds, and it was on the verge of rain. I wanted to make sure it was not a doe, as it is forbidden to kill a doe during the hot months. Once I got close enough, I was sure it was a buck; it had two points. It was young and small but a buck.

I had my bow and the new arrows I had just made. I needed to see how well they worked, and what better way than to kill a deer? I wanted to make Father proud of me for bringing home fresh meat. I spotted the deer grazing in a field of clover. I hid behind the brush. Not making a sound, I eased closer and closer. I was so proud of myself. I had done it. I got my bow out and nocked an arrow. I remember saying to myself, "Wait. Wait. *Now.*" Just as I was about to release the arrow, I heard the loudest crashing noise on the side of the mountain. There went my deer.

I could see smoke, so I ran to get Father. Father gathered a few men, and we went to scout it out. We found a bird made of metal that had fallen from the sky. It was small and broken in half. The front of the bird was smashed in, and two people were inside. The man looked as if he had died instantly, but the woman had lingered, for she had tried to crawl out.

The fire was almost out when we arrived. The men got down off their horses and stomped the remaining flames out. We looked around but could not find anyone else. I spotted some small footprints and started tracking them. I knew I had to find whoever made the tracks soon. There were wolf prints everywhere, and they were close. I followed the footprints to the river. I could hear a soft cry. I did not know at first what it was, but it sounded like a child calling out the name Kati.

As I got closer, I knew it was coming from beneath a river boulder. There you were, hiding from me. I jumped down and crawled underneath the boulder to get to you. You were so afraid. You were bruised and covered in blood from your cuts. When you saw me, you went deeper under the rock. I reached for you, but you would not come. I reached into my pouch and handed you some dried meat. You took it and ate it as if you had not had anything to eat in days. After a few minutes you took my hand and came out to me. When I spoke to you, you seemed not to understand. You spoke words I had never heard before. I asked your name. All you would say was Kati. So we said no more.

I reached into my pouch and took out some cloth. I wet it and washed the blood off you.

You were the prettiest thing I had ever seen, and I felt a connection to you right then. I knew you had been given to me by the spirits, and I felt our bond. You followed me back to Father and the men.

You were still afraid and hid behind my legs. You could not have been more than three years old. When I looked into your crying eyes, I knew then that we had a bond. I just did not know how much of a bond until many years later. I knew you were special. Father took you to our hut, and you lived with us there.

Father knew we had a connection and that you were different. He once told me that the moment he saw us together that day, it was in our eyes. I believe that is why he let us do as we pleased. We were so close, we never left each other's side. Father never objected that we were not the same color. I guess he figured there was no reason to stop us, for that would have been impossible.

Once you started to know us better, you spoke English and taught us all you knew. As you got older, you could get into my mind and see me, and I too could talk to you in your mind, but I did not have the power to see you. That was okay by me. As long as we could talk, that was all that mattered. Every time one of us got hurt, we knew it and came running. We were like one person. As children, we were inseparable and there was nothing anyone could do about it. I loved you so much. Do you remember the day we were in the valley and found a tree? We carved our names into the bark. It is still there. I visit it often. Oh, how I miss you.

We were not afraid to go in our bare skin. Everyone did it, and you understood our customs. I love the way you accepted our way of life. I remember the day I sat you down when you were nine and told you about me becoming man. I can remember word for word what I said.

"Kati, next week I will be of age and I will become the maker. I love you so much. I cannot stand the fact that you are not ready. You know I love you with all my heart, soul, and mind. Father has no choice but to make me the maker, and I no want to mate with another before you. You are a part of me, and I want you to be my first."

Remember what I did? I ran away. That was my plan. We decided that we would talk to each other daily until you were ready to become a woman. You agreed to wait for me.

You told me once we mated, I would then become the maker. You told me how much you loved me. You said you loved me more than ever, with your whole heart, soul, and mind. I was your true love, your soul mate.

I broke the rules and went to live with the white people to learn your ways. I sent to you the things I learned, and in return, you taught my people English. When it was time for you to become a woman, you had a vision and sent for me. I was so happy and excited to be back with you again. Oh, how I missed you then and still do.

You were eleven. I came as fast as I could, leaving everything behind. I will never forget the look on your face when I returned. You ran to me, and I ran to you. We mated that night. We were not afraid to be bare skinned in front of the villagers, for we were used to it. You were so beautiful as you got up on the table, all dressed with flowers. I could not wait to have you.

I was so proud to wear the mating ceremony headdress and accept my first feather. Whatever happened next was from the spirits; I am sure of it. You felt it, as I did. You were not tied as all others are. We were free to touch each other as we pleased. It was like we had never seen each other's body before. Neither of us knew what to do. It was our first time, but it came naturally. The spirits took us to another world. We explored each other's body with all the new feelings we felt. We made passionate love to each other without hesitation. It was as if we were glued together. We were one person in all ways.

Father did not stop us. He allowed us to be together. It was the most wonderful feeling to hold you in my arms and enter your body. There had never been a mating in that fashion before. Our love was so great, and the spirits blessed you with child. We were so excited about becoming a family. Father and some men helped build our hut. We were going to have many children.

You were so happy when we moved in. We had more privacy than in Father's hut. It was ours. You fixed it up, and we had many special nights and days together all alone. We spent days deciding on the name for our child, Teka for a boy and Aika for a girl.

It was time for the yearly hunt, when all young men from age fifteen to age twenty-five go out to hunt for three weeks to provide food to last the winter. I am so sorry I left you. I should have stayed and protected you. You told me to go; it was not time for the baby. You even told me that babies were born every day and that I was not to worry. I was worried the baby would come before I returned. I wanted to be there with you.

We had done everything together, and this was no different. I had a sickening feeling when I left. If I had only stayed, you may still be here with me.

I remember you saying, "Matete, it will be fine. If I need you, I will call you. We will talk in our minds every day. Do not worry about me. Now go make your family proud."

So I against my better judgment, I kissed you and left with the rest of the men. I still did not feel right about it.

We had a great start. I killed two deer and was tracking a third. I sent some men back to the village so that the women could start preparing the meat and hide. If only I had been the one to take the deer back to the village. You would still be here.

I will never forgive myself for not coming back when I could have. I became sicker to my stomach as days went on and I had not heard from you in my mind. All I could think was that the baby had come and you were too busy for me.

When the hunt was over, I hurried to you. Something did not feel right. You were not there to greet me as you always did. I ran to our hut to see if you had delivered the baby, but you were not there. Our bed had not even been slept in. I wondered where you were. I knew something was wrong, so I went to see Father. When I went into his hut, Mother was sitting on her bed with an infant in her arms. I asked where you were. When I saw her face, I knew you had left me. I felt life leave my body.

"Son, I am so sorry. Kati fell, and the baby came early. The baby survived but not your Kati. Before she passed, she told me to name him Teka. She said you two had worked really hard on coming up with this name, being from both your names."

I fell to my knees and sobbed. I hear it every day, the way I screamed, "No! No! Not my Kati. She is my life. So beautiful, kind, sweet, and loving. All she ever wanted was to love me and have many children."

I asked Mother why the spirits took you from me. I didn't understand, and I turned from the spirits. Mother assured me that the spirits had not turned on me, but I could not believe they would let this happen.

Mother handed me my son. She said, "Here is your son. He looks like you, but Kati gave him her eyes. She lives in him all his days. The spirits blessed you, son. Open your eyes and see."

I remember all of this every day of my life, like it happened yesterday. I died inside that day. I promise to never have another and to visit you every day to bring you a flower. You are not dead to me. You will always be my life. Please forgive me. Someone has come into my life, and I have been unfaithful to you. I miss you so much, and I am sorry. I was weak. Will you ever forgive me?

Anna was in tears. She'd had no clue what Mat had been through. She knew she had heard too much, so she decided to go to him. He was in such pain and needed her. She had not realized just how special Kati had been to him.

When she got within ten feet of him, he stopped her. "Stop. Stop, Anna. Please leave. This is no place for you now. I need my time alone. Leave!"

Anna stopped for just a moment. Then she went to him and standing behind him, placed her hands on his shoulders. Her hands were so soft, it made chills run down Mat's back.

"Mat, my heart breaks for you. I know last night was hard for you, as it was for me. This was my choice, not yours. You only did your duty as maker. It was not your fault. Please, Mat. Do not blame yourself. I can feel your pain, and I cannot stand to see you this way."

"Anna, I have ruined you. You've told me so. I did not

want to mate with you last night. I could have stopped it. I never wanted us to come together like that. I know how hard it was for you. I do not understand why. Why did you put me in a position I could not get out of without punishment? If I had refused, Father would have taken my place. The ceremony must go on."

Anna sat beside him and reached over to turn his face toward her. He had been crying. She wiped the tears from his eyes.

"Mat, it is not your fault. I did it to protect Lilly. I asked you to postpone the ceremony, and you know I am a stubborn woman. You would not work with me on this, so I made the decision. It was the only way I knew to save Lilly for Teka. You too are a stubborn man and would not listen to me. What would it have hurt to just wait a while?"

"Anna, I have betrayed my love for Kati."

"How so?"

"During the ceremony, you already woman and you no bleed. High chance of making you with child. I have child with Kati, and I will not make another."

"What are you saying? You already made many children."

"No, Anna. You no understand. I not make child with love during the mating. During the mating, it is quick. I did not mate you; I made love to you. Much different. Because of my feelings for you, I got overexcited. I no do during the mating. By being weak, I have betrayed my Kati's love. I need time to ask her for forgiveness. Anna, I wanted you so much, and I know you felt the same. I could see it in your eyes."

"Yes, Mat. The cuts and rope burns on my wrists are not from me fighting back or trying to get loose. They are from my need to hold you."

"Yes, Anna. I knew that. We made love, and I am so sorry to publicly humiliate you that way. I wanted that day to be special, when we both were ready."

"Mat, it is okay. It was my choice. You did what you had to do. I expected no less. Thank you for not making me with child. Not that I don't want a child, just not today. And thank you for not refusing. I could not live with myself if Father had done the mating."

"What are we going to do, Anna?"

"We are going to move on with our lives and see where my God takes me and where your spirits send you. You are going to add my feather to your trophy headdress and have no regrets."

"You are a strong woman. I have misjudged you. Can you forgive me?"

"Yes, and don't ever forget how strong I am. I forgive you, but I do want my feather next to the first feather to represent your first and your last. Can you forgive me for putting you in this position?"

Mat burst out laughing. "Anna, you always have a say back. You put sunshine into me on a cool brisk morning, warming my heart, never knowing which way the wind will blow. You do have the gift to calm people. I always feel better when we talk. Go get breakfast. I will be there soon. I need a little more time with Kati."

"Take your time with Kati. I know she understands and forgives you. I will be waiting for you."

Chapter 19

Secret

All Anna could think about was how Mat had been with all the girls in the tribe who had become women over the last fifteen years. Soon his son would take over and do the same. Teka seemed like a sweet boy, but there was something about him that she could not shake. She could see it in his eyes.

He must have his mother's eyes, for they were different than Mat's. They were not cold and black; they were brown. She could see he was going to be big and strong like his dad. In fact, he was almost there now. Would this becoming a man change him, she wondered.

As she worked with the babies, she wondered how many of them were Mat's. Did some have his eyes, his smile, his cry, his nose, his toes, his fingers? *What is wrong with me?* she thought. *It is all about Mat. I need to get over him. We have no future together."*

Mat came by to see how she was doing. She looked at him with so much curiosity that she just had to ask, "Are all of these yours?" She made a sweeping gesture with her hand across the room.

He smiled. "No. Is that what is on your mind?"

"Well, you did have your way with all of their mothers first."

"What?"

"Surely some of these are yours?"

Mat went to Anna and gently sat her down. "Anna, some are mine and some are not. I do not have claim to any of these children."

"How do you know the ones you fathered?"

"Does not matter. I will be Father to all of tribespeople."

"Mat, I am serious. How can one tell?"

Mat took a child into his arms and showed Anna the brand. "Here is where the mother's brand goes, and here is where the father's brand goes. When children are promised to one another, we make sure their brands no match. All children are branded with both parents' brands."

"So what is your brand?

"Anna, please. You do not need to know."

"But I want to."

"No, Anna. Let it go. Please let it go. It no matter. You will make crazy more than you already are."

"I am not crazy."

"That depends on who's talking."

Mat continued to refuse to show her his brand. Then he told her he was going hunting and would be back in a few days.

"Why do you feel the need to tell me?" Anna asked. "I am not your keeper."

"I thought you would like to know. I be gone maybe six to seven days."

"Thanks," she said. "Be careful."

"I thought you no care."

"Well, I have to keep up my good image, don't I?"

He just shook his head and said, "You impossible."

"You too," she replied.

The more she looked around the sick hut, the more she wondered. Who had the most brands alike? This was impossible. Then she remembered Teka had the brand. That is where she would find her answers. She went to find Teka. She looked in their hut and then went to see Mother to see if she knew where he was.

Anna walked into Mother's hut just in time to see a birth. A young girl was in the final stages of delivery. Her pain was so great that Anna started to take it away.

Mother said, "No, Anna. She has to do this on her own. If you take her pain away, I cannot do my job. I need to know when she needs to push. Anna, don't!" Mother said again.

Mother noticed Anna had drifted away. She was having

a vision. Mother became worried because it was a long one. Anna watched the rest of the birth in a daze. She saw the branding. When it was all over, Anna was still standing there, not knowing what to do.

Anna looked at Mother and said in a whisper, "You lied. You told me I had not been with a man."

Mother said, "Not lie. No, Anna. I did not lie. I said you had not been with another man."

Anna said, "Yes, to Matete you lie. Both you and Father."

"Anna, dear, look at me. Tell me what you see."

"Mat is hunting."

"Yes, I know. Mat is hunting."

Anna began to shake. "Matete is hunting. The baby comes." Anna looked away. "It was a boy."

"Yes, dear. It was a boy."

"The girl did not die."

"No, Anna. She did not."

"Matete was not here. Mother, you were here."

"Yes, I was there."

"It was a beautiful boy, with lots of black hair like his father."

"Yes, Anna, he was."

"I looked to see if he had all his fingers and toes."

"Yes, you did."

"He was beautiful. I was so happy, I cried. Matete was hunting."

"Yes, he was," Mother said. "You did cry."

"Then they branded him and I named him. Matete and I had thought for a long time on the name. Part his name and part my name. *Te* from Matete's name, and *ka* from my name, Kati."

"Yes, dear. Teka. Yes, a beautiful name, Kati," Mother said.

"What have you done, Mother?"

Anna walked out, still in a daze, and went to Father's hut. She walked in without announcing herself. Father could see in her face that she knew.

"Father, what have you done?" she demanded.

"Anna, sit."

She shouted, "I do not want to sit. I want to know why I am here and who I am!" Anna slapped Father. "I have a son!"

Mother had walked in just as Anna had started screaming at him. Anna was hysterical. Mother tried to calm her. Anna was so loud that Teka came running in. Mother told Teka to leave.

Teka stood up to her and said, "No, Mother!"

Father slapped him. "You no talk back."

Anna jumped in. "You keep your hands off him. I

want some answers now, and if I am right, he needs to hear them too."

Teka turned to Anna and said, "Mother, are you okay?"

Anna tilted her head as she looked at him with teary eyes. "You called me Mother?"

"I know, Mother. I have known from the first day you came."

"How?"

"You have my brand on your leg. I saw it when you were sick."

"Why did you not say something?"

"It not my secret to tell."

"I did not know. What must you think of me?" Anna said.

Teka looked at Father and said, "It seems someone has some explaining to do."

Mother looked at Father and said, "I told you so. Stubborn old man does not listen. Tell her and Teka. Tell them now."

Anna calmed down, and she and Teka took a seat.

Father started from the beginning. "Twenty-five years ago, a bird fell from the sky. Lots of smoke. We search the forest and found a little girl no more than three years old. She was covered in blood and crying out, "Kati." We found the bird that fell with Kati's parents inside, both dead.

"We took the child home, and she lived with us until she was twelve. Kati and Matete became very close. They did everything together. There was a bond between them that no one could break. They both shared their spirits. She knew him in every way, and he knew her. When it was time for her to bleed, I let Matete perform the ceremony. Matete has blamed himself for her death because he went against the spirit. Kati was his first, and they married. They loved each other deeper than anyone I have ever seen. There was no way to separate them. While Matete was on the yearly hunt, Kati gave birth to a boy.

"Matete and the group of men were gone for three weeks. During that time, a man who had been searching for the bird that fell from the sky for ten years found it. He searched and searched for anyone who knew what had happened. We found him wandering in the woods. We told him that we had found the little girl, Kati. A puzzled look came across the man's face, for Kati was his daughter-in-law's name he said.

"We took him to you, Anna. You did not know who he was because you were too young at the time of the accident to remember. We knew you were his granddaughter because you knew who your parents were from a photograph he carried with him.

"We knew you would never leave the tribe, for your love

for Matete was that strong. Mother knew you had special powers, a spirit she had never seen before. We were afraid of that spirit and made the decision to let you go back home with your grandfather, without the baby.

"Mother mixed up a potion that would remove your memory. She slipped it into your drink. It worked. You did not remember anything. Your grandfather was so thankful, he promised to give us this land in return for saving you.

"We decided that if you and Matete had not found another love by your twenty-seventh year, before your spirit matured, we would reunite you to see if it was true that you were meant to be together. Matete went mad when we told him you had died in childbirth. He blamed himself for going against the spirit. He swore he would never love another. He was close to Teka and made a promise to bring him up right for Kati.

"In this box is a unity necklace that Matete made for you. I placed it in your grandfather's box, and he gave me the key."

Father opened the box and gave Anna the necklace inside.

"Matete has the mate to this necklace. This is proof of who you are, and with that necklace, Matete will believe you are truly Kati."

Anna spoke up. "Kati was my mother's name. I was calling out for her. I remember seeing her face covered in blood.

Both of you are fools. Did you really think the spirits would allow us to not be together?"

Teka and Anna compared their brands.

"Teka, you are so much like your father. He has done a great job with you, just as I would have wanted him to."

She looked at both Mother and Father and said, "I am not dead. What is done is done, and you will suffer the rest of your days with what you have done. I hope he forgives you when he finds out."

Mother said, "We did what we thought was right, Anna. You would have never left on your own with a child. Matete would have followed you, and he would not have survived in your world. If your grandfather took you, Matete would have searched for you for the rest of his years."

"So you would let his soul die over a lie? I cannot see that," she said. Then she spoke out in a harsh tone, "I do not want any of you to tell Mat. Do you understand? Teka, promise me."

"I promise, Mother."

"I need to trust you on this."

"I promise. I do not lie. I will not tell him. It is your secret. You tell him when you are ready."

Anna sent Teka away. Once he was out of hearing distance, she looked at both Mother and Father. "I understand what you did. I probably would have done the same to save my family from pain. You did it for land and for all your people. It was a sacrifice you made for your people at Mat's expense. I see that. Now, if you want to keep this land, then I have some things I want. First, I do not want you to tell Mat about this. I need for him to love me for who I am now and not who I was. I mean what I say."

She continued, "If he finds out from anyone, I will destroy this land with the snap of my fingers. I will get back to you on the other things I want. I have to give great thought to how to tell Mat. Do not speak of this again."

Father agreed.

Anna left the hut, and Mother ran after her.

"Anna, wait. Please."

Anna turned to her and said, "Have you not already done enough damage? You have destroyed Mat's and my life. My son grew up without the love of his mother. You took that away from us all. We will never get that back."

"I know," Mother said. "You need to hear me. Mat is a proud man and strong willed. He will fight you. He will feel that you are trying to take Kati's place. This could backfire on you. Your plan to win him over is not going to be easy."

"Don't you think I know that?"

"No, Anna. His spirit will be fighting too. In fact, both your spirits will fight you both for what they want. He will resist because he feels the spirits have turned their backs on him. He will reject the spirits and die."

"Yes, and whose fault is that? Looks like we have a situation, don't we?" Anna said. "It looks to me like he has been dying for the last fifteen years."

Chapter 20

The Confession

When Mat returned from his trip, he could hardly wait to see Anna. While on the hunt, he had come across the luggage he had thrown out that belonged to Anna. He had gone through a few pieces of luggage and brought back some items for her. He could not wait to see the expression on her face when he showed her what he had found.

Mat was sitting on his bed when Anna came in to put her laundry away. She looked at him, not knowing how to handle the news of him being her husband and the fact that she was Kati. How was she to win him over? She knew it would be tricky and she would have to do it over time. She had thought about it all night.

When she saw him sitting on the bed, she noticed the sneaky look on his face. Had he already been told? What was he up to?

"Hi. I see you are back in one piece. Did the hunt go good for you? Did you find a helpless bear to kill?"

"Yes, the hunt went good. I killed eight deer and two wild hogs. And no animals were helpless. It was a fair hunt. But I did come across something I no understand." Mat held up two small pieces of flowered fabric. "What is this used for?" he asked.

Anna smiled. "That is my bathing suit. Where did you get that?" She went to snatch it out of his hands.

"I found on side of road."

"Really? I wonder how it got there."

He just smiled at her and asked, "You bathe in this?"

"No. I swim in this."

From the smug look on his face, she could tell he had something else to share with her.

"What else did you find?"

He pointed at the end of her bed. She looked at him with a grin on her face.

"That is a teddy." She held it up to her body and said, "This is what I sleep in to have fun."

He raised his eyebrows twice and said, "Much better than that gown. You wear teddy for me?"

"I wear for you when you can touch."

"You sleep in tonight?"

She just rolled her eyes at him.

That night, when she went to get dressed for bed, she saw

the teddy lying on her bed. She picked it up, wadded it up, and threw it at him. "Not tonight," she said.

He smiled and said, "Soon, Anna. Soon."

She smiled and rolled her eyes at him again.

"Anna, your eyes will roll out of your head one day if not careful."

The next day, after his morning run and breakfast, Mat asked Anna to return to their hut with him. When they got inside, Mat handed her the bathing suit.

"We swim today."

She agreed and sent him outside while she changed. He took her to a beautiful place deep in the woods. There was a lake surrounded by mountains, as well as a picture-perfect waterfall.

"Wow, Mat. You amaze me. There are so many places out here that are breathtaking."

It was a warm day, and the air was so clean. She remembered how bad the air smelled in New York City. She sat on a rock and admired how beautiful it all was. All she could hear was the water flowing down the waterfall and the sounds of nature. It was so peaceful.

"Mat, this place is so nice and peaceful. Why have you not shown it to me before?"

"No bathing suit."

"Mat, you are too funny."

She lay back on a rock to sunbathe. He did not understand and asked her if he should lay with her. She explained that she was sunbathing. She could see he did not understand.

"I lie in the sun to make my skin darker. Not as dark as yours, but darker."

"Why you want dark skin? Your skin is nice and soft. Too much sun makes skin tough."

"I do not want too much sun. Just enough to fit in with your people. Look at me. I am white as snow. If I get a little darker then maybe I would not be referred to as white meat."

"You will always be white meat no matter how dark you get. Your skin smells different, sweeter than women in my tribe. There no way you can hide being white."

"Do I taste different?"

"Your kisses are sweeter, so yes."

"No, Mat. That is not what I was talking about. Is my wine sweeter?"

"Anna, we said we would not talk of this again." He just smiled at her.

Mat looked up and saw an eagle fly past them. He got on his knees and looked as if he was praying. Anna looked at him with curiosity. Before she could speak, he told her how the eagle was a sacred bird to his people.

"They very powerful and fly closest to the spirits. They

carry our prayers and messages on their wings to the spirits. The eagles and the red-tailed hawks are both respected, and their feathers are used in our ceremonies."

Just then, the eagle lost one of its feathers, and Anna caught it before it hit the ground.

"Anna, this is great. You have in your hands a feather from the great bird, a feather that has never touched the ground. This feather very important. You must never let it touch the ground. To hold one of these feathers is of great honor. It means the eagle is watching over you. You have been blessed by the spirits."

Mat cut a piece of cloth from the dress she had worn over her bathing suit to wrap the feather up in to protect it.

"Father will honor you at the next ceremony with this feather. I will help you come up with a way to display it, either in jewelry or a headdress. This is a great honor."

"Mat, I do not need to be honored."

"Yes. This is very special in our world. You will be honored, for you have been blessed by the great eagle."

Mat sat beside her and watched as she began to sweat under the heat of the sun.

"Anna, you get hot. Need to cool off."

Anna stood up and spotted Missy on one of the mountain cliffs.

"Mat, look. There is Missy. She is a beautiful dog."

"No dog, Anna. She is wolf. I tell you she very dangerous. I think she is watching you. Wolves have spirit, and she feels your danger. You need be careful around her. She no friend."

"Oh, Mat. I do not believe she will hurt me. You do not have to worry. I do believe she is watching us and keeping us safe."

"Anna, you have such an imagination. You must have special spirit to have the spirit gods, the eagle and the white wolf watching over you."

Then he pushed her into the water. Anna screamed because the water was so cold. He dove in, thinking something was wrong, and swam to her.

"You okay?"

"Yes. It is just cold. I will be fine."

Anna swam away, and Mat swam after her. Mat got out of the water on the other side of the lake to climb the mountain so he could get to the top of the waterfall. Then he dove off into the lake close to her. Anna waited for him to come up to the surface, but he did not. He was under the water for a long time, and she started to get worried. She did not think about his ability to play wind instruments and how it made him able to hold his breath much longer than most people.

He has been under too long, she thought and started screaming for him. She dove under several times but could not find him. Anna was panicking. She shouted, "Mat! Mat!"

He jumped up behind her and grabbed her, scaring her to death. She screamed and turned around. They were face-to-face. Water dripped down their faces, and he pushed back the hair that was covering her eyes. He could see the fear in her face.

She pushed him and told him he had scared the living daylights out of her.

"So you do care?" he asked.

"Mat, I never said I did not care for you. I do very much. I wish no harm to you. You are a good man. Just because I do not sleep with you does not mean I don't care. I cannot say I do not love you, for I do, with all my heart, soul, and mind. There is no question about that. If something happened to you, I do not know what I would do."

Mat took Anna by the hand and led her to the bank and up the side of the mountain to the top of the waterfall. Once they got to the top, Anna could see for miles. The sky was so clear, she felt as if she was on the top of the world. Anna could see the ocean all around and realized they were on an island. In the far distance, she could see a small town and the surrounding villages. She had no idea that there was so much land. *Do I own all of this?* she thought. "The town, is that where you went to school?"

"Yes, white people live in town."

To her surprise, Mat suddenly grabbed her hand and

jumped off the cliff toward the lake, taking her with him. She screamed the whole way down.

"Are you trying to kill me?" she demanded when they surfaced. "That was a long way."

"Anna, I no try kill you. I love you, and you know how I feel about you. Why you no sleep with me?"

"Mat, you know how I feel. I want someone who loves me back, as I love them."

"Anna, I love you."

"Yes, I believe you do, but I need someone who loves me with all their heart, soul, and mind. You are not ready for that. Your love for Kati is too strong for you to open your heart to anyone. It is not fair that you choose not to love another. You are only hurting yourself, Teka, and your family."

She continued, "Your family loves you very much, and it kills them to watch you suffer the way that you do. Kati is gone. She is dead, and you choose to love the dead. Mat, you are still young and have time to make a family."

"Anna, you no understand. I promised. Teka will soon be man and take my place being the maker. I have no one after that. I need woman for my needs. You are mine."

"Yes, I may be yours, but that is a promise you made to someone who is dead. Kati would not want to see you suffer. If I die before my husband, I would want him to carry on and love another. I know if she loved you that much, she would not want to see you suffer the rest of your life like this. It is the choice you made.

"I do not want to be with a man who just wants me to fulfill his needs. I need a man who has no other and does not think of another when with me. My man must put me first and love and care for me. I want to be his life, forever. I want to share my life with him and for him to share his with me. We will do everything together. Your heart is closed, and I am not sure I am the one who can help you. Kati is always going to be with you. I know that. She is the mother of your son.

"Kati was very special to you, and no one will ever take that away from you. But you need to give love another chance. You will not allow another to get into your heart. In my world, we love till death do us part. Do your spirits tell you to stay behind or move on?"

"The spirits have turned their backs on me," Mat said. "I disobey the law. Kati was not ready to mate when I turned of age, so I refused to mate until Kati was ready. I left the tribe and went to white school during that time so I did not have to mate others. We had a connection like no other. She could talk to me in my dreams. One day she sent for me when she was to bleed. I hurried back and Father allowed me to mate with her. Now the spirits angry with me and took her away."

"Mat, it is you who has turned your back on the spirits.

The spirits never left you. The spirits blessed you and Kati with a wonderful baby boy, and you have done a great job with him. Kati would be so proud of you. You just have to forgive yourself and open your heart before it is too late."

"Anna, I am afraid it is already too late for me." Mat took her by the waist and pulled her to him. "Anna, I want you so much."

Anna looked him in the eye. "Mat, you know I am going to leave."

"No, Anna. I need you. I need you to stay with me."

He pulled her closer. She did not resist. He kissed her. She returned the kiss. It was long and hard.

"Anna, stay with me as my wife."

Mat and Anna were still dripping wet. Their eyes locked. Mat lifted his hand and gently brushed the hair out of her face and placed it behind her shoulder. Then he pulled the bathing suit tie behind her neck loose to expose her breasts.

As her top fell down, he watched her response, but she did not move. She continued to look him in the eye and did not object. She was ready for him. He kissed her neck. Anna leaned back, lifting her chest, and gasped.

He watched her deep breaths raise her chest up and down as he slowly kissed her shoulder and then her soft breasts. He cupped them in his hands. They fit perfectly. Anna held his head in place and tilted her head back, closing her eyes.

Realizing that she was ready to give herself to him freely, he slowly slid his hands to her hips. He hooked his thumbs in the waist of the bottoms of her bathing suit and stopped. Was she going to call his bluff? Still she did not reject. Then he knew she was calling his bluff. He wanted her so much that he was shaking. He looked into her eyes, and she knew then that he was not ready to give up Kati.

He removed his thumbs and slowly covered her breasts with her suit top and tied the strings back in place.

Anna knew how he was feeling, and she knew he was thinking of Kati. She had hoped he was going to give himself to her. She knew they loved each other. How was she to get him to let go? She saw the pain in his eyes. He wanted so desperately to give himself to her, but he could not because the love he'd had with Kati was so strong. She was always going to be in Anna's way, even though she was Kati. To him, she was so young and innocent.

"No, I cannot be your wife. In your mind, you are still married to Kati, and I will always be second. I am never second. You will have to let her go before I can be with you as your wife. You need to let Kati go. I must be the first thing you think about when you wake up and the last thing you think about when you go to bed. I must be in your dreams while you sleep and with you when you are away. I would have to be all you want and all you need.

"I am selfish and have only one love. It is not fair to you or to me if I stay and you cannot give us that love. I understand you have needs, but love is different than needs and desires. I too have needs and desires. Love to me is forever and always, as long as we both live. Kati is gone. You must save yourself and let her go."

"I love you, Anna."

"I know you think so, but your heart tells you differently. I want you to love again. When I settle down, I want a man who respects me, who listens to me, and who values my opinion. I want a man who will take me as I am, and we are joined as one unit. We will be together through the good times and the bad, we will have no secrets, and we will share our lives together as one. Mat, you are not ready for that type of commitment. I feel Kati is keeping you from moving on."

"Do you love me, Anna?"

"Mat, please don't ask me. I have told you how I feel."

"Do you love me, Anna?" he asked again.

Anna kissed him on the cheek and swam to the shore and returned to the village and her hut without him.

Mat did not understand. *She says she loves me but cannot not be with me. Why? I do love her. Could I love her the way she wants me to? How could I love her with all my heart, soul, and mind? I have already had that love. I am not sure I could ever love another. Does she love me or not?*

Anna knew she had left him not understanding what had just happened. She loved him so much and knew he loved her. But she was not that little girl anymore. She had grown up differently than he had, and she did not have the memories he had of their time together. How was she to win him over? She said all those things to him to get him thinking. Could he love her as she was now?

Chapter 21

Taken

When Mat started back, he carried her feather with great care. While traveling on the trail, he noticed fresh footprints around the waterfall. Someone had been watching them from the woods.

When he got back to the village, he went straight to Father to give him Anna's feather and told him about the footprints around the waterfall and lake. Father called a meeting with the warriors at the stomping grounds. Mat told them that he had been with Anna down by the falls and on his way back had come across some fresh footprints nearby.

"Someone was watching us. We need to increase our scouts and be ready for a fight."

All the men went out to train some more.

Mat knew it would be soon. A fight was coming. They would stop at nothing to get their hands on Anna. He had to do whatever it took to keep her safe, even if it meant taking her back to the white people himself. He knew that she understood her time here was short.

Teka had met Anna not far from the waterfall to lead her to her hut. When Anna entered, she noticed that Teka did not follow her in. She called for him. He walked through the door with a knife against his throat. Behind him was a savage, the same one she had met on the trail with Mat.

"*Shh,*" the savage said. "Or I will kill him."

Anna's heart fell. She had just found Teka and now someone was going to take him away from her. She would do anything to save him, but she froze.

Teka got into Anna's mind. "*Mother, do not do anything crazy. They are here for you, and they are going to kill me. Take care of my father. Heal his heart. I know you can do it. Tell him the truth. I have seen it. You will be mother of all. Save yourself. Use your spirit to help you. The spirits are on your side. Forgive Mother and Father for what they have done in the past. The spirits know what they are doing, and all was done for a reason.*

"*Listen to the spirit. Do not shut them out. Do not worry about me. They will not succeed. Mother, please do as I say. Use your spirit to send for help. Mother, you are a great person. I could not ask for a better mother. I sent for you through the spirit. I know what you have done and why you are here. It is time for you and my father to be together. Do not take too long. He is dying. He does not have much time. Be patient with him.*

He needs to adjust. I know you can do this, Mother. I have seen it."

Two more savages came into her hut. One took Anna and tied her hands together. The other tied her feet so she could not run away. They put a gag in her mouth so she could not scream. Anna did not resist for fear they would hurt Teka, so she did as they said. Then the one with Teka slit her son's throat. Anna nearly fell to the ground. One slapped her in the face, pulled her up by the hair, drug her out to their horses, and off they went.

Anna was devastated. Her heart was broken, and tears streamed from her eyes. *My son*, she thought to herself. She prayed to God to have mercy on him and protect him and to take her life instead.

Mat was returning from the meeting with the warriors when he got a sickening feeling. Something was wrong. All he could think about was Anna. Standing in his path was the white wolf. In the middle of the day and so close to people, Mat thought. What was this about? He threw a stick to scare her away, but she did not go. She just stood up on her hind legs and started jumping up and down. Mat saw it in her eyes.

The wolf's eyes looked like the deer's eyes on the trail when Anna was talking to it. Could this be Anna calling for him? No. That was impossible. He threw another stick at her, and the wolf continued to stand her ground. The wolf looked as if she were motioning Mat to follow her.

"What is it, Missy? You want me to follow you? Show me."

The wolf turned and led Mat back to his hut.

The wolf went straight into Mat's hut. The door was open. Mat thought, *How many times have I told Anna not to leave the door open? Now there is a wolf inside.* When Mat entered the hut, he saw the wolf standing over Teka's body. His throat had been slit, and he was gasping for breath.

Mat screamed, "No no no! My son!"

Mat picked Teka up and carried him to Mother's hut. She started working on him at once.

Teka whispered, "Anna, savage, help!"

Mat knew then that the fresh tracks by the falls had been the savages. They had followed her home to take her. He knew exactly what they were going to do to her. He had to stop it.

Mother told Mat, "Hurry. Anna needs you. Teka will be okay."

Mat gathered some warriors and said, "Missy, show me where she is."

Missy led the way as they rode off to find Anna before it was too late. Mat could hear Missy's pack howling and knew they were after something. Could this wolf have sent her pack to watch over Anna? All he could think of was Anna.

How could this happen? I swore to protect her, and now she is gone again. What good am I to her? he thought. The feelings he had for her were so strong even after just a few months of knowing her. He did not know if he could live without her. How could he care for her? What was wrong with him? He knew when he got her back, he was going to have to let her go and send her back to where she came from.

The savages had taken Anna to a clearing, where they dismounted and threw her to the ground.

The leader said, "Now! We do it now!"

The other two men took Anna to a tree, laid her on the ground, tied her hands to the tree trunk, and held her down while trying to hold her legs apart. Anna kicked as hard as she could to get them off. The leader took out a knife and sliced her dress all the way open to expose her body. She knew what was coming next. What was she to do?

Use spirit, she thought, *but how? I am not strong enough to use at my own free will.*

The leader undressed himself from the waist down. *My life is over*, she thought. This was the end of her being pure. Mat was the only man she had ever been with and now this ugly savage was going to destroy her and she would never be the same again.

She prayed to her God. *Lord, forgive me for my sins. Take my pain away. I will do your will and be strong if this is your will. If this is what you have in store for me, I accept. Keep Mat safe and heal his heart. Save Teka, for he is innocent. Mat and Teka need each other. Thank you for all you have done for me and for giving me strength to get through this. In Jesus's name I pray. Amen.*

Anna fought back hard. She kicked and twisted her body. They had a hard time holding her down to get to her. She could smell their stench.

Anna tried to use her spirit, but she did not know what to do. She looked around and saw the wolf pack. *Where is Missy?* she thought. The wolves were growling as they surrounded the men, but that did not stop them. Anna was fighting for her life. *Why is Missy not here? She has always been near when I need help. Oh God, please help me!*

The leader took a knife and stabbed her in one leg to secure her to the ground. She nearly passed out. When he saw how well that worked, he stabbed her other leg. The pain was more than she could bear, and for just a brief moment, she thought she passed out. Blood ran from her legs and her body shook. Now she could not move, giving him the chance to have his way with her.

Then she spotted Missy. Missy gathered her pack and left. "No! No! Missy! Attack!" she cried. "Come back! I need you more than ever. Come back!" Anna could not believe Missy would leave her and not attack. The wolf was going to let the savages have their way with her. "Please, Missy, come back and help me!"

Missy kept on going with her pack while Anna cried.

The savage got on top of her and just before he was about to enter her, he fell onto her chest and across her shoulder. Anna looked out over his body and saw a knife in the middle of his back and Mat running toward her. Mat pulled the savage off of her and covered her body. He reached over her head and cut her hands free. She grabbed him by the neck and held him. She could not control her body from shaking all over. She could hardly move.

"Anna," Mat said, "I am going to leave the gag in. You are going to need it. I am going to remove the knives, and you will need to bite down."

She nodded.

"Okay. Here goes one." He jerked it out fast.

Anna nearly jumped out of her skin. He stopped the bleeding and wrapped it up.

"Anna, look at me." He held her face between both of his hands, looking into her eyes to take her mind off of it. Both of their eyes were full of tears. He put his arms around her and gave her a hug. "You are going to be okay. I need you be strong. You can do this, Anna."

She shook her head.

"Yes, Anna. You are the most fearless, loving, caring, strong-minded, and stubborn woman I know. Teka is alive."

She smiled as much as she could with the gag in her mouth. In that second, he jerked out the second knife, and Anna passed out.

He kissed her on the cheek and said, "You be fine now. I promise."

He stopped the bleeding and wrapped up her leg. The warriors killed the other two savages as Mat picked up Anna's limp body and took her to Mother.

When they were in Mother's hut, Mat laid Anna in the center of the table. She was still unconscious.

"Mother, the savage was on her. Can you see if they damaged her in any way?"

"Mat, she would want privacy. Go check on Teka while I examine her." When she was done she told him, "No, son, there is no damage. Son, what wrong with you? You have not had your way with her I see."

"No, Mother, other than the mating."

"Why? She is yours."

"She is not ready."

"Really! Maybe it's you who is not ready. Mat, fifteen years is a long time. You must let it go and let someone back into your life. You must move on, son."

"Mother, we no talk about no more!"

Mother shook her head at him and went to check on Teka. Mat sat with Anna, holding her hand, until she woke up. Anna called out for Teka. Mat assured her that he was all right. He pointed to the other table where Teka lay. He was going to be fine.

"How did you find him?" she asked.

"It was the white wolf, Missy."

"She did come."

"You spoke to her, didn't you?"

"I spoke to the spirits, and they sent her to help."

"It did, honey. Smart girl. Use spirit on your side," Mother said.

Anna smiled at Mat and said, "Thanks to Mat. He saved me again."

Mat just looked at her. He knew what needed to be done, and it had to be done soon, not only for the sake of the tribe but for Anna's as well.

Chapter 22

Joined Spirits

That night, Mat and the other warriors were each honored with a feather for killing the savages and for saving Anna. Father came into Mother's hut with the elders and as many tribal members that would fit. Mother danced around Anna to help her heal faster, and then Father, with Mat by his side, all dressed in their ceremonial clothing, stood by Anna's side to honor her with the eagle feather. Father and the elders danced and chanted around Anna. Father touched Anna's body from head to toe with the feather she had caught by the lake. He held it with care, cradling it on with both hands, lifting it to the sky, and blessing it.

Anna remembered how Mat had received her feather after the mating and the way he had blessed it. Father held the feather out to Anna. She held out her hands palms up, held the feather toward the sky, and said a prayer. Mat was pleased that she had remembered and had accepted the feather with such grace.

It took a few weeks for Anna to heal enough to go outside. Mat went with the men to hunt again. When he returned, she was much better. Father had gone with them on the hunt, as he often did. He was not feeling well, so Mat had to make the rounds in the tribe that day. Mat sent Father to go see Mother so she could check him.

"Old man, it is time for you to slow down and let the young ones take over," Mother admonished him. "You rest. You have been blessed with many years now and have served your time. I love you and would like to have many more years with you before I leave this earth."

"Old woman, I am fine, just a little tired. Need to rest awhile. You need not worry about me. I love you too. You worry too much."

Mother checked him out, and he seemed to be okay.

Anna was glad to see Mat, but he had been a little standoffish since his return from the hunt.

"Mat are you okay?" she asked. "You have not said much in the past few days."

"Yes, I am fine."

"Then why do you seem so down? It hurts me to see you with a heavy heart."

"Anna, I am not down. I am a busy man and have things to do."

This was not like Mat. He was always making a play for

her. She knew something was weighing heavily on his mind. Later that night, she followed him when he went to pray.

He turned and looked at her. "Not tonight, Anna."

"Mat, stop this now. What is wrong?"

"Anna," he said and then walked away.

"Do I have to use spirit to get my answers?"

"You do what you please."

She was speechless. He had never acted this way before.

After Mat prayed, he went to Kati's grave. Anna followed him and placed her hands on his shoulders.

"It is not your fault. Mat, you need to let it go."

"Anna, you know how I feel. Just leave me alone."

"Mat."

"Anna, why you not obey? Please leave."

"No," she said. "You hurt, I hurt."

"This damn bond!" Mat said.

"Mat! You never talk like that. What is going on in your head? Let me help."

"Anna, you make me crazy. I no good for you. I violated you, I whipped you, I mated with you, I let you get attacked, not once but twice, and now I let you get kidnapped and stabbed. You too much woman for me to protect. I no good for you."

"Mat, you have to forgive yourself. You have saved me all those times."

"How? If you had stayed home …" He did not finish his statement. "I told you the first day you would hate me, and you have. I told you that you would not survive, and you nearly died four times. You must go home."

"Mat, you are a good man, and you have protected me at all costs. Look at me, Mat. We are all here on this earth for a mission. It is not for us to question but to serve. You serve your people very well. You have loved and have a child. The only thing missing is you. You must stop feeling sorry for yourself. Open your heart and love again."

"Anna, I am doomed. The spirits are against me."

"No, they are not. You have shut the door on them. Like your mother did. Open the door. Let love come back to you. People love and care for you, but you only shut them out. Please, Mat. Try before it is too late."

"Anna, I fear it already is too late for me. I have told you this before. Why can you not believe me?"

"Because, you are wrong!"

There was a shout from Father's hut. Anna and Mat ran to see what was the matter.

"Mother, what is wrong?" Mat asked.

Father was holding his chest.

"He is having a heart attack," Anna said. "He could die."

Mother told Mat, "Hurry, go get Teka."

Mat ran as fast as he could and brought Teka back, along with two guards.

"Anna, Teka, hold hands," Mother said.

Mat shouted, "What are you doing?" He stood back and saw Anna starting to hurt.

"No, Anna," Mother said, "do not take his pain. We need you to heal. Hold Teka's hand. Think good thing of Father. Concentrate. Harder! Harder!" Mother shouted. "Join in, Mat! It is going to take all of us if we are going to save him."

Mat did. He could feel pain tingling in his body, and then they all started to glow. Father's pain stopped, and they all fell to the floor.

"Everyone okay?" Mother asked.

Mat said yes, but no word came from Teka and Anna. They had passed out.

"It takes a lot out of them, Mat. I feel that one of them has the grand spirit and the other one has a great spirit. Neither one is strong enough to heal. Together their spirits work as one. It is more challenging to heal, and they are drained. They must rest."

"How is Teka a great or grand spirit? This is not possible!"

"Remember when I told you your mother had a spirit and refused to use it? We did not know what spirit she had. It could have been a great spirit. She could have passed it down to you. The spirits are with you, and that is why you are drawn to Anna. She too could be a great spirit. We do not know for sure until it is fully developed."

"But Anna has nothing to do with Teka."

"No, but Kati did. We knew she had spirit at a young age, and that is why the two of you were so connected. If she did have the great spirit and you had the great spirit, it is understandable that your child would have the grand spirit. Or maybe Anna has it. We do not know for sure which one has the grand spirit."

"Mother, are you saying if I mate Anna, her child would have the grand spirit?"

"No. You have already passed on the spirit to Teka. Spirit is only passed to the first child. Anna is still in danger."

"I love her, but my heart says no. Mother, what am I to do?"

"It's not your heart, son. It is your pride. Your heart is ready to move on. Your spirit longs for it. You choose pride. That is what is in the way. Grow up. You were so young when you found your true love and started a family, only to lose the one love you had. This is a lot for a young man to deal with."

"I did okay."

"Do you think so? Then why do you have such a heavy heart?"

Mat looked at Anna and Teka. "Will they remember when they wake up?"

"I not sure. Up to the spirits. The more they mature, the more they are able to control and remember."

Mat stayed with them both until they woke up.

When Anna opened her eyes, she said, "Did it work? Is Father okay?"

Teka and Anna both remembered but had to rest that day and night because using so much spirit had drained them. Teka's powers were maturing faster than Mother had thought they would. She knew it was time to teach them both how and when to use their powers.

Mat continued to work with the warriors on protecting Anna and the tribe. He could still feel danger coming, and it was getting stronger every day.

Anna was still bound and determined to put a stop to the mating. She started visiting the girls' huts to prevent others from knowing that they were bleeding. She knew she would be whipped if they found out, but it was a chance she had to take. Anna talked to the women of the tribe about how to please their men and how to work it in order to get the things they wanted.

Anna and Teka also met every day to practice their skills to control their powers. Mother was there most of the time, showing them how to control the spirit. Mind reading was what Teka wanted to learn most. Mother did not have much experience in that spirit, but Anna did, so she worked with him on it in private. Anna's first experience with mind reading had been on the trail with the savages. She knew she had the power, but she could no longer read Mat's mind.

"Mother, I know I can get into people's heads, but why can I not get into Mat's when I choose? I have read his thoughts once but cannot now."

"It is because of the bond. You would be able to talk to each other only if the other allowed it. You can shield out his thoughts yet still communicate with each other."

"I have seen the future and know I will be leaving soon. I will have no choice. Teka has seen it too. I do not know how to leave Mat and Teka. I just found them and want to stay with them forever. I have seen Mat turn on me. I will fail trying to change his heart. He is never going to let go of Kati, and I do not know if he loves me for who I am now."

"Anna, you are her. He will come to love you once he knows the truth. I know he loves you now. He has told me many times. Anna, you are the only one we have that can bring him back. He will not get close to any of the other women here. He only wants you, but it is his pride that is standing in the way. Don't give up yet. The future can be changed. That is why you see it. So you can change it if it needs changing. You have been blessed with the power to change the world. Use it, understand it, and stay true to your heart."

Mother continued, "Seeing the future shows you the path you want to take. You have free will to make things happen to your advantage. Mat needs you, Teka needs you, and we need you. Keep trying harder. You are woman. Use what you have to wake him up. He will not resist."

"I do not feel right tricking him. I need him to be willing on his own to love me. I cannot use my womanhood to lure him into something he is not ready for."

"Try, dear. He does not have much time left. I feel it. You are his last chance. You must use all your power and strength to save him. Try harder. Save him."

That night Mat, Anna, Teka, and Mother were honored with a feather for saving Father's life. Now that Anna had two feathers, she was going to make a headdress. She braided some leather to go around her head with the two feathers and some beads hanging down to one side. She was proud of herself for learning the craft of Mat's tribe. She was the one who made the headdress, along with a little help from close friends.

Chapter 23

The Trade

It was two weeks before Teka's fifteenth birthday. On that day, he would become a man and the maker. He would start mating on that day, regardless of who bled. Anna had given this great thought. How was she going to pull this off? She knew it was time for Lilly to bleed again. It was going to be an exciting day for him when he became a man, but not if he mated someone other than Lilly.

Anna saw Teka at the breakfast table, looking a little down, so she went to him to find out what was wrong. This should be a happy time for him.

"Teka, why are you so blue today?"

"Lilly bleeds today, and she will be mated tonight. Then she will be promised to someone."

"You mean she will not be promised to you?"

"I am not sure."

"She will not mate with your father tonight. I will take her place."

"Mother, you do not understand. I will not be able to mate with her until she bleeds again."

"Yes, I do understand. You will just have to wait until that day comes."

"No, Mother, you do not understand, I will have to mate all others until then. Lilly will not be my first."

Anna had not thought of that until now.

"I see. Don't worry. I have a plan. No one has bled this month as far as they know, and I will continue to hide it. If you will keep my secret, we can get past this."

"Mother, I cannot lie. I need not know of what you do."

Anna sighed. "Don't worry. I will work on that. I will need to talk to Father. I will make him understand."

Teka took Anna by the hand. "No, Mother. You have to stop. You cannot trade places with everyone. This is not fair to you. I know how strongly you feel about the mating. I feel it is killing you."

"I am your mother, and I will take care of this. Lilly will not be mated tonight, and no other girl will either until you are ready for Lilly. It will only be two weeks. How many will I have to do in two weeks if I continue to hide it? I will not tell you who bleeds, so you will be faithful to the law. You will just have to catch me, won't you? Let me take care of it, my son. Please, Teka let me take care of it. I have a plan, and I know what I am doing."

"Mother, they will be expecting you to interfere, and they too will have a plan."

"What can they do? It is law. I can trade places with her three times. They cannot change that. Once I do this tonight, she will be yours forever. Trust me, son. Lilly will be your first mating in two weeks. I promise."

Teka could not understand how Anna thought she had the power to change their customs. His spirit was maturing faster than expected. He could get into the minds of others just as Mother had told him and with Anna's help. He had learned he could control it more by sending only the information he wanted to share with another.

He knew it had something to do with the papers on the land, but he did not know everything. He knew when Anna came that she owned the land. He thought, *She must be holding the land over Father's head.*

Teka went to spend some time with Father to see if he could find out and ask to delay Lilly's mating tonight. Father was not in his hut when Teka got there. He remembered the time of the day. Father was out making his daily rounds. Father spotted Teka with a long face and went to him.

"My son, why are you not excited about becoming a man in a few weeks? This is great honor for you. It is the beginning of the process of becoming chief one day. All firstborn males in this family have been the maker for generations. Our bloodline has been passed on with many spirits."

"My girl, Lilly, bleeds and will mate with my father to-night. I wanted her to be my first like my father did with my mother."

"It is in the spirits' hands, son. We do as the spirits tell us. This custom has been passed down for thousands of years. Your father broke the custom to be able to mate with your mother. Your father was older than Kati and was to be man before she bled. When he came of age, he refused to mate with another. He ran away until Kati bled. This why he cannot let go. He believes the spirits have turned their backs on him."

"Father, we know she did not die. He needs to be told."

"No! We are men of honor. We promised Anna we would not tell him. We always keep our word."

"My father is dying inside. He must know if he is to live. I hate keeping secrets from him. If only Anna would tell him, he would wake up and be able to love again."

"It is in the hands of the spirits. It is not for us to tell. The spirits have a plan, and we need to leave it alone and let them work it out. They will not take your father after all that has passed. Anna was sent here to bring him back to life."

"Yes, Father, but at what cost? Her life? I just now found my mother, and I fear she is up to no good and it will cost her her life. He cannot lose her a second time. That would be the end of him. I know it. I have seen the future. It does not look good for either of them. Father, I am worried."

"Son, it is what it is, and we must accept what the spirits have given us."

Teka knew now was the time to get into Father's head. He tried hard, but nothing came. He could not understand, for he had gotten good at this by now. He tried again and still nothing came.

Then Anna walked up to them and put her hands on Teka's shoulders and said, "I need to speak to Father."

Father rolled his eyes, for he knew she would be asking him for favors again.

When Anna touched Teka's shoulder, it happened. He was in Father's head. He could see Father's concern. He was right. Anna was holding the land over Father's head. Teka could see the papers in her hand and her waving them in his face.

It was the land she threatened him with. If they wanted to stay here, he had better do as she said. She had one year to decide. Father was afraid Anna would take their world away as they knew it. It scared Father very much. What would his people do in the real world? The tribe would be lost.

Anna knew what Teka had seen. She whispered in his

ear, "I have a plan. Do not worry, and do not tell. It is going to work out. Trust me, son."

He smiled and nodded as he walked away.

"Anna," Father said. "What can I do for you today?"

"I understand Lilly is to mate tonight. I want you to extend the time for two weeks so Teka can mate with her in private as husband and wife."

"Why would I do that?"

"I want Teka to experience the love Mat and I had. Instead of a mating ceremony, I want a wedding. After they are wed, they are to be put into a private hut to start their lives together as one with no one watching, just the two of them. I want him to feel her and her to feel him. When you open a woman, she loses that feeling. It's a feeling she will never have again. They need to be gentle with each other. He needs to know that she is willing to endure the pain he puts on her and be with him all his days."

"No!" Father said.

"Then I ask to take her place."

"Anna, you cannot do this every time."

"Yes, I can, for it is written in your law. I have that right. No matter what Mat says, I will take her place and everyone else's."

"So be it," Father said.

"One more thing," she added.

"What is it now?"

"I want the wedding to take place in two weeks whether she bleeds or not. Teka and Lilly will be wed and have their privacy."

"Anna—" Father said.

"No! It will happen—do you understand?"

Father knew what she was doing, but he did not have much of a choice.

"I get a mating ceremony, and you get a wedding. Seems like a fair trade. Agreed," Father said.

"Agreed!"

Chapter 24

The Second Mating

Anna knew if she had Father's permission, Mat could not refuse. Anna went to tell Lilly about the deal she had made with Father. She would be wed in two weeks to Teka.

Lilly said, "No, Anna. You cannot take my place again."

"It is okay, Lilly, I will be fine. Trust me."

Lilly agreed and went to tell Teka.

Teka came running to Anna. "Mother, what you are doing? My father too smart for this. He will refuse."

"I have Father's permission, and Mat cannot go against Father."

"Mother, you know not what you do."

"It will be fine," she said. "Go now. Prepare for a wedding. We only have two weeks. Say nothing to your father or he will try to stop it."

Later that day, Mat came to Anna. "You stay in tonight."

"Why?" she said.

"I believe you know, Anna, and you no interfere."

"What are you going to do to me? Are you going to tie me to a pole to stop me?"

"Anna, this is no game we play. Some things you cannot change. Teka will be man in two weeks. I am sorry Lilly bleeds now, but that is the way it is. She will mate with me tonight. Teka mates with others until Lilly is ready. Lilly will not be his first."

"Not acceptable," she responded.

"No come tonight!" he shouted. He needed to know Anna's intentions. Why was she against the ceremony? He would find out tonight; he was sure of it.

It was time. Anna and Lilly walked out in matching robes. There stood Father and Mat, both dressed in bearskin robes with their headdresses that reached the ground. Mat knew Anna would take Lilly's place again. He had to know how far she would go to get what she wanted. Anna thought this was different than the last time, but as long as she could save Lilly tonight, it would be worth it.

She looked at Father and said, "Agreed?"

Father spoke out, "Agreed."

Mat said not a word.

That was strange, Anna thought. Mat did not refuse. What was he up to? She expected him to protest or at least tell her to leave or have her escorted back to her hut. But he did nothing. She knew he was up to something, and that bothered her.

Anna went to the table, turned to the tribe, and stated she was to take Lilly's place. Then she walked over to the end of the table.

Mat asked, "Tied or no tied?"

She looked into his eyes and said, "No tied."

Mat had a feeling she would choose to be untied. Mat walked away, and Father approached Anna. Anna was confused. Why had Mat walked away? This was not how it went. What was going on?

Father looked at the tribe and announced, "I mate tonight."

Anna's eyes widened and she looked over at Mat. He smiled back at her.

"Mat," she said. "No! I mate with you! Mat, Mat, stop this."

He stood tall and still.

"Why, Mat? Please stop this."

Father said to Anna, "Our agreement was that you take Lilly's place. Here we are. The ceremony begins."

Anna was going to use her powers to stop Father as she had with the savages. But she decided not to, for they would beat Mat. What was she to do?

Anna was not going to cry.

Lilly yelled, "No! Anna, I will do it."

Anna shook her head.

Teka went into Anna's head. *"No, Mother, please don't do it. My father would never forgive himself. You have only been with him. Please don't break the bond."*

She responded back in his head, *"I give myself so that you and Lilly will be as happy as your father and I once were. Your father is already dead in his heart. I fear I will not be able to return his love again. Let it be, my son."*

Anna looked at Mat directly in the eye. He saw the look she had when she was in someone's head, so he turned away. She could not reach him.

She shouted, "Mat, you look at me."

He refused.

"Mat, look at me now."

Still no response.

Anna shouted, "Matete, look at me now!"

That got his attention. He looked straight into her eyes, and she was in. He could not move. She had a grip on him. He could hear her, but with the great spirit in him, he had the power to keep her from reading his mind.

"Mat, please. Do not let this happen. Kati would not like it. Please, Mat. I will do anything you want if you mate with me tonight. This mating will end my life. I will be impure. Please, Mat. You said you loved me. How can you let this happen? Mat,

I love you and I do not want another inside me. You are the only one I have been with. Please, Mat, I beg you. I cannot do this."

Mat didn't respond.

If he would allow this, he had no love for her. She knew it now. She would never be able to look at him or have a relationship with him. This was a deal breaker. It was over, and she would have to leave. Kati would always come first. And then there was the picture of Father being inside her.

She was doomed. But first, she would see her son married, clean and happy. That was all that mattered to her. She would do anything for her son.

A tear fell from one of her eyes. Mat was still watching her. She maintained eye contact with him. Her bottom lip quivered, but she was not going to cry out. Mat could feel her heart pounding inside him. It hurt him as much as it did her. He could not show any emotion in front of the tribe. It would be a sign of weakness.

Anna stood at the end of the table, still looking at Mat. She opened her hands and closed them and forced them, shaking, down to her side. She took a few deep breaths and breathed out slowly several times. Her heart was beating so hard it hurt. Her chest visibly rose and fell with every breath she took. She was shaking all over when she dropped her robe. Father dropped his robe as well.

I will not cry out, she told herself. *I will not show them a sign of weakness. If this is how he wants it to be, then let it be. It is all on him.*

She swallowed hard, trying not to cry. Her eyes welled up again. *No crying, no crying. Get yourself together. Be strong. It will soon be all over,* she thought.

Anna held her head up high, got on the table, and said, "Tied."

She laid down and closed her eyes. She could not bear the thought of the memory of Father's face looking at her every night.

She would never be with another again. She would let her spirit die. What choice did she have? The guard lifted her hands above her head and tied them to the pole. She waited for them to tie her legs, so she put them into position, but they did not tie them. She felt him on top of her. Not wanting to see his face, her eyes stayed closed. She did not want this stuck in her head for the rest of her days.

But something was not right. He did not smell right. He climbed onto the table, across her chest, and reached above her head to untie her hands from the pole. She could feel his long silky hair draping over her body. *Wait,* she thought. This was not Father. She opened her eyes and saw Mat.

She cried, "Why did you do this to me?" She could not catch her breath.

"I needed to know how far you would go for what you believe in."

"You broke my heart, Mat."

"I am sorry, but I had to know how far you would go and at what cost."

"I would give my life for the ones I love. He is your son, Mat. I love you, and I love him. He is part of you. I love everything about you and your family. I want your son to have what you had with Kati."

"Look how that ended," he said.

She did not tell him who she really was. It was not the right time. She knew she had to use extra care to keep him from losing his mind.

"Yes, and what few years you had together will last you a lifetime. Mat, you must let the past go. Give Teka those memories you have. Even though they were cut short, they will always be with you. Cherish them, but do not let them smother you. Kati would want you to live again. She would hate seeing you like this. Let me show you how Kati would want your life to be now."

"Can you talk to her?"

"At times."

"Is she with you now?"

"Yes, Mat." Anna took her hands and led his face to hers and kissed him. He could feel Kati.

"This how she would kiss me," he said. "Is it true? Kati is with you?"

"Yes."

His heart swelled, and he kissed her again. Father knew it was time to dismiss the tribe. Anna had work to do if she was going to free Mat. He sent them all home to give Mat and Anna some time to reunite. Father was sure that when Anna got done with him, he would be a changed man.

Anna slowly caressed Mat's face, kissed his neck, and rubbed her hands on his chest. Then she kissed him with all the passion she had been holding inside her, and he did the same to her. They felt every inch of each other's body. Mat tasted her wine as she indulged him. It was getting hot. They were both breathing heavily and sweating.

"Mat, I want you now. I love you so much."

He looked into her eyes and then entered her. He could feel her excitement, and she felt his. Anna squeezed his back as she pulled him closer to her. She wrapped her legs around him and caught her breath. She felt him inside her as they moved as one. Their breathing became erratic. It was the most powerful feeling Anna had ever felt. Then they released together.

He laid on top of her after collapsing and said, "I love you, Kati."

Anna said nothing. She knew he had not made love to

her. It was Kati who he thought he was with. Anna could not be second in his life. This confirmed it. She would be going home soon.

Mat carried her to his bed, and they slept together all night. Anna had a heavy heart, but she was not going to ruin his night. It was probably the best night he'd had in fifteen years. She owed him that much.

Chapter 25

Betrayed

The next morning, Mat was still holding Anna tightly.

"Anna, you are in my bed? Tell me I no take advantage of you in night."

"No, Mat. You are fine. It just got so cold last night that I am here to keep warm."

Anna knew he had been in the spirit world last night and did not remember what had happened. He had not made love with her. He had been with Kati.

Teka was still in his bed. *"Mother,"* he said in her head. *"You need to tell him. He loved you last night. He really loves you. Tell him before it is too late."*

Anna responded, *"No, Teka. He made love to Kati, not to me. He does not remember. Just let it be. He will find out soon. I have seen it. You have to promise not to tell him. The spirits have a plan, and we must let them bring us back together. If he refuses to go with the spirits, we cannot save him. No matter what happens, I want you to know I love you and your father."*

"Mother, what have you seen? You are worrying me."

Anna would not answer. She had already blocked Teka from her thoughts. She got up to start her day.

When Mat came back from his morning run, he noticed men standing at the entrance of the stomping ground. The men waved to Mat to come, and they all went inside. Mat followed.

"What is the meaning of this meeting?" he asked

The men all started talking at once.

"Stop!" Mat shouted.

A man got up and told Mat, "It is your woman."

Mat rolled his eyes and said, "What has she done now?"

"She tells our women not to lie with us. They hold back. Your woman tells them to lie at their own choice. She tells our women they lie when they are ready, not for our needs."

Mat shook his head.

"Your woman make our women cover themselves, and we no touch as we please."

Mat smiled.

"Your woman make babies come in our beds. Cannot have way with woman with child in bed. Then there is your son."

That got his attention. "Teka? What with Teka? What she do with him?" Mat asked.

Another man replied, "She sneaks off to woods be

alone with him for hours. She always holding his hand and whispering in his ear. She stares at him, and he stares at her across the way. This not look good. Once I heard him call her mother. Then last night, she stared at him and he at her and then at you. After that you mated her. Father sent us all away, for it was more than mating. She put a spell on you. You were all over her."

Mat was upset to hear about last night. Anna had not told the truth. She said nothing had happened. Had she put a spell on him? What happened? Why could he not remember? All he could remember was a dream he had about Kati.

This was disturbing to him, so he started to watch them both more closely. It was true. Teka and Anna were always together. Did she want Teka and not him? Is this why she turned him down? So many questions went through his mind. She was going to have to go. There was no way she was going to take Teka from him. With her powers, she could brainwash him to do what she wished.

Mother had warned him about getting caught up in her spell. What was she? Was she a witch? Why had she lied to him? What else had she hidden from him? *She said she loves me and wants a man she can share everything with. But she lies. She could not love me like that.*

Did she want Teka? He was younger and pure. He did have spirit. What if they both were great spirits and Mother was mistaken? Did she want to mate with Teka to create a grand spirit? Did she have Teka under a spell? Had she brainwashed him into making him think she was his mother? That make no sense. So much to think about. He needed some time to get his thoughts together.

Mat was going crazy. He needed the spirits' help, so he went to talk with them in the cave.

"Spirit of the earth, I come to you. I know not what to do. I feel Anna has betrayed me. She has been playing with my heart and soul. I am confused. I have been told she has lied and has feelings for my son."

Mat waited for the spirit to speak to him. Nothing happened.

"Speak to me!" he shouted. "I come to you for help, and as I have said, you have turned your back on me. When I ask for help, you are nowhere. Why have you deserted me in my time of need?"

Mat was angry and stormed out of the cave. When he got outside, he smelled something rotten, and then someone was in his head.

"The girl must go. She is not here to help you. She will destroy you. She lies. She withholds secrets from you. She has a spell on you and that is why you are so attracted to her. She is evil. She is only here to destroy you and your family. She has come to you on false pretenses. She will destroy the tribe and all other tribes. She

does not love you. She only wants to use you, to have power over you. You have been warned before. She plays with your heart, tempts you with her womanhood. It is all part of her plan to win you over and take all you have. You must send her away. She has evil powers and is just waiting for the kill. Send her home. Don't waste any time. She is working her magic on your son. Once she gets her claws on him, you are all doomed.

Mat had been frozen the entire time the voice was in his head. He could not move. He was cold and felt death upon him. Once the person got out of his head, he fell to the ground and slept for hours. The old woman Anna had seen at the cave was there.

She went to Mat and placed her hand on his forehead. "Go, do as you were told."

Anna knew her time here was being cut short. During dinner, Mat did not sit with her. He looked withdrawn. She knew he was up to something and that her vision was coming true. She needed to see Father and make her final deal with him to save his land. It was going to be the hardest thing she'd ever had to do and hard on Mat and Teka as well. But she knew what she had to do, and she was willing to make the sacrifice to save them both.

Anna met with Father and made the deal. "Father, whatever happens, I need you to make no exceptions for me. Stick to your customs. Do not go easy. I have to do this, and then I will go home. Promise me."

He agreed.

Anna knew the box was the key, so she went to get the necklace. On the beaded length of cord was half of a broken arrowhead. She put it on. If it did not bring Mat back, then she knew there was no help for him. She was too late, and he was too far gone.

Mat was furious. All kinds of thoughts ran through his head. Was she a witch? Had she come here to destroy the village? Had she come to destroy him? What lies had she told? He was so angry with her that he could not think straight. He went to Father and asked for a tribal meeting. Father agreed, keeping his promise to Anna. Anna had seen this coming and needed to make her last deal with Father. If this did not work, he would know what to do.

When Anna arrived at the tribal meeting, she could see it in Mat's eyes. He was so upset. She knew he had turned on her just as she had seen in her vision. Mat called Anna up in front of the tribe.

"Our men are not happy with you clothing their women. You tell their women not to lie with them."

Anna replied, "No. I did not tell them to not lie with their men. I told them to lie with their men when they are ready and not on demand. Men do not own them. They have the right to choose to give themselves to their men."

"Tell them to remove their clothes."

Anna said nothing.

"Anna!" he shouted. "Tell these women to go home and lie with their men."

Again, Anna refused to speak.

"You do as I say. You are my woman, and you must obey."

She gave him a sharp look but still said nothing.

"Anna, this is no game. You are in my world now. This is how we do things around here. Tell them now or be punished."

Mat gave a signal to the guard. The guard approached Anna and twisted her arm behind her back.

Anna cried out. "Why, Mat? How can you allow them to hurt me?"

Teka spoke up, "Stop, Father. This is not right."

Mat held up his hand and said, "Speak no more, son. I am your father, and you do as I say."

Teka stepped back. "Anna, tell him now!" he shouted.

The guard twisted her arm harder.

"No!" Anna screamed as she fell to her knees. "Stop, Mat. You know how I feel about this, and you know how this is going to end. Have I not proven to you how I feel?"

Mat knew it was hopeless. He motioned for the guard to stop.

"Father!" he said. "What is the punishment for disobeying?"

Father looked at Anna. Anna nodded.

"Two lashes," Father said.

Mat stated, "Let it be known, she will receive two lashes for disobeying her man." He turned to the women and told them to go with their men and remove their clothes. None of them got up. "I demand you women to leave now."

One woman stood up and said, "I will take my two lashes." And then others started standing until all the women were standing and claiming their lashes too.

Mat turned to Anna. "Look what you have done! Are you proud?"

Anna smiled and said, "No, Mat. This is your doing."

"Anna, I shun you from the tribe. Receive your punishment and leave tonight."

Suddenly, Mat noticed the necklace around her neck. "Where did you get that necklace?"

Anna said nothing.

"I am talking to you, Anna. Answer me now."

He went to her and jerked the necklace from her neck, cutting her skin. Blood trickled down her neck. "That is mine. You steal from me."

Anna had not expected that. She thought that if he saw the necklace, he would remember, but the look in his eyes told her a different story. What was happening? *This is not working as I planned. He is being unreasonable*, she thought.

Mat asked, "Father, what is the punishment for stealing."

Father said, "Three lashes." He looked at Anna, and she nodded.

She took a deep breath and let it out slowly with her head held high.

Teka stood. "No, Father! Do not do this. Stop this now. That is five lashes. She will not survive. Please, Father, she is my—"

Anna cut Teka off. "Teka, you are a man of your word and know better than that."

"I am sorry, but he needs to know now, Mother. Stop, stop," Teka said.

A guard struck Teka to keep him from coming up to Anna.

Anna and Mat both went crazy. "Do not touch my son!" they shouted at the same time.

"You know who he is. You never strike anyone of my family," Mat told the guard. Then he looked at Anna. "This is my son. What do you have on him? He is nothing to you."

Anna knew at that moment that there was no hope. His heart had died.

She looked at Teka and said, "We only work on spirit. I have nothing on him. Believe me, Mat. There is nothing going on between him and me. I would never."

Mat stopped her and said, "This woman is a witch. She cast a spell on me last night, lied to me about it, and now she brainwashes my son, telling him that she is his mother. The men tell me she sneak off with my son. Your punishment is now set for five lashes, and then you are to leave and go back to where you came from, never to return."

Anna said, "Let it be as stated, I accept the three lashes for stealing and two for disobeying, and I want to take the five lashes Mat took for me. I do not want to owe him anything. That makes a total of ten lashes, and then I will leave, never to return."

Teka ran toward her, but Mat gave the signal for the guards to hold him back.

"No, Father. She is my mother. She has the brand. She will die. No one can take that many lashes and survive."

"Stop now!" Mat stated. "Teka, she has used spirit on you. She is not your mother. I am sorry, son. She will be punished."

"Please, Father, let me take the lashes. I will take her place. She does not deserve this. Please, Father, open your heart and see what it is you are doing."

Anna shouted to Teka, "Stop! You are the son of a great

warrior. Stand tall and strong. Honor your father and obey him." Then she looked at Father and said, "Deal."

Father signaled to the guards to stand by Mat. They had been instructed to restrain him if need be.

Mother spoke up. "Son, do not do this. She will die. No one can survive ten lashes."

Mat answered, "Mother, we all know she can take pain away. She will not feel it."

"Son, it does not work that way. She cannot use spirit on herself. She will not make it. Think! Think, son. You do not want to do this."

Anna repeated herself to Father, "Deal."

Despite his sadness, he nodded.

Teka looked at Mother. "He needs to know. Tell him, Mother. Please. He needs the truth."

Anna said, "Stop. That is enough. Stop this now. You promised."

Mat looked confused. "What is going on? What truth?"

Mother looked at Father. "Tell him."

Father refused. "We have promised."

Then Mother said, "I did not promise."

Anna shouted, "No! Mother, no!"

Mother went to Mat, opened her hand, held it out to Mat, and said, "If she steals from you, then whose necklace is this?" She held the second necklace from Mat's room in her hand.

Mat looked at the necklace and said, "What is going on? Where did you get this?"

Teka looked at his father and said, "Father, she is my mother and your true love."

Mat took the necklace and matched it with the one he had taken off Anna's neck. They fit perfectly. He went to look at Anna's leg and saw the brand. How had he not seen it before? He looked into her eyes and then he saw it. "You are my Kati."

Anna looked at Father and nodded. They took Mat away. It took four men to hold him back. He screamed, "No! Let me go! Let me go! You know who I am. Father, stop this. It is Kati."

Anna could feel his heart pounding, and it hurt so badly. Anna had made an agreement with Father to hold Mat for twenty-four hours before they released him. She did not want him to see her get whipped or watch her die.

As the guards carried Mat away to Father's hut, Anna said, "Mat, I am so sorry."

They took him away. In his head, she told him that she loved him with all her heart, soul, and mind. Mat fought as hard as he could but could not get away.

In the distance, Mat could hear Anna screaming with every lash she received. He cried, "Please, Father, let me go to her. Stop this."

"No!" Father said. "It is done."

Chapter 26

The Sacrifice

Mat could have killed Father when they got back to his hut. It still took four men to hold him down long enough for him to cool down.

"Father, what are you doing? I need to go to her. Let me go. She needs me. She is Kati. Please, Father," he said, tears running down his cheeks.

"No, my son, I am a man of my word, and I made a deal with Anna. She requested me to hold you here for twenty-four hours. I honor that request."

"No, Father. Let me go now. Let me go now. Now, I say. Let me go." Mat fell to his knees as he collapsed in sorrow. "She is my life. I need her. I need Anna. Please."

When they were through with, Anna, she fell to the ground, gasping for breath, trying to stay awake. She could hardly move. Her back was sliced up, blood was everywhere, and overlapping gashes of all sizes covered her back. There was not much left of her skin when they were done.

She pulled herself together and in her mind spoke to Teka. *"Stop taking my pain. I know you are trying. I love you. Take care of your father. He will need you more than ever. Tell him how much I love and care for him and for you. You are my sweet little boy. Grow up and be strong like your father, and never forget to pray and love. Love Lilly and have many children. You are going to be a great man. I am your mother always. Now stop taking my pain."* And he did.

She nearly passed out as she felt the full force of her pain. A guard placed her dress back on her, trying not to hurt her. Then he put her on a horse that they had prepared for her and whispered to her softly, "Thank you for all you have done for us. You did not deserve this. Mat must be under some other influence. You have always been kind to me, and your spirit will live with us forever. I will miss you."

Anna smiled at him and said, "Thank you. Watch after him and keep him safe. Everything happens for a reason, and this is what the spirit has in store for me. I will miss you. Tell him I love him." And off she went.

The guard's heart was heavy. They were all sympathetic to Anna. He felt Mat was wrong, but he could do nothing. Anna had always been kind to him and to their people. He could not understand how Mat could turn on her like that. He knew Mat loved her. Someone must have put a spell on him, but it was not Anna.

Anna could hardly sit on the horse as it walked along. She tried to hang on as long as she could. The pain was so bad, she could hardly breathe. Anna had not gotten far before she fell off the horse. She was ready to die. She managed to slowly pull herself next to a tree and sit up. She knew Mat would soon be on his way. She could feel him fighting and knew it would not be long before he broke loose. She did not want him to see her this way, but there was nothing she could do to stop him from coming. She could feel her powers quickly draining away. She did not even have the strength to send Teka a message. She knew she was dying. She closed her eyes and asked for her death to come quickly, before Mat could come. She did not want him to see her die.

Mat was still fighting to get out. There were too many guards. They were holding him down when Teka came in. He too started to fight off the guards so that they would let Mat go. Mother joined in and hit one of the guards on the head with a clay pot. Mat got free, gathered some supplies, and went after Anna. He rode as fast as his horse could go, in search of her. His horse became wild at the sight of a black wolf on the path, growling, ready to attack. He thought he saw a woman dressed in black standing next to a tree. Was it Anna? Was he too late to save her? Before he knew it, he was on the ground and the wolf was at his throat, ready to bite down. But Missy appeared and fought off the black wolf.

As Mat remounted his horse, he could smell Anna, but her scent was getting weak. He could tell her spirit was leaving her body. Anna was not far away. She tried to be as quiet as she could. Missy came back and led Mat to her. When he reached her, she was hardly breathing. He cried out over and over as he held her in his arms and rocked her back and forth. Blood seeped through her dress.

She had lost a lot of blood. Missy licked at the blood that had dripped down Anna's legs as Mat held her. She was almost dead.

"Anna, I am here now. Why did you not tell me you were Kati? I am so sorry. You are my life. You must hang on. You will not die on me. Remember you have work to do. Teka needs you. He has been so long without a mother. Please, Anna." Mat knew he had to do something and do it quickly.

Mat looked up to the sky and asked his spirits to take his life instead. She did not deserve this, and it was his fault entirely. He was not worth keeping with the living. He asked them to spare her life, since he had died many years ago. Then he spoke to Anna's God and asked him to heal her. He did not know what to do. He knew he did not have much time. He picked her up and took her to Mother as fast as he could.

"Mat, she has lost too much blood. She is not going to

make it. We need the spirit." Mother told him it was up to the spirits. "Let us put our spirits together."

They tried. Anna opened her eyes and touched Mat's face and smiled.

"I love you with all my heart, soul, and mind," she said.

She caressed his face and then reached for Teka.

"Son, honor your father and keep him safe. He will need you more than ever. I love you so much."

Then she looked into Mat's eyes and smiled once more. "You must love again. Do not hang on to my memory. I set you free."

Then after taking her last breath, Anna died.

Chapter 27

The Deal

Mat grabbed her lifeless body and held her close. He breathed into her mouth, but nothing happened. He tried to breathe for her again, but again nothing happened. He began to cry with his whole body. He looked up to the spirits and asked for forgiveness.

"She is all I have. Please do not take her from me. I cannot live if I have lost her twice. Please, I beg you."

Still nothing happened.

Mother came to him and said, "She is gone, Mat. Let her go."

Mat gently placed Anna's body on the table, collapsed to his knees, and wept.

Teka ran to Anna, saying, "No no no! My mother will not die today. I will not let it happen, not now." Teka then breathed into Anna. Nothing happened, so he tried again. Still nothing. She was truly gone.

Mat held Teka as he cried over his mother's body. Mat

leaned over Anna's lifeless form one more time, crying, as they both held her. He kissed her goodbye.

One of his tears fell into her mouth as he said, "I love you with all of me. You are my life. Without you, I die. I will see you soon in another life. My sweet Anna, I love you, Anna, with all my heart, soul, and body. You are the only one for me. You are first in my life. You are my true love, my soul mate. I will love you forever."

When he said those words, she opened her eyes.

"Mat," she said. That was all the strength she had.

He held her, trying to be gentle so he didn't hurt her back, and cried while kissing her face. Mother told him that she needed to clean Anna's wounds and Teka was going to try to help Anna heal. Mother told Mat that they needed space to work and that he needed to leave.

Mat stood back while Anna screamed in pain. He could not stand it. Mother sent him out of the hut until they were finished.

Mat went to see Father. He burst into the hut and said, "I want to know now! What just happened? What was this deal Anna made with you? I want the truth. Old man, you will tell me now."

Father motioned him to sit, so Mat did.

"She owns our land. She came here to see if it was to stay

as it is or if she would sell it to be developed. She has been holding this over me all this time."

"So this is the hold she had over you?"

"Yes. She is very smart."

"But, Father, how was she to give us this land if she is dead?'

"She did not know who she was when she arrived. While you were hunting she remembered her time spent with us. I told her how we had found her and that while you were hunting, her grandfather came searching for her. Mother and I decided to erase her memory. We kept the baby and told you she had died. Her grandfather gave us this land for caring for her for all those years. We made an agreement that before her spirits matured, if neither of you had found love, we would bring you two back together to see what the spirits had in store for you. You turned your back on the spirits, son."

"How could you do this, Father? You know how I have mourned."

"Yes, son. You were dying."

"Why did she not tell me?"

"That is something you need to ask her. She tried everything she could to win you over, and still you refused to let someone into your heart."

"What was the deal she made with you?"

"She asked for us not to hold back the punishment. She

was to be treated as one of the tribe members. She asked that all be clothed, even the children, at all times, except in their private homes. Teka and Lilly will be wed when he comes of age, and they will go to their private home to mate. There will be no more mating ceremony, and we were to hold you back for twenty-four hours to give her time to die. In exchange for all this, she gave us the land forever. It is in our names."

"Can I see the papers, Father?"

Father gave him the papers. Mat read them and looked at the chief.

"Did you read these?"

"Yes. She gave them to me before the meeting."

"But, Father, did you see the date on them?"

"Yes. She is a smart woman."

"She gave us this land before she came. She did not have to come."

"Yes, son. She did it of her own free will."

"But why? She did not have to go through all this suffering. Why would she do that?"

"Son, you will have to ask her. I feel that her spirits sent her here. They had unfinished business with the two of you."

Mat shook his head, bowed it, and said, "I have been such a fool." Then he went to be with Anna.

He stood at the door to Mother's hut as Teka and Anna talked.

"Mother, why you do this?"

"You know. I have already told you why, and you will understand once you and Lilly start your lives together."

Mat cleared his throat and told Teka that he needed some time alone with Anna.

"Anna, you are going to be the death of me," he said.

"Yes. You have told me many times."

"Why you do this? Why did you not tell me when you found out?"

"You would not have believed me. You were so wrapped up in Kati's memory that you would not let anyone in."

"But if you had told me—"

"Mat, you would not listen, and even if you did, I needed to know you loved me the way I am now and not the memory of who I was. I needed to know you loved me. Me! Just me."

"Anna, I loved you the first day I saw you."

"Is that why you were so rude and did not speak to me?"

"You noticed?"

"Yes. How could I not? You went into the store for a long time. What was I to think?"

"Anna, I had to pull myself together before I could talk to you. You were so beautiful, and your scent was killing me. I wanted nothing more than to take you home with me forever. The time we spent on the trail was more than I could handle. I knew I had to be strong and stay away."

"I felt the same way, Mat. It was hard for me too."

"Anna, why did you do this? You made that deal with Father. Why?"

"Mat, you turned on me. There was nothing I could do to get through to you. I knew your love for Kati was too strong, and I knew the only thing I could do was go home. I made the deal with Father in exchange for the land. I want Teka to share the same kind of love we had for each other with Lilly. I would do anything to see that happen, even if it means giving my life.

"That night we made love on the mating table, I thought it would wake you up, but it did not. You drifted off into a world of your own, and you called me Kati. The necklace was my last chance, and you accused me of stealing. I had instructed Father what to do if you did not see. I knew I had failed, and it was time for me to leave and never bother you again."

"But, Anna, you had already signed the papers before you came. Why come?"

"I have always lived under the shadow of my grandfather's name. I was looking for a purpose in life. I just felt it would be a great adventure, and it was. I would do it all again if I had to. I have no regrets. When I came here, I had no idea of what lies ahead. When I saw you get out of the old rusty beat-up Jeep, my heart skipped a beat."

"Why make such a sacrifice for people you knew nothing about?"

"I felt it in my heart. I love this place. If it were not for your people, I would not be here, we would have not have loved, and we wouldn't have Teka."

"Father told me the deal you made, but I do not understand. What about the whipping pole? He did not say anything about it."

"No, he would not. I told him we would keep it. How else am I to keep you in line?"

"Anna, what am I going to do with you?"

"I am sure you will find something, but now we have a wedding to prepare for."

"Yes, we do."

"I love you, you know."

"I love you too."

Chapter 28

Wedding

It took Anna over a week to heal, even with Teka's help. Mat stayed by her side as much as he could. There was no more mating, but he did not mind.

"Anna, we are still married. When will we be together?"

"I want to see Teka married first, and then we will see. We need to learn to love each other again."

"But, Anna, I need you."

"You always need me. After Teka is wed. I promise."

"Anna." He took her by the hand and said, "Will you be my wife? Will you marry me again?"

She looked at him and said, "What took you so long? I told you a long time ago I would."

"You know you did not mean it then. You were trying to get yourself out of trouble."

"Well, I think being your wife would be more trouble."

"Will you?"

"Yes, Mat. I would love nothing more. Let's get married at the same time as Teka and Lilly."

As soon as Anna was able, she started preparing for the weddings. She gathered flowers, and the women prepared all their wedding clothes. Anna even went to Father to prepare the vows. She found the perfect hut for Teka and Lilly. She cleaned it, and she and Lilly decorated the inside. Anna went to the cooks and planned a huge feast. Mat and Teka worked on carving the wedding bands. They would party all night.

"Anna," Mat said, "you have done a wonderful job."

She looked at him and said, "Your English is getting better. I am so proud of you."

"It is all you, Anna. You are improving our way of life. I am glad. Will you dance with me tomorrow night?"

"I do not know. It seems like they do not turn out so good. I seem to get into trouble every time I dance with you. I do not want to spoil the night."

"Anna, you cannot spoil any of my days or nights ever again."

"Oh, I am sure there will be days."

"After all we have been through, I think we can get through anything that comes to us."

The next morning, everything was ready. Teka was soon to be wed, and it was his birthday too. Anna went to him and gave him two necklaces like hers and Mat's. She had Mat make them each one, just as he had for her when they were wed.

"Here is something for your birthday and a wedding gift. Give the other half to Lilly. Wear these necklaces to represent the two of you being joined. When together you are whole, one person united together. Love each other and keep each other safe, not only in the flesh but also in your hearts and souls. Cherish your love together and always remember it takes two to make a family. Keep Lilly next to your heart always. She is your other half and in everything you do you carry her with you. You have been blessed with a special and rare spirit. Use it wisely."

She continued, "Always remember what comes first in life: your God or spirit, family, and love. I am so proud of you. You have turned into a wonderful man. You are strong, handsome, brave, and wise. You are going to be a great chief one day. I love you, son."

Teka turned to Anna. "Mother, you have already prepared us a place to live and made it possible for Lilly to be my one and only."

"Still not enough," Anna said. "I have missed so many birthdays. I want this one to be special."

Mat asked Mother about the grand spirit. "If Teka has

the grand spirit and mates with someone without a spirit, will he be like my mother when her spirit died?"

"No, son. The grand spirit can mate with anyone. His spirit will not die, and he cannot pass the grand spirit to his firstborn. It will be thousands of years before the grand spirit reappears. Teka will have much power and be a great warrior. He will do well for his people, and thanks to Anna, we can continue to live here as it has been."

Mat went back to Anna. "You are so beautiful and have thought of everything."

"Look how handsome you are. We wed tonight," she replied.

"Yes, we do. And then you wear the teddy for me."

"Yes. It will be the right time for me to show you what you can do with a teddy."

"I think I like the sound of that."

"I am sure you will not forget it."

"Anna, you once said you could eat me up."

"Yes. I remember."

"Tonight will you show me what that is?"

"Oh, yes. I will eat you up. I cannot wait. You will have to wait a few more hours. Trust me—you will not forget this night. You told me that if you had your way with me, I would remember the next morning."

"Yes. I meant that."

"I hope so."

"Oh, you will, you will."

Later that day, Mother had an errand to run. Anna thought, *How unusual. Mother never leaves the village.* Anna watched Mother go down the path next to Father's hut, the one that led to the beach. What was she up to? Anna decided to follow her and see for herself. Anna stayed back far enough that Mother had no clue that she was behind her.

Mother met up with a savage woman on the sandy shore. Anna could barely hear what they were saying.

"Sarah, why have you called on me? You know it is not safe for you to be here."

"Mother, thank you for coming. I understand Teka becomes man today. I would like to have your permission to attend the ceremony. I know I am not welcome, but could you make an exception?"

"He knows nothing of you and will question your appearance. Besides, there is no mating tonight."

"No mating? How is this possible? How is he to become man?"

"Father has allowed him to be with his promised one. They are to be wed tonight and go off to their new home and mate in private."

"Teka is so much like his father. I see that. So strong,

brave, and handsome. He is going to be a great chief one day, like his father. How is his father? Has he changed?"

"Yes. He has a new love, and she has opened his heart. All of this is her doing. She is making changes for the better. The maker is no more. Men will take on wives when the women are ready. No public mating anymore."

"Do they have spirit?"

"Mat's mate does, but Teka's does not."

"No, Mother. Teka will die if not wed to one with spirit."

"No, he will not. The spirits have approved their union. He will be safe."

"Do you think I could stand back unseen in the woods to see weddings? Mat's mate, is she the white girl I saw by the cave?"

"You were there when Matete was attacked?"

"No, not during the attack. I came later. This girl has strong spirit and asked for help, so I helped her. I sent her powers to help Matete. She has not learned to direct her powers yet."

"She has been practicing. Her spirit is getting much stronger each day. We do not know what spirit she has. I suspect it is the great spirit."

"If she mates with Matete, their child will have the grand spirit."

"No. Mat has already passed his spirit to Teka."

"Then she is in danger to one trying to mate with her to produce the grand spirit. Matete will never have peace, having to constantly protect her. I hope he is up to that challenge."

"Don't worry about that. He knows what he is up against. Sarah, I cannot allow you to be at the ceremony, but I cannot stop you from watching from the woods. Stay safe and keep your distance. I know how important this is to you. Take care."

"Thank you, Mother. I will be careful. Do you think he will ever forgive me?"

Mother returned to the village, not knowing Anna had seen and heard everything. That was the woman she had seen at the cave. Who was she and why the interest in Mat and Teka? No time for that now. She had a wedding to get ready for. There would be time to get answers later.

Soon it was time for the weddings. On the stomping ground was a large circle made of sticks. Both Teka and Mat stood outside the circle. Anna and Lilly walked slowly to the circle and stood by their men. Father gave each couple a stick to hold during the ceremony. The couples walked side by side around the inside of the circle, holding on to their sticks. The entire tribe stood around the outside of the circle.

Father was in the circle with them. He held a smoking bowl and a large eagle feather wing fan. The elders, dressed in their ceremonial clothing, stood behind them and placed a blanket around each couple. Father fanned the wing to send the smoke toward them. Each person reached into the smoke to grab a handful and then released the smoke in his or her face. Then they reached in again and released the smoke onto their hearts. The last handful of smoke, they released down the length of their bodies.

Father blessed them as he tapped each of them on their shoulders and then four times on the head. Father chanted and sang throughout the ceremony. He held his arms up to the spirits and blessed each couple. No one else made a sound throughout. Mat and Anna poured sand into a gourd, as did Teka and Lilly.

Father honored Mother Earth and asked for their marriages to be abundant and grow stronger through the seasons. He said, "Fire is for the union between each couple. Be warm and glowing with love in your hearts. Wind, we ask that they sail through life safe and calm in the Father's arms. Water is to clean and soothe their relationships so that they may never thirst for love."

Father gave each person a medicine bag and instructed them to exchange the medicine bags with their mates. Anna gave hers to Mat, and Mat gave his to Anna. Lilly gave Teka hers, and Teka gave his to Lilly.

Then Father stated, "Woman is to protect their home, and the man is the spiritual leader of that home."

Mat faced Anna and Teka faced Lilly as they exchange rings. The rings were made of turquoise and silver and had the symbols of their heritage and their union brand carved into the stone. Then they each shared words to express their love for the other and stated that they belonged to each other forever. Once the rings were exchanged, Mat turned to the tribe and announced. "This is my wife; she will be called Katiann from this moment on. All the people chanted and sang as the couples walked around the circle, shaking everyone's hand. When they were finished shaking hands, the party started, and everyone knew it was going to last all night.

"Katiann," Mat said, "I love you so much."

They ate and danced for hours. As the party started to slow, Teka and Lilly left to go to their hut to be together. Mat took Katiann by the hand to lead her toward their hut.

Katiann smiled at Mat and said, "It was a great party. Thank you for allowing them to marry."

"Katiann, you know you held the land over our heads to get this to happen."

"Yes, but look how it worked out. You could have taken the land and sent me away to continue living your way of life."

"No Katiann, we are men of our word."

"I know, and I love you for it."

He kissed her, but she pushed him away as she started to see a vision.

"What is it, Katiann? What?"

She stared into the air. Her facial expression was different than he had ever seen before. It was not like when she went into his head or when she talked to the animals. This expression was one of fear. Something fearful was coming.

Chapter 29

The Fight

"Mat, they are coming, a dozen or more of them on horseback. They are close, coming to raid the village. They are coming for me and to take revenge."

Mat had known he had killed four of them and that they would come. That is why he had the tribe prepare for war.

"I'll go get Teka."

"No!" she said. "This is their night. Do not get him. I have shielded his powers so that nothing can come between him and Lilly. Leave him be."

Mat reached over and gave her a big kiss. "I must go."

"I know. Be careful and come back to me, you hear. You better come back to me!"

"Katiann, nothing is going to come between me and you having fun tonight."

"You have it bad, don't you?"

"It has been a long time."

"I am glad you saved yourself for me," Katiann said.

Mat left her standing there as he yelled for the men to get ready. They gathered their gear and painted their faces.

They meant business, she thought. She had not seen them in action like this before. The women also started preparing for what was to come.

Mother came to her and said, "We must be ready. If they get to us, they will take our women and children and kill the rest. Go find something to fight with. Katiann, stop shielding Teka. He must prepare if we are to survive."

"Mother, why is this happening? It was to be our night."

"Mat has been expecting it. We are ready for anything. They will not win. They come for you, Katiann. Mat has been preparing for this day for a while now."

"He has? Even before?"

"Yes, even before. Katiann, you are the only one he cares about. He has always loved you."

"I see that now."

Katiann ran after Mat and found him just before he mounted his horse. She stopped and he ran to her, picked her up, and kissed and hugged her. She told him that they had just found each other again and that he had better come back to her.

"Katiann, I love you, and I will be back."

She smiled at him and nodded. "Katiann. I can live with that," she whispered.

He just smiled back at her and off he rode. Katiann was so scared. Her vision of Father's heart attack had come true and they had to bring him back to life, but Mat's heart had yet to stop. In her vision, she remembered Mat dying because his heart stopped. She prayed that this was not that time. She got a lump in her throat, swallowed hard, and started to cry. She knew something was wrong.

Katiann had a feeling she was not alone. She turned around and saw two savages standing behind her. They had already entered their camp while the men were getting ready, waiting until she was alone. She had not seen this coming.

Why? she thought.

Then she realized the old woman had spirit. She was strong with spirit; Katiann could not move. The old woman had frozen her. What was she to do? She did not know how to work that power. The man walked up to her and looked her up and down.

"Very nice," he said. "It looks as if you were waiting for me."

Katiann could not cry out, but she did have the power to send a message to Teka and Mother. They were too far away to get to her before the savage took her for himself.

It was dark. She knew the night animals would be out, so she reached out for help with her mind to the animals that were near. Katiann had been kind to the animals during her stay, so they all got together and surrounded the savages.

The old woman looked at Katiann and said, "So you speak to them. Very strong power. I can speak to them as well."

Her powers were stronger than Katiann's, and she put the animals to sleep. Then she got into Katiann's head and sent pain so that she could not speak to the animals anymore. Katiann fell to her knees.

The savage took her by the hair, drug her to her hut, and slung her on the bed. He ripped her clothes off. She could not fight back; her body was still frozen. She looked to the spirits and asked for help. Then she broke free of his hold and the old woman's power and started to fight back. She knew she had strong power, but she was not sure how to use it. She asked the spirits to take over her body and save her from this savage.

Katiann raised her hands, and the man flew across the room. He looked at her in fear. "What spirit you have? I never seen before."

"I have all the spirits on my side. I am of great spirit."

"Yes," the old woman stated. "I too have great spirit, but I no do that. Your spirit different in some way. What are you?"

The man started toward Katiann again, but she stopped him in his tracks this time and got into both their heads.

"You are a very bad man. I curse you for the rest of your life. You shall never have spirit again. You use spirit in a bad way; therefore, the spirit has been taken from you and your offspring. I will spare your life so you can tell your people to change their ways or I will cast down doom upon them.

"Go, leave these people alone and do not come back. You will let our people pass through your territory or I will take that away as well. I am being very kind to you. Do not cross me or my people again. No one in your tribe will cause us harm. Do you understand? You have not yet seen my powers, for I am the grand spirit of all. Go. Never come back."

The man ran out, but the woman stayed.

"I know you are his mother," Katiann said to her.

"Yes," the woman said.

"Then why do you want to cause harm to a tribe you were part of at one time?"

"Yes, I was. I never intended to hurt Mat or Teka. I have always been close to protect them. I was there at cave and helped you get through to Mat. I helped Teka escape when he traveled too far in search of deer."

"You were the one who got into my head. Those men were your people. They wanted to take me to your tribe as they did you. You protected both of us. The men who assaulted me, did you send them?"

"No, they came on their own. Many want your powers.

Lots of men carry great spirit to mate with another of their kind. Only a few women have the spirit."

"Wait, you passed it to Mat. What about the man who just left? He too is your son? How did he get the great spirit?"

"He got from his father. I can only pass once, and since I had passed it to Matete, the great spirit was passed to my other son by his father. He was his first child. This is why you are so special. Even if you do not mate with another great spirit, your offspring could."

The old woman continued, "The savages came and took many women while men were away hunting. My tribe never did come for us. They told my husband I had died. The savages had their way with us. Some died, some survived, and many became with child. I never wanted to use spirits, but at that time to survive I was forced to, and so I did. They realized I had power, and I was mated with another spirit. The man who was here is my husband's firstborn and has the great spirit. Now you have taken that from him."

"Why did you not come back?" Katiann asked.

"I was with child, damaged goods. This tribe would no accept me with a savage child inside me. I could never return. My tribe needs your child to be strong. You will bring the grand spirit to our land. But I no realize you are the grand spirit. The grand spirit has already arrived. We have no use for you now. We will no bother you anymore."

"I am sorry things happened that way," Katiann said. "Mat has missed you so much. I think it best for us to keep this secret from him. I see no good coming from him knowing. Agreed?"

"Yes, agreed. We will not cause you any more trouble. I go in peace."

Katiann could not believe what she had just done. She did not have that much power, and she knew she was not the grand spirit. What had just happened?

Teka came running in. "Mother, are you okay?"

"Yes, son. But you will not believe what just happened. I asked for the spirits to help me."

"Yes, Mother, I know. The spirits came to me and told me to get into your body. I did not know I could do that, but it worked."

"Son, that was you talking through me?"

"Yes, Mother. Are you all right?"

"Yes, but I did think this was my last day." Katiann gave Teka a big hug. "Is your father back?"

"No."

"Can you see what he is doing?"

"No, Mother, I cannot."

"I cannot either. Something is blocking us from seeing what is going on."

"Do you think father is blocking us?"

"I hope not, son, for I fear if he has, then it must be really bad and he does not want us to see. Teka, we cannot tell your father what happened here tonight, okay?"

"Okay, Mother," Teka said.

"You do realize she is your grandmother?" Katiann asked.

Teka said nothing.

Then Katiann grabbed her heart and fell to the ground. She looked up with wide eyes to see Mother in the doorway. Katiann's nose started to bleed. Mother came to her and held her.

"I feel it too, my dear. Just hold on. It will all be over soon."

"No no no!" Katiann rocked back and forth. "No no no!" she screamed. "He is dead!" Katiann laid on the ground and sobbed. She would not get up or move. She wanted everyone to just leave her alone. Her love was gone. The bond had been broken.

"Why?" she asked the spirits. "We just found each other. You put us through all this and now take him away from me. I do not understand. Why?" she cried.

Teka ran to Katiann with a heavy heart and tried to hold her.

"Please, Teka, go to your wife—hold her. I need to be alone. I feel him no more. He is gone."

"Mother, we need each other."

"Not now. I need to be alone. Leave and go love your wife. She needs you, and you need her. Don't ever let her go. Go, Teka."

Teka did as his mother instructed.

Mat had been fighting for his life and to save Katiann from being taken. He fell off his horse when a savage struck him in the chest. His heart stopped, and he fell to the ground. While Mat was on the ground, a savage pulled out a knife to scalp him. He grabbed Mat's long hair and raised it up to cut it. Just as he put the knife to Mat's head, the white wolf and her pack attacked.

It was about an hour before the warriors got back to the village. Katiann knew they would bring back his body. She went to claim him. She was numb all over. Her eyes were swollen from crying. She felt like she was walking in slow motion as she went to see where the warriors were. There were several bodies on horses.

"Which one is Mat?" she asked.

The warriors looked confused as Katiann walked passed them. She looked at the first body. It was not Mat. She went to the next body and looked. It was not him. Katiann frantically searched each body to find him.

She shouted, "Where is he? Where is he? I demand to know now! Where is Mat's body?"

Father came to her, and she collapsed in his arms.

"What have they done with Mat? I need to see him."

"He is with Mother in her hut."

"I forgot. He is ruler. They would not keep him with the others!"

Katiann and Father walked toward Mother's hut. By now, fog had filled the sky. She could hardly see her way. Her eyes were almost swollen shut. How was she to live now that her heart, her soul mate, the love of her life, was gone? She had not and would never be with another man.

She now knew how Mat had felt when he thought he lost her. This was the greatest pain she had ever felt. How could she have been so insensitive to his feelings about Kati? No one knew until it happened to them. What was she to do?

She looked up and saw someone coming toward her through the fog. It was a man, but who? He was too far away, and the fog was so thick, she could not recognize him. He had a bandage around his waist and one on his arm. It had to be one of the wounded. And then his face emerged. She could not believe her eyes.

She whispered, "Mat, is it true? Is that you, Mat?" No, she was seeing things. Mat was dead. She was sure of it.

The man saw her and started to run toward her. It was Mat! She ran to him. He picked her up and held her tightly.

She wrapped her legs around him and said, "You were dead. I knew it. I felt it. My nose bled. How?"

"I was hit hard in the chest, and my heart stopped for just a second. When I fell, the blow from the ground must have started my heart back up. When I woke up, the strangest thing happened. There was a wretched old lady kneeling over me as if she had given me breath. She smelled of savage. Her son came and saw her kneeling over me. He took out his knife and threw it at me, but she jumped in front of me and took the knife. She looked into my eyes and said, 'I love you, my son.' Her son came and held her until her last breath."

Teka came running to Katiann, shouting, "She is dead!"

"I know, son. She gave her life to save Mat's."

Mat looked at them both with a puzzled look. "Do you know her?"

"She was here earlier. She came to do us no harm. She told us that her tribe would not bother us anymore."

"Why would she give her life for me? She knows nothing of me."

Katiann started to tear up. Mat demanded answers, and he wanted them now.

Teka jumped in and said, "She was my grandmother."

Mat looked at Katiann. "What is he saying?"

"Mat, when she said, 'I love you, son,' she was talking to you. She was your mother. I looked into her mind when she was here. She was taken by the savages and left for dead. After they had their way with her and she became with child, she knew she could not return to you. I feel she has watched over you and Teka all your lives. She loved you very much."

"She gave her life for me. Why?"

"Yes, Mat. That is what mothers do for their children. They would put their children's lives before their own."

"Now I understand how deep a mother's love is and why you did the things you have done. I love you, Katiann, more than you will ever know."

"Mother, she is on her way here," Teka said.

Mat looked up to the edge of the woods and saw a black wolf standing beside the savage who had tried to kill him. The man carried the woman's body in his arms. Mat reached for his knife, but Katiann stopped him.

"Mat, we must help him. He is your brother."

"My brother? I have no brother, Katiann."

"Yes, Mat, you do, and we must hear what he has to say."

Katiann motioned for the savage to come to Mother's hut. He looked at Katiann and spoke to her while Mother translated.

Crying, he said, "This is my mother. She does not deserve to die. Please help her. We know the grand spirit is within you. Bring her back to life."

Katiann looked at Mother and then at the savage. "I

cannot bring her back. I do not have that power. Teka must do it."

Teka looked at Katiann. "Mother, I cannot bring her back. I tried with you, and it did not work."

"Then who brought me back?"

"It was my father. After I tried, Father spoke and cried over you, and you woke."

Mother looked at Mat and then at all of them.

"Mat does not have the power to bring back life. It has to be something else," Katiann said.

Mother took Katiann's hand and placed it in Mat's, and Teka joined in.

"It takes all three of you to bring back life," Mother said. "When Katiann died, her spirit was still with her. Teka's spirit came to Katiann. The circle was completed when Mat joined in. With all three spirits, then and only then can life be restored. In all our years, no one has experienced the bringing back of life until now. Hurry. She does not have much time to be revived."

"Mother, why should we bring her back? She is dead. Let it be," Mat said.

Katiann looked at him and said, "She is your mother, and we do all we can to save family."

"Why? She left me as a child. I owe her nothing."

"Yes, you do. She has given you life twice. You owe her that much. She was left for dead. It was no fault of hers. She was violated and could not return to you. She has been watching over you all these years in ways you do not know. She is Teka's grandmother. You owe it to him. Please, Mat. We must do it," Mother told him.

"It is like with my God," Katiann said. "It takes three. In my world we know this as the Father, Son, and the Holy Ghost. We must complete the circle, and then and only then can we save her. Mat, come on. Hurry. We don't have much time."

The three laid hands on Sarah, and Mother chanted around the room, calling upon all the spirits. She shook rattles and shakers as she danced while looking upward. The air in the hut became fresh, like it smelled after rain had washed away all the impurities. Everyone in the hut could feel the goodness around them.

Their hands hovered up and down her body three times. Then their hands began to glow white and blue. The more they passed over her body with their hands and the more Mother said blessings, the brighter the glow became. Soon, it was almost too bright to look at.

Katiann looked up and saw it—a round glowing ball floating in the air, descending into Sarah's body as her body began to glow blue and white.

As the glow diminished, they lifted their hands from

Sarah, and she gasped for breath, still unconscious. Mother checked her and announced that she was truly alive. They had done it. They had brought her back to life, all three of the spirits together.

"Mother, is it true? Is she my real mother?" Mat asked.

"Yes, son."

"Did you know all this time and did not tell my father?"

"No, son. We believed she had died. We would have fought for her if we had only known. It was when your father died that I suspected she was alive. I saw her in the woods during the ceremony when we buried your father. I went to her, and she confirmed my suspicion. She made me promise not to tell anyone. Sarah was ashamed and thought it best if you believed she was dead. When you and Kati got married, she came to see me. She was very proud of you and the way you stood strong on your belief to be Kati's first. She supported the union. She has always been close and was there when Teka was born. She loved you so much but did not want to bring disgrace to you and your family."

"My father died of a broken heart. He loved her with all his heart, soul, and mind. She let him die."

"No, son. She was a prisoner for many years. It was after she had a son that they let her roam free. When your father passed, she grieved as you did. She had no choice but to go back and let you live an untainted life. She felt that if she returned, it would disgrace the family and you would not be the man you are today. Your father loved your mother as you love Katiann."

"Mother, will she be okay?" Katiann asked.

"I believe so. It will take some time. I have never cared for someone whose life has been returned before."

The savage man who had brought Sarah to the village looked at Mat and said, "This is your mother and mine. I am called Kowl."

"Yes, it looks to be so. We are brothers."

Kowl went to Mat and held out his hand. Mat looked at Katiann as if asking for her permission. Katiann smiled and nodded, squeezing his hand softly. Mat reached out and shook his brother's hand.

"We are now brothers. No more fighting. We live in peace."

Kowl nodded and then went to sit by his mother's side.

"Mat, are you okay?" Mother asked. "You and Katiann need to go celebrate your union. I will watch over Sarah. It may be days before she wakes up. Go now."

Mat was going to be fine. He took Katiann to their hut and whispered in her ear, "Is it time for teddy now?"

They stayed there for two days.

Chapter 30

The Wolf

"Katiann, it is time for us to get up. We have been in here many days. It is time to see the sunshine."

"Do we have to? Can we not stay in here one more day?"

"I would love to, but I am acting chief and I have work to do. I need to help Father do his rounds today, and besides, what will people say if we stay in another day?"

"They will not say anything. They know how long we have been waiting for this. Please lie with me a little longer. I love feeling the warmth of your body next to mine."

"Okay, a little longer and then we have to get back to the real world. People are expecting us, or they will think you really did eat me up."

"I will take as much time as you can give me. Do you think you will have time today to take me to the falls? I have something I want to show you."

"Will I come back alive?"

"I am sure you will feel alive, but I don't know how you will come back."

"What am I to do with you, woman? Okay. After lunch I will come with the horses. Be ready."

Katiann waggled her eyebrows. "You best be ready for me."

After lunch, Mat went to get the horses and picked Katiann up in front of their hut.

"Where is your gear?" he asked her. "You never go anywhere without a bag of something to carry."

"For what I have to show you, we do not need to bring anything but ourselves."

Mat looked puzzled. He could not imagine what she had to show him that he had not already seen. This was a mystery to him. He could not believe she did not carry anything with her, not even her bathing suit. She said not to bring anything, so he didn't. He helped her onto her horse and rode to the falls.

"Mat, I cannot believe how beautiful this place is. I am so glad I saved this land from ever being populated by outsiders. I do not want to see anything happen to any of this." She waved her hand in front of her at the land. "Come sit with me on the rocks and listen to the water flow and the birds sing."

It was not long before she began to get hot and started to sweat, and so did he. She looked at him, took him by the hand, and stood up. They stood face-to-face as she removed her dress.

There she stood in her bare skin and said, "I am yours, and my body is for no other eyes. You are mine, and your body is for no other eyes. We are one now." Then she jumped in. He undressed and followed her.

It was late afternoon when they decided it was time to go back. Katiann and Mat got out of the water and got back on the rock. She put her dress on, and Mat put on his pants. Mat noticed something was going on in her head.

"Katiann, tell me what you see."

"It is Missy. She needs me. I feel her calling me, and she is hurt."

"I was afraid of that. When the fight was over, I saw her leave. It looked like blood on her white coat. I was not sure if it was hers or from a savage she had torn apart."

"What do you mean from a savage she tore apart?"

"She led her pack to help us in the fight. If it were not for her and the other wolves, we would not have succeeded. She saved us."

"Oh, Mat, I sent her there. I believe she does have a spirit. I think she has been watching over you and then over me when I came back. We must go to her and help."

"I do not know where she is. We have never been able to find a wolf den. They are too smart for us. I do not know where to start. There is a lot of land out here. She could be anywhere."

Katiann stood for a few minutes with her eyes closed. "She is over the mountain, in the cave, the spirit cave. I am sure of it. I can see her plain as day. She is dying! Mat, we must get to her quickly. Let's go, please. Hurry. She does not have much time. She calls for me to come."

They got on their horses and rode until they reached the protected area. Mat signaled to the guards that they were coming and to let them pass. They signaled back that all was clear. Mat made a torch from a rag he kept in his saddlebag to give them light in the cave. All around the edge of the woods, they could see the wolves gathering. None made any effort to attack. It was as if the wolves were waiting for them and they were welcome there. It was cold, but Mat and Katiann would have to endure it this time. They found Missy back in the corner.

Mat held Katiann back. "Katiann, it is too dangerous for you to get close to her. She is hurt. She will attack you. Don't be foolish. Listen to me on this."

"Mat, when will you ever learn to trust me? I know what I am doing. She is calling for me to come. I must go. She will not hurt me or you. She is of spirit, and she cares for us."

Mat let go of her hand, and she went to Missy. Katiann sat beside her, and the wolf laid her head in Katiann's lap. Then

Mat saw it, as did Katiann, a white glow that turned into a woman. Katiann did not know what to make of it until the woman started to talk.

"Katiann, my love. You were such a brave little girl when our plane crashed. I have always known you were special. When my powers started to emerge, your father did not know what to do with me. He took me to many hospitals, but they could not help me. Then one day I remembered a place that believed in spirits. I knew I had to find these people to help me and to save you. You see, my great grandmother was an Indian. I knew I had to find out what her people were like. So your father and I decided to come here to see if the tribe could help me control my spirits."

Katiann started to speak, but the spirit said, "No, Katiann. I do not have much time to answer your questions. Listen to what I have to say. During the transition is the only time I can speak as I do. Our plane crashed not far from here. You survived. Your father died instantly, but I lingered long enough to tell you goodbye. A wolf came to my aid.

"With my spirit, I spoke to the wolf and asked her to watch over you. Find a safe place for you to stay. When I took my last breath, my spirit left my body and went into the wolf, and she turned white. She is old now, and her time has passed. She has been a good guardian to you—and to you too, Mat. I was with you, Mat, when your father died and when your heart was broken when Katiann's grandfather came and took her away. Now I leave the wolf's body and go to another. I will still be with you all the days of your life. I love you, Missy."

Katiann's eye welled up with tears, and then she saw a white mist drift over to the other side of the cave. Katiann was still holding the wolf as she took her last breath. Katiann wept. Mat went to see where the mist had gone. It was dark, but he managed to see it. Far, far back in the cave was a little white pup, shivering in the cold. Mat picked her up and took her to Katiann. Katiann wiped her tears away. She knew then that her mother's spirit had gone inside the pup. Mat knew there was no way Katiann was going to leave her behind.

Mat helped Katiann up onto her horse and gave her the pup. He built a fire and burned the wolf's body. All the wolves gathered around and howled throughout the night. When Mat and Katiann got back home, Katiann made the pup a bed inside their hut. Mat was reluctant, but this was Katiann he was dealing with, and he knew he would not win this battle.

"Thank you for letting her stay with us. I think I shall call her Little Miss. What do you say?"

"She won't be little long, but she will be a good guardian for our tribe. Teach her well."

Chapter 31

Forgiveness

It took a few days before Sarah was able to speak. She moved slowly and was ready to get out and get some sunshine. Kowl stayed with her the entire time she was in the village. They stayed in Mother's hut.

"Mother, I think I should go back now," Sarah said. "I am better, and Mat has not once come to see me. I fear he wants nothing to do with me. I am nothing to him, and he will never forgive me. He thinks I abandoned him as a child. He will never get back what he has lost. Mother and son always have the closest relationships. We missed having that bond."

"Sarah, he needs time, and besides, he has just reunited with the love of his life."

"What do you mean? Kati died years ago and this girl has stolen his heart."

"No. She has always had his heart. Katiann is Kati. Father

and I thought it would be best to send her back to her people, so we told Matete she had died."

"All these years he has been suffering and you let it happen. Why?"

"Her grandfather traded the land for her. It was for all of us. They could have come and destroyed everything we had and the others tribes as well. We had no choice. If Mat knew she was alive, he would not have stopped looking for her."

"He and Kati had a child?" Sarah looked into Mother's eyes. "She does not have the grand spirit does she? Teka has."

Mother did not say anything.

"Your silence speaks for itself. All of this could have been prevented if you had not lied. Four men have died, and Matete and Kati have been tormented. Losing Kati was the worst. I have watched him grow up without me from a distance. Losing Kati was uncalled for. That did not have to happen. I am sure something could have been done. I am very disappointed in you and Father. I thought what I did was to save him pain, but you only caused him pain. His soul was dying. How could you do that to him?"

"It was Father's and her grandfather's decision. They made a deal to reunite them if they had not found another love before her spirit emerged. Her coming back was all in the plan. I erased her memory, so they had to fall in love with each other once again."

"I do not approve of what you and Father have done, but who am I to judge? The spirits will cast judgment on your souls when it is time."

"Sarah, you are not innocent in this. You let Matete's father die, my only son. How do you speak this way of us when what you did cost a life too? We would have fought for you. Mika would still be here. My son died of a broken heart because you did not come forward."

They both cried together.

Mother told Sarah what was done was done and that now it was time to heal. "Sarah, you know you can stay and live with us."

"Maybe I can visit without having to hide in the woods. I have a family of six children, and I love them as any mother loves her children, and many grandchildren."

"I know it will be difficult for our tribes to adjust. All I ask is that we be peaceful toward each other. I will talk with Father to see if you can visit as you please. I cannot promise. I am sure Mat will have some input in that decision."

During breakfast the next morning Katiann carried Little Miss with her. "Mat, you have not said anything about your mother. I hear she is better and is able to leave. You should go see her," Katiann said to Mat.

"Katiann, I have nothing to say to her. She left me as a child. What am I to think? She let my father die."

"She did what she thought she had to do to protect you. It was not her choice. Look at you. You are a powerful man, strong and smart. You are next in line to be chief. You are much respected in all tribes. She knew if she came back it would have destroyed your life. You are who you are because of her. As a mother, I know I would do anything for someone I love to be happy and live a prosperous life, no matter the cost. I cannot blame her for doing what she thought was right."

"This is different. None of this would have happened if she had come back."

"Mat, you do not know that for sure. There would have been a war, and you could have lost it all. She did what she had to do to protect you. You cannot condemn her for that. I would have given my life for your or Teka's happiness. She has done no different than I would have done."

Mat looked at her, and she embraced him. She knew it was heavy on his heart. What should he do? He had been without a mother for all these years. He needed some peace.

"Katiann, I need time with the spirits. I will be back in a few hours. Do not let her go home until I get back."

"We will be waiting on you. Take as much time as you need."

Mat rode out to the cave and remembered the last time he was there and how someone had been in his head. Then he remembered seeing a dark shadow of a woman with a black wolf. Why would she tell him all those things and send her wolf after him? Then he remembered that she sent the wolf away so that no harm would come to him. She had been protecting him, and she had been there to take the knife her son had thrown at him. She had been willing to give her life to save his.

When he went into the cave, he felt different. It was as if his heart had been lifted. He could feel the spirits. He had not a care and felt safe. This was truly what he needed. Then he realized the spirits had made all this happen to get his attention. They knew he was a stubborn man; the spirits had to use drastic measures to get through to him. He had in fact turned his back on the spirits. Throughout everything he had been through, the spirits had always been there for him. They sent Kati back, protected him during all his battles, gave him a son, and now had given him his mother.

Mat got down on his knees and cried, chanted, and sang to the spirits. He could feel it deep in his soul. Then the spirits formed a haze that spun and twirled around him. He could hear drums beating in his head.

"We watched over you and kept you safe. We have never turned our backs on you or your family. You have been blessed, blessed above all others, with spirit. Cherish what you have and pass it on. You are like the eagle soaring above your people. Keep them safe. Never underestimate the power to believe. You have great spirit, and we are always here.

"Watch for the eagle, and send your prayers upon his wings. You have free will to ask for anything. Continue to look after your people, and never be afraid of change. Your bloodline will inherit the earth with your kindness and spirit. Stand behind your belief. You are the wise one.

"Everything that you have been through has only made you stronger and was in our plan. Learn to forgive. Forgive yourself, as well as others. Everything on this earth has a purpose in life. You may not understand it at times, but in the end it will all be known to you.

"Never forget where you come from or that we are here for you. You are the steward of the land. Keep it safe and respect it and the animals that live upon it. Teach your people to do the same. We have been here thousands of years. Never forget we are here for you and your people for thousands more to come.

"Go share your love with all. Watch over your people, and lead them down the right path. Never forget who you are. To say you are sorry, you must forgive yourself before you can forgive those you feel have done an injustice to you. Always look up to the sky. We will come down to you when you need it. Go with love and peace in your heart."

Mat on his knees sobbed, and then he prayed, "O great

spirit, heal my heart. Forgive me. Open my eyes so that I might see the road you lead me on. Forgive me for not trusting in you. I walk the earth only to serve you. I bless the animals for all they give to me. The sunshine is the light of my day, and the moon is the light of my night. The love of a woman completes me. You give me fire to keep me warm and the water to cleanse me. The air I breathe is the breath of the spirits, which keeps me alive. All these things you allow me to have. I have been such a fool.

"I have not opened my heart to you in many years. Please forgive me. Guide me in the direction you would have me go and to serve you in all ways. Give me wisdom to make the right choices in my life, as well as for my family and for my people, as it would be in your will. Continue to send the eagle to take my prayers to you and to watch them soar through the air as a constant reminder of where I have come from and where I am to go through the spirit. Without you, I would be nothing and have nothing. Thank you, spirits!"

Mat chanted and sang once more to the spirits. He was a changed man and now knew what he had to do. The spirits had forgiven him, and now it was his turn to do the same. He had some people to see.

When Mat reached the village, he went to Father's hut.

"Father, I understand why you did what you thought you had to do with Kati. I know it was a hard decision to make, but you did it for our people. You are our leader, and we trust your leadership to protect the whole tribe. I would have done the same to protect all we have. I forgive you. Can you forgive me for giving you so much worry? You were right. I had turned my back on the spirits."

Mat reached out to shake Father's hand. Father took his hand and pulled into an embrace. "Forgive me too, son."

They both cried and patted each other on the back.

Next, Mat went to Mother and asked for forgiveness. She asked for Mat to forgive her as well, and they embraced.

Now he went to his hut, where Katiann and Sarah were waiting on him. He opened the hut door and saw no one. *Where could they be?* He looked around the village. He went to the children's hut, but they were not there. He went to the dinner tables, but there was no sign of them. Then it hit him. "My father."

Mat went to his father's grave, and there the two women stood. Katiann had her arm around Sarah. They had both been crying.

Mat went up to them and starting chanting and singing. Sarah joined in. They held hands. Mat turned to his mother and said, "Mother. May I call you that?"

"Yes," she said with tears in her eyes.

"At first I could not understand how you could have left me like that. I have been searching my heart to understand.

In the last few months, Katiann has taught me how to love and live again." He looked at Katiann and smiled.

"I could not understand how or why she would go through all the pain and suffering she did for me. She was willing to die so that I could continue to hang on to Kati's memory. Today I went to see the spirits. They explained what true love is all about. It is when you are willing to give up your life to save someone else. I would do that for her, as she has demonstrated that she would do for me. I have been such a fool."

Katiann was about to cry. She stood next to Sarah as he spoke about her.

He held her gaze and said, "I love her more now than I can imagine. Someone who is willing to give up their life for another is true love. Mother, I have nothing to forgive you for. You have shown great strength and wisdom in protecting me all these years. You have only done what you thought was right. I understand you have never left my side. I need you to forgive me for turning my back on you and the spirits. I remember at a young age you told me that when I am down, I should turn to the spirits. I did not until now. I have spoken to the spirits, and they have forgiven me. Now I need you to forgive me."

"Son, there is nothing I need to forgive. You were the perfect little boy who has turned into a great man. I could not be more proud of you than I am now. You have been so sad for so long, and I blamed myself."

Sarah took Katiann's hand and placed it into Mat's hand. "She is the one who completes you. You are whole now. If it were not for the love you two share, we would not be here today."

Sarah placed a hand on each of their cheeks and smiled.

Katiann told Sarah she was welcome to come visit anytime and that, if it was okay with Mat, maybe one day the family could sit together for a meal to get to know each other.

Sarah smiled. "I think I would like that someday."

Mat walked Sarah to the edge of their territory, where his brother, Kowl, was waiting for her. Mat and Kowl shook hands. Sarah kissed Mat on the cheek. And then off they went into the sunset.

Mat returned to the village about an hour later and went to see Katiann.

"Katiann, I meant every word I said. I told you the spirits had sent you to save me, and you did. I saw the spirits in the cave. They spoke to me and said they had never left me. You were right all along. I love you so much."

He kissed her long and hard. Then he picked Katiann up and carried her into their hut.

Chapter 32

Months Later

Screaming came from Mother's hut.

"Katiann! Katiann! We need your help. Do not take the pain away. We need to know when to push at the right time."

"I am trying, Mother, but there is so much pain."

"I know, Katiann. It will be over soon. We need this pain."

"I am trying not to, but, Mother."

"No, Katiann, stop now. It is almost time. I can see it. Okay, push."

There was one more scream.

"Come on—push. You can do it. This should be the last one. Push! Sarah, help hold her up."

Then it was over, and the baby cried.

"Look, Sarah. He's beautiful," Mother said.

"I never thought I would ever be a part of this. Thank you so much. I would not have missed this for anything, even if I had to hide out in the woods to see it," Sarah said.

Teka turned to her. "Never again will you hide from us. You are our family and are always welcome at our table. Never forget that, Grandmother."

To have him call her Grandmother was worth it all. Her eyes started to tear up. This was the happiest day she'd had in a long time, other than the day she got her family back.

Mother took the baby and handed him to Katiann.

Mat walked in when he heard the baby crying. "Is it over?" he asked.

"Yes, Mat. Look. Isn't he beautiful? All ten fingers and all ten toes. He looks just like his father," Katiann told him.

"He does."

"Here. You hold your grandson."

Teka was holding Lilly. For a short moment Katiann envisioned how it should have been when she and Mat held Teka for the first time. She had accepted the many years she had lost, but she would cherish every moment of the present and was so thankful that God had watched after them all through the years.

"Katiann, I love you with all my heart and soul," Mat said.

Katiann looked at him. "Mat, you are still so full of it. If I did not know you better, I would think you wanted to play with teddy tonight."

"That sounds like a plan."

"Let's leave these kids alone with their new family," Katiann said. "We will see if teddy will let us practice increasing ours. Come on. You might just get lucky tonight."

Mat handed the baby to Teka and Lilly and put his arms around Katiann. Their one-month-old daughter was asleep in a pouch on his back.

"Did she give you much trouble?" Katiann asked.

"Not today, but I am sure if she is anything like her mother, I'll have my hands full eventually."

"Do you think?"

"I love you, Katiann."

"I love you too. Come, Little Miss. Let's go home."

Epilogue

Back in the US

Knock, knock, knock.

"Come in. What can I do for you?" said Mr. Peterson.

"Good morning. I am Detective Martin. I understand that you are Miss Anna May's attorney and handle all her affairs. There has been a missing person's report filed, and I thought you might have some information on how we can locate her. Could you tell me the last time you spoke to or saw Miss May?"

Acknowledgments

I never in a million years would have thought I would be writing a book. Yet it happened one day, out of the blue. I found myself in a place in my life that I no longer wanted to be. I was too young to feel this old. I knew I had to make a change, for me. I want to thank my doctor, Courtney, for encouraging me to think about my family and the things I wanted to do with them. With her help I received therapy to keep my joints moving. With diet and exercise, my life started to change. I walked each day while listening to Native American Music performed by Alexandro Querevalú, that relaxes me. After my walks I told a co-worker my thoughts, thank you Debra, for insisting that I write them down. Each day I would come back with another, another and another thought until one day, I had a book.

I would like to thank my family for putting up with me, talking about the book so much, I am sure they were tired of my every word being about my story. To my husband who suffered countless headaches while listening to the pecking of the keyboard. To my friends who helped read, read and read again, until they were sick of it, but yet wanted more, and for editing, which seemed like a hundred times, Sue, Debra, Chrissie, Wendy and Caitlin, and for not getting mad as I laughed at their expressions while reading, I thank you. I would have given up if it weren't for your need to want more. Thank you so much. Then there is my sister, Pat, who said, "What took you so long? I knew you were always a writer." I would not have been able to continue if it was not for a very special friend who had to listen to all my plots, my ups and downs, without complaint and built me back up when I got discouraged, Tammie.

I want to thank the editors of Archway for fixing my hot mess. They did a wonderful job.

But most of all, I want to thank Alexandro Querevalú, a brilliant performer of Native American Music that has touched my soul in ways I cannot express. His music is like no other, music that relaxes you and takes you away, free of stress. He plays his music with his whole heart, body, and soul. Walking to his music every day has truly saved my life. His music was the inspiration I needed.

Thank you, Alexandro.